INSIDE

D.M. SICILIANO

The Parliament House Press Edition, October 2019

INSIDE

All rights reserved. Published in the United States by
The Parliament House, a division of Machovi Productions Inc.,
Florida.

ISBN: 978-1696577434

Cover & Interior Design by
Shayne Leighton | Parliament House Book Design
machoviprods@gmail.com

Edited by
Live Knudsen, Megan Hultberg, and Ashley Connor

Published by The Parliament House
www.parliamenthousepress.com

Printed in the United States of America.

INSIDE

D.M. SICILIANO

1674

The man lifted his head and arched his shoulders back, revealing what was in his arms.

His baby.

Flames licked at the man, delicately lacing around his shoulders, coaxing him forward.

The fireplace grew, looming high above the man and his baby, surpassing the walls and the ceiling. As the scene unfolded, it appeared as if the fireplace could never have fit inside the tiny house at all.

Perhaps the house existed within the fire.

The man willingly accepted the flames, like a friend leading him forward.

As an offering, he held the baby out toward the fire. Flames extended to greet the child, and wrapped wisp-like tentacles around the baby's arms, legs, and neck. The baby wailed—a gurgling wet scream which held desperate sickness. The drowning cries of the near dead.

The man didn't flinch, didn't notice or care about the baby's cries. He moved forward with even, guided footsteps, not once looking at his helpless and doomed child. His face was blank, devoid of emotion. Empty of everything human.

He bent forward and gave his baby to the fire.

The baby's screams grew tight and muffled as the flames crawled down its throat. Like an octopus, the fire reached out with too many greedy hands and enfolded the baby, first cradling and rocking it, then wrapping each blazing arm tighter around the infant until it was nothing but a bundle of fire. The flaming arms withdrew back into the fireplace, taking the baby with it.

From within the fire, faint voices echoed, crackling within the embers.

"The fire consumes, the fire cleanses.
The child is yours, the child is ours.
Forever bound."

The man straightened his posture and smoothed his hands down the front of his trousers. Finally he blinked, unaffected as if he hadn't a hint of guilt for the sacrifice he'd just committed.

2

1987

T he house sat alone, deep in the woods, dark and quiet. It crouched at the end of an old dirt road, undisturbed for longer than it could recall. Content to wait, as time had no meaning from within.

Its old wooden door and window were loosely boarded up, a flimsy deterrent at best. The house needed no deterrent but its own reputation. Its story and its walls held strong through generations, hundreds of years.

A wind from nowhere burst through the inside, kicking up years of dust. The house shivered, the walls and floors shifting. Invisible footsteps paced the floor. Darkness drifted and a shadow crept across the ceiling. A crackle from a long since dead fire sounded from the fireplace, though no spark danced within.

The flutter of tiny wings flapped from somewhere inside.

And then, in the dark of night, the glow of fire emanated from within the uninhabited house. A single flame to light the darkness.

The house was waking.

And waiting.

PART I

1987

Chapter 1

Anxiety pulsed through Alex and hung heavy in the humid New England summer air. As he pedaled behind Reid in the dark, the beam of the flashlight strapped to his friend's bike bobbed like some strange drunken firefly, darting this way and that. The ripe funky smell of a skunk somewhere nearby wrinkled Alex's nose. Hectic cries of cicadas in their nonstop buzzing played in his eardrums.

Alex thought back to their conversation earlier in the evening and cringed, wishing he could've stopped this awful plan. Not only were they sneaking onto private property, they were doing it at night in the dark woods, through a path that barely existed. A path which led to a house no one else dared go near.

He gripped harder on his bike's handlebars as he followed behind Reid. No one else wanted to go through with it. It was all Reid's doing. Big bully.

Alex clenched his teeth to stop them from rattling in

his head. He wondered if it was fear or the rough terrain that shook him so much.

There was a reason that creepy house had stood for three hundred years, untouched, unspoiled. *Undisturbed.*

"Hurry up, Alex," Reid yelled back over his shoulder. "We're almost there!"Reid yelled back over his shoulder.

A small branch reached out and slapped Alex in the face. The dirt path turned sharply, and Alex swerved to avoid running into a tree. His wheel skidded as he yanked the handlebar to the side, barely in time to straighten out and hold himself up. A terrifying thought popped into his head which made him shudder despite the heat of the night—maybe the path and the woods were trying to give them one last warning. *Stay away.*

"I can't see, wait up!" Alex cried out. He pedaled faster.

It was almost impossible to keep up and see what remained of the path ahead with just Reid's light to guide them. He hoped he wouldn't have a run-in with that skunk.

There were no streetlights this far past the outskirts of town. A heavy film of clouds blocked out any chance of moon or stars. The humidity draped itself over Alex's shoulders like a blanket. Sweat soaked through his U2 t-shirt and clung to his chest as he rode on.

The old dirt path was rough at best and wouldn't have been easy to ride even in daylight. That is, if anyone else was ever dumb enough to come out here. No one had come out this way in years. Everyone knew to stay away. *Everyone but us.*

The last spot of civilization they'd passed was Old Miller's Bar down on King Street, and that was well over ten minutes ago. That bar was one of the oldest buildings in the town, full of some of the oldest drunks.

No one to know we're here. Alex wiped the sweat from his brow.

The grass grew in uneven patches, sometimes spreading across the path entirely, erasing all signs of it. Branches jutted out from trees. Some reached far over the path, like skinny jagged claws in the night, waiting to snag any trespassers. It gave Alex the willies.

He tried to imagine what the path might've looked like years ago, before the trees and bushes and grasses took over, back when the house could be seen from the road. He tried to picture a clear, even road leading up to a small house surrounded by trees. Sun shining through the leaves, dancing across the wildflowers strewn across the lawn. Instead of the house they were headed toward, this one would be full of life. Maybe there was a little girl in a yellow dress playing outside with her fluffy dog. Mom might be inside making lemonade, and Dad trimming the hedges, taking breaks to laugh and play with his daughter.

Hard as he tried, though, Alex couldn't complete the picture. All he could see in his mind's eye was a rotted old house. Dark and smelly, neglected and ancient. Rats and cockroaches scurrying across the floors. Termites eating away at the centuries-old walls. No one came here. No one lived here. It was haunted. Everyone knew. As if at some point there'd been a silent agreement within the town to let it get overrun, to block out all sight and hopefully all thought of that dreadful house.

Reid brought his bike to an abrupt halt in front of Alex, skidding it to the side, kicking up dirt and pebbles.

The glow of the flashlight stopped its dance, giving Alex a better target to follow. He pulled up a little ahead of Reid and sent up a spray of dirt through the beam of light.

Reid nodded in the direction of the beam. "Cool." Then his face got serious and he folded his arms over his chest. "It's just you and me."

"No, they're coming."

Alex wasn't sure that was true, but it made him feel better to think there'd be four of them stepping inside that creepy old house instead of just him and Reid. Like, a whole two-percent less creepy.

Reid had gotten off his bike and walked in front, straightening his posture. Blocked out the beam of light, casting an eerie shadow over Alex. It made Reid appear even taller than his five feet ten inches.

"No, they're not." He laughed and then dragged out the final word for effect. "They're wicked scared."

Alex shook his head. "Just give 'em a few more minutes. I know they'll come. They said so." He took a step to the side.

He didn't like the way Reid's face looked in the dark. Ashen, gray, empty.

"And get outta my light."

Reid moved back to his bike and the light shone past him once again. "Fine, but I think we're wasting time for nothing." He paused. "You better not be stalling 'cause you're scared, too."

But Alex wasn't listening. He thought he saw a shadow, something dark dart into the bushes, just out of the corner of his eye. He blinked and doubted he'd seen anything at all. Still, he couldn't shake the feeling there was someone else—no, some*thing* else there with them.

"Hey, Alex, what's wrong with you? Are you even listening? You look like someone just made you eat shit." The last word lifted the side of Reid's mouth into a crooked smile.

Funny he should phrase it that way, because it didn't feel too far from the truth. This plan was shit. Yeah, it was pretty damn tough to swallow. And Alex wasn't just being a coward.

He licked his lips before answering. He had to choose his words carefully. Even though Reid was his best friend, sometimes he could be a real dick. And Alex knew Reid could easily lay him out flat if pissed off. Good guy to have on your side in a fight. Ugly to get on his bad side. Reid was bigger, tougher, and a lot quicker to anger. It wasn't his fault, though, and he hadn't always been that way. The mean in him only came to the surface since his mom died a few years back. Before that, he was more lighthearted and playful. Alex couldn't imagine losing his mom the way Reid had lost his.

Alex swallowed down his true thoughts on the plan and hoped he sounded convincing.

"Nah, I'm cool." And he threw in a shrug for good measure, all nonchalant-like.

He considered adding in a casual whistle while they waited, but he didn't want to lay it on too thick because he was anything but cool. It seemed like the night had grown hotter the closer they got to the house. Like sitting by a crackling fire. The heat pushed at Alex. He wiped sweat from his brow and felt it beading up above his lip.

The night in this part of the woods both pushed

and pulled at him. Daring him to get closer to the house, yet begging him to stay away.

Even though they'd been friends since forever, Alex couldn't deny that Reid's bullying was the one thing about him he disliked.

There hadn't been many times in their lives when Reid's ideas ended well. One time when they were ten, Reid talked Alex into climbing the giant old pine tree in his backyard. Alex knew it was an absolutely stupid thing to do. If it was such a great idea, why didn't Reid climb the tree? Why'd it have to be Alex? But as with so many other things, he went along despite his better judgment.

It didn't take Alex long to climb up that tree. Up is never the problem. After a few cautious steps, he grew bolder, reaching, pulling up, then finding a safe step to heave himself up farther. Finding a rhythm, Alex reached, stepped, reached, stepped, and before long he was near the top of the pine. He made the mistake of looking down when Reid called out, and that was it. Alex was struck with the panic of being what looked to be a good fifty feet in the air. He found the nearest branch and wrapped his body around it, probably looking like some clumsy sloth as he hung there.

This sent Reid into a fit of laughter and shouting. With all that commotion, Reid's dad came out and saw Alex stuck up there. By this time, Alex was crying, scared stiff. It was both good and bad that Reid's dad came out, then ducked back inside to call the fire department. Good because Alex never would've made it down alone. Bad, really bad, because Reid caught a sound whooping for embarrassing his dad and pulling a stunt like that. Mr. Thompson had released a stream of words so crass it'd make a sailor blush. Something like, *"Rotten son of a bitch, dirty no good little fuckhole shit-for-brains ass…"* His words weren't the worst of it, though. Reid showed up at Alex's house the next day with a black eye.

Still, Alex wasn't about to mention how rotten of an idea it was to sneak into that house. A fool of a friend he was.

"I don't think they're coming," Reid said. He glanced down at a watch-less wrist. "I bet Danny's home on his couch eating ice cream, watching MTV, or playing Atari." He raised his hand, made it into a fist and shook it in the air, doing his finest Billy Idol impression. "I want my MTV."

"They'll be here."

"They better. Those two morons better not screw up the plan. I'm staying at your house, you're at mine, and they're staying over at each other's. Parent lies are all covered." A shadow fell across his face again, making him look dark and ashen. "We'll be in and out before you know it just to prove once and for all this place isn't haunted. It's a sham. If we do this right, no one will ever know we're gone."

Those last words echoed in Alex's head.

Chapter 2

Danny hated this plan. There was a whole list of things he'd rather be doing than riding his bike with Clint through the darkness to meet up with Reid and Alex. He'd rather be home playing Atari with Clint, sitting on the couch, with some fresh snacks delivered by his forever-loving mom. When he thought about it, he'd rather go to the dentist than this. But there was one thing he wouldn't rather do, and that was not go and have Reid kick his ass, tease him, or call him a big fat baby one more time. Besides, he wasn't really fat, he was just big-boned. That's what his mom called it, anyway.

"Tell me why we're doing this again?" he whispered, and glanced to the side at his friend.

As he did, the clunky headlamp strapped to his head cast weird shadows behind Clint, making it look like little creatures were dancing around his feet.

Clint gave an audible sigh. "It's a thing. You know, to prove we're awesome. We're going into high school next year, and what better way to make a grand entrance?"

"How does Reid talk us into all this crap?" Danny's words came out choppy as he hit a rough patch of dirt.

A rock kicked up and grazed his knee.

"Cause, well, he's Reid." Clint shrugged.

Danny's bike skipped over a broken branch laying across the path.

He moaned and took a deep breath. "Crushed my gnads. Gotta stop."

He halted his bike, drew in another deep breath but couldn't bring himself to lift his leg up and over to step off it. Instead, he brought his hands over his crotch, leaned forward and tried to shake off the wave of nausea.

"Dag, man, you OK?"

"Totally. Just gotta catch my breath. Can we walk?"

Danny slowly slung his leg over the bike and stepped off. He grabbed the handlebars and started pushing it as he walked. Clint hopped off his bike and pulled up beside him. The path was wide enough in some spots, but in others, one of them had to fall back in single file or risk getting swiped by a branch or tripped by the bushes. Like the woods were alive, reaching out for them as they pushed onward. Danny shook off the thought.

"We shouldn't go to the haunted house." Danny cast his eyes to the ground as if it were going to reach up and drag him down into the darkness. "It's probably not haunted anyway. Who knows how long it's really been there."

He was just making noise to keep from freaking out. If he kept talking, the darkness wouldn't scare him so much, the idea wouldn't be so stupid, and he might be able to keep going. And he also knew that Clint would go into Mr. History mode. That was his thing, after all.

As if on cue, Clint nudged his glasses high onto his nose and launched into the story. He was an ace at reciting facts, and this was one story the whole town was well aware of.

"Pretty sure it's been there at least since the 1600s." His voice deepened. "Legend has it the troubles began during King Philip's war."

"The Indian dude, right?" Danny stumbled over a rock and then found his balance. "Feather, not dot, right?"

"Uh-huh. From the Wampanoag Tribe."

Danny nodded. "Yeah, Reid's cousin or whatever."

The light of Danny's headlamp flitted across Clint's face just in time to catch a massive eye roll.

Clint sighed. "Not quite a cousin. Duh. A distant relation by like three hundred years." He straightened up. "They fought against the colonists and burned down all their houses. Every one burned to the ground, except that one."

The beam of the headlamp cast from side to side as Danny glanced off into the woods and then looked over each shoulder. No matter how many times he'd heard the story, it never got any less scary. And the darkness felt like it was pressing in on him. Even with the light, the night seemed to grow darker in the telling of the tale.

Clint said, "It was like the fire couldn't touch it, couldn't burn through."

"Nuh-uh. You're shitting me." Danny squirmed.

Clint raised his palm. "I swear. I shit you not." He

dropped his hand. "Even though they set it on fire, the flames rose and surrounded the house but couldn't destroy it." He leaned in and whispered over Danny's shoulder. "Since then, no one has dared to go near it. The house is cursed, haunted. Some say the devil himself resides there. It's said that when the fire enveloped the house, screams could be heard from within. Thousands and thousands of screams." He recited the words from rote, a story passed down to him from his father, and his father's father. From everyone's father. "In fact, those screams, the evil within grabbed hold of the hearts of the fearless Indians and drove them away. But it was too late. A shadow had sneaked its way into King Philip's mind. Fear had taken over his men, and that eventually led to his madness and his capture and death."

Danny whipped his head around and mushed his hand over his friend's face, forcing him back. "It's a lie, a stupid story."

Clint dropped his bike and pushed Danny away, intent on finishing his lecture. "Sometimes, in the dark of the night—"

A branch cracked and Danny scanned the darkness for the *thing* that had brushed past. Clint seemed unconcerned, and Danny wondered if he'd imagined the sound.

Clint continued. "The glow of a fire emanates from within."

A rustle of leaves drew both of their attention, but then there was nothing.

"A single flame to light the darkness."

"Stop!" Danny cringed at his own outburst.

Clint shrugged, then leaned down and picked up his bike, and they both continued walking.

It was too late though. Danny could feel the fear seeping into him. It raced over his skin like little spiders. Pricked at him and brought every hair on his body to attention. He rubbed his arms, trying to relieve the goosebumps. His headlamp flickered. Breath caught in his throat before the light came back on. He hadn't realized until then how terrifying the woods would be in the full dark. He started to hum like he always did when he got nervous. Except the humming didn't help, so he started singing.

"Carry a laser down this road that I must tra-vel. Carry a laser through the darkness of the n-i-i-ight!"

Clint laughed. "I really don't think those are the words."

"Yes, they are."

They stopped dead in their tracks.

Clint shook his head. "But the name of the song is *Kyrie*."

He wasn't going to budge. He never did. Danny was used to it. This type of stuff had gone on between them for years.

"But he has to carry a laser down the road and through the night," Danny said. "It's like a weapon or a flashlight so that he can see in the dark."

He felt good about his argument. Made sense to him. But these were the kind of arguments his dad had told him to avoid at school. The nuh-uh, no how, no way, I-know-you-are-but-what-am-I childish jabs that he'd surely—hopefully—grow out of by fourteen. He only had a few months to sort that out.

"I really don't think so." Clint stifled a giggle. "The

name of the song is *Kyrie*. He says *Kyrie Eleison*. It means lord, have mercy."

Danny shook his head, unwilling to lose this battle. "Not even. Who'd write a pop song about that?"

Clint laughed even harder.

The anger overtook Danny's fear. "I know it's carry a laser. If you don't believe me, ask my mom when we get back."

The laughter from Clint only increased. "Your mom."

"Your mom!" Danny yelled.

Another rustle from the bushes. Footsteps. Getting closer.

He froze, terrified of what might be following them. His mind created all sorts of terrible things—vampires, werewolves, Bigfoot, witches, demons, ghosts.

The bushes parted and a figure stepped out. It had a girl's snarky voice.

"*Your* mom. Ya momma's so stupid she thought meow mix was a record for cats."

Danny recognized the voice as the girl snorted.

"Wicked fucking morons."

Chapter 3

Heather stepped out of the bushes and into the light of Danny's headlamp. Both boys were wide-eyed, their faces struck with fear. They looked ridiculous and Heather couldn't help it, so she burst out laughing, bent over, holding her stomach. Her dark curls fell over her face, tickling the leaves on the ground.

She finally took a deep breath. "Ooh, that hurt." She looked straight at the boys again. "Douche nozzles." She stifled another giggle. "You should see your faces."

"Oh, dag, what are you doing here?" Clint pushed his glasses up higher on his face. "You're not supposed to be here."

The light from the headlamp illuminated the path ahead. Heather was glad for it. Plus, now she could see the boys' stupid reactions.

"Man, you guys should try this in the dark. Wicked hard." She pulled a twig out of her hair. "Well, what're we waiting for? Let's go." She reached into the bushes, pulled out her bike and set it on the path. Straddled it and kicked one foot at the pedal and then turned back to look at the boys. "Seriously, let's go. Either start moving or gimme the headlamp. I feel like I'll be picking leaves and twigs from my hair for days." She reached up and untangled another twig from her tight curls. As she pulled it out, she felt a trickle of blood run down her palm. "That wasn't a twig." She licked the trail of blood and the metallic penny-like tang hit her tongue. The taste made her smile. It was one of those weird things she secretly loved. "Thorns got me."

Danny shined his light at Heather. "You're gross." He shook his head and the light went flashing side to side. "You can't come. Alex'll kill us if you tag along."

She groaned. "Way I see it, you got two choices. Either all three of us meet up with Reid and Alex, or I go home and narc you all out."

"We're not gonna win this one, Danny," Clint said. "Let's just go. We're already late."

The boys hopped on their bikes and pushed past Heather.

She thought the whole thing was a stupid idea, too. The difference with her was that she hadn't been invited. If they'd have asked her, she would've said yes, but not before telling them what jackasses they were and that it wasn't going to make them any cooler even if they pulled it off. Unlike most of the others, she wasn't afraid. Wasn't afraid of most things. Growing up with two brothers saw to that. She was two years younger than Alex and about ten years more tomboy than all the boys combined, minus Reid.

They were always trying to get rid of her. Even

though she was arguably the best all-around athlete of all of them, they didn't give her enough credit. Besides, it wasn't like there were any girls in the neighborhood to play with. Sure, there was Jessica Karsen, her mom's best friend's daughter, but all she wanted to do was play with Barbies, get into her mom's makeup, and talk about boys. And there was Danny's little sister, Rebecca, but she was only ten, and, well, a big, whiny baby. It ran in the family.

Heather thought back to the night before, overhearing Alex and Reid discussing their plan to invade the haunted house. She had sat patiently outside Alex's bedroom door, ear pressed to it while the boys plotted. She'd had a plan of her own, and she knew they'd never see it coming.

So after Reid and Alex had hopped on their bikes and taken off, she'd hopped on her own and headed down to King Street to travel in the dark without a flashlight. It wasn't quite as easy as she had imagined, but she'd never tell the boys that and she'd never in a million years back down. The farther out from town she got, the harder the ride had become, with hardly any light to guide her way, and the trees and grasses grew wilder and thicker. It was as if the trees were reaching out with hundreds of fingers, grabbing at her hair, getting her tangled and matted. Convinced it would take her too long to get to Alex alone, she tucked herself in the bushes, waiting for Danny and Clint. She knew she could convince them to let her follow.

The anger from getting shut out of the boys' plans once again made her blood boil, as if it wasn't hot enough out there already. The sweat dripped down her forehead, into her curls.

Pedaling behind Danny and Clint, she grumbled, "Those shit-for-brains think they can close me out like that. They got another thing coming."

"What'd ya say?" Clint called back.

She frowned. She hadn't meant to voice her thoughts out loud, and the constant buzz of the cicadas were driving her mad. The farther they got down the path, the more cicadas there were. Like they were shouting at her to go back. Even the cicadas didn't want her to come.

"They think they're so tricky," she yelled to Clint. "Fucking morons, what they are!" She nodded, agreeing with herself. Then she lowered her voice so only she could hear. "I'll show them."

"Guys?" Danny shouted through labored breaths. "You notice it's getting harder to ride the farther we get? I feel like the woods are closing in around us."

He slammed his bike to a halt, and Clint and Heather almost ran into him.

"Dude, what was that all about?" Clint butted his bike into Danny's rear tire.

Danny turned his head back toward the path they'd come, shedding some light. "Look, it's like there's no more path." He gulped. "Like the night ate it all up."

"Don't be so stupid." Heather turned to look at the way they'd come.

The path did seem smaller. It made her wonder how they'd gotten their bikes down it in the first place. The bushes and leaves reached across, locking with the branches on the opposite side of the so-called path. *Like, no going back.*

A chill ran up her spine. The salty copper taste of her blood still sat heavy in her mouth. She absently

24

brought her hand up and sucked the wound on her finger again, then plucked it out of her mouth with a popping sound.

She sniffed the air. "I think we're getting close. I can smell the *Aqua Velva* coming off Alex from here."

Chapter 4

"I'll give them five more minutes," Reid said, "then we're going with or without them."

He leaned back onto his bike seat, one foot in the dirt to prop him up. He swung the handlebars back and forth, the light making strange shadows shift around them.

Why it was such a big deal, why everyone was so afraid, he'd never know. It was a chance for glory. The house was haunted, everyone in town knew it, but Reid didn't care about that. He didn't really understand what that meant exactly. And it didn't scare him. He'd faced too many real-life monsters to be afraid of something no one could see or explain. From cancer to death, from alcoholism to abuse, there were much more frightening things in the real world.

A rustle came from back down the path. Reid swung his bike and light in the direction and illuminated Danny and Clint.

"Oomph!" Danny grunted as his bike ran over a large rock, and flew headfirst over the handlebars.

Clint ran over Danny's back tire and fell over him. There was a crunching sound and Danny's headlamp went out.

"You ride like a bunch of girls." Reid snorted and turned to Danny. "Smooth move, Ex-Lax."

A third, unexpected voice said, "Why ya gotta shine the light in our eyes?"

"Who's there?" Reid stared, mouth agape as another bike came into view.

"Who else would it be, dickweed?" Alex's younger sister, Heather, brought her bike to a smooth stop just in front of Reid's. "Some of us girls ride better than others. Now wipe that shit-eating grin off your face." She got off her bike and crossed her arms.

"Oh, no. No fricking way! Nuh-uh." Alex dropped his bike to the gravel, marched up to her and pointed his finger inches from her face. "You can't be here!"

He turned to Danny and Clint, who still sat in the dirt, watching the show.

"How could you guys let her tag along?"

Reid sighed at yet another distraction. Heather was always tagging along. She was two years younger than Alex but just as tough, if not tougher. Everything the boys did, she had to try to do better. And though Reid would never admit it to her face, she often succeeded. Like she had to one-up them being a boy. She never backed down from a challenge or dare or a rough round of any sport, and she wasn't afraid to get dirty or her hair messed up. She was the girl who didn't know she was a girl. Reid would never tell her, but he liked her

28

toughness. Although, in this instance, it was exasperating and slowing them down.

Danny said, "It's not about letting her—"

"She blackmailed us." Clint climbed to his feet and dusted the dirt from his jeans. "Plain and simple." He shot Heather a wicked glare and shook his head. "It's your fault, Alex. She heard you and Reid planning it all, then ambushed us when we came to meet you. She was just sitting there waiting in the freakin' bushes. She told us if she couldn't come, she'd rat us all out."

"Give me one of the extra flashlights." Heather held out her hand to Reid. "Don't know why you gotta bogart all of them, anyway. You know how hard it was riding up here in the dark?"

"I'm keeping them for when we get to the house. Plus, we don't want anyone to see all our flashlights out here and wonder what we're up to. Use your brain." Reid gave Heather a light knock on the top of her head. "We're sneaking onto this property. Have to be *sneaky* about it."

"You wouldn't know sneaky if it bit your ass." Clint looked at Reid as he tapped himself on the chest. "Gimme a break here, we need some light. And Danny just busted his headlamp."

"Hands off my sister, Reid." Alex shoved him.

As much of a bully as Reid was, he'd never hurt Heather. She was the only one who got away with the crazy shit she'd say to him. She might act like a boy, but he still knew she was a girl.

Reid shook his head and swung his backpack off his shoulder. "Just one more flashlight until we get to the house."

He plucked one out and smacked it against Clint's chest.

"Gnarly," Danny said. "I think I lost some serious skin. Gimme some light here." Danny still sat in the dirt path, checking his wounds.

Clint shone the light on him, and one body part at a time, Danny looked himself over.

He stopped when he got to his left elbow. "Ah, man, that's gonna leave a mark. Serious road rash." He was bleeding from elbow to wrist. "Shit burns."

Alex reached out a hand. Danny took it and scrambled to his feet.

"You gonna make it?" Alex gave him a playful punch in the arm.

"Yeah, I'll live. Let's go."

"Bunch of girls, I'm telling you. Does anyone need to fix their hair, too?" Reid stood with his arms crossed, head tilted.

They all climbed back on their bikes, and this time it was a little easier, having two flashlights to work with.

The path ended about twenty yards from the house, where the weeds and grass had run so out of control they couldn't to see through it. The path was completely swallowed up by the living mass of greenery—one final warning to stay away.

Reid shoved his hands deep into the bush and tried to part it enough to see through to the other side. Branches and leaves pressed back at him, and it felt as if they were intentionally keeping him out.

He turned to everyone. "We'll leave our bikes here, do the rest on foot. Come on."

Everyone followed silently as he pushed through the growth, leading them to the house.

The closer they got, the hotter it seemed to get. *Like marching into a damn oven.*

Reid wiped the sweat from his brow. It definitely got quieter, too. The cicadas and their constant buzzing had faded to nothing. There were no crickets, no anything. The smell of the skunk from earlier was gone, and there seemed to be no smell at all. It was like the night in this part of the woods devoured everything else. Or maybe no other living creature was stupid enough to go that close to the house.

It was a small, dark timber-framed house, if it could even be called a house. *More like a glorified box of wood.* Standing one story, about sixteen-feet-by-fourteen, it looked like it could fit inside Reid's living room. The chimney stood out of the center of the roof. The one visible casement window was closed tight, rotted old two-by-fours nailed carelessly over it. As Reid looked closer, the house seemed to be leaning to the left, yet the door stood straight. A fleeting wave of disorientation overtook him, and he swayed as the house was abruptly straight and even, as if it never leaned at all. Despite some ashy smudges here and there, it was surprisingly intact. Just outside the front door, a few scattered boards looked to be all that remained of a long-since gone porch.

"Impossible," Reid mumbled.

Heather leaned over his shoulder so close he could feel her breath on his neck.

"What's impossible?"

"That it didn't burn down. Look at the hunk of crap."

Heather brushed past him to the window. "I don't see the flame."

Reid watched her balancing on her tiptoes, trying to see through the cracks of the boarded-up window.

She nodded and turned back to Reid and the others behind him. "Nope, no light."

"Because there's no flame, dumbass. It's just a story. Nothing scary about this house."

Reid placed his flashlight under his chin, trying to light his face with the eerie glow. He bugged out his eyes and grinned widely, hoping to scare them and make them realize how ridiculous they were being.

"Maybe if you're afraid of rats or spiders. But there's no unholy, freakish being floating around in there. It's all a crock."

Danny said, "No, my uncle told my brother that he saw it one night, coming home late from a party in the woods when he was a teenager. He saw the light shining out from the cracks of the house like there was something in there. Something or someone." He scrunched his nose and squinted.

"My mother's uncle's brother's aunt's cousin's dog's owner's friend's neighbor said…" Reid cracked himself up. He couldn't finish through a fit of chuckles.

The only thing that interrupted his laughter was a burst of sneezes coming from Danny.

"Damnit! There's got to be a ton of ragweed out here." Danny wiped at his nose.

"Maybe it is all just a story." Alex slid up beside his sister to get a better view as well. "A stupid story to scare kids. Maybe it's just—"

A crack and a crunching sound came from near the front door. Reid turned to see Clint's foot caught in between the broken boards. No amount of windmill-arming could stop Clint from falling forward and crashing into the front door. A collective gasp came from the gang.

"I'm OK," Clint muttered. "Bumped my head, but I'm cool." He rubbed his head where it had knocked into the door.

Reid held his breath, waiting, though he didn't know what he was waiting for. The house wasn't haunted.

But from inside, he swore he heard the flutter of tiny wings. *They've been disturbed.*

"Holy shit, did anyone else hear that?" Danny took a step back.

"Like something flying around in there?" Heather asked.

"Yeah, I heard it," Alex said. "Maybe it was cockroaches?"

"Cockroaches don't fly," Clint said, after finally getting to his feet.

"Yes, they do, dip-shit," Alex said.

Reid felt another wave of disorientation come over him, but he shook it off. *Must just be the heat.* His heart thrummed in his head like the steady beat of drums.

"Enough dicking around, guys," he said. "Let's go inside."

He swung his backpack around and rummaged through it. He handed out the remaining flashlights so that everyone had their own, and stuck his hand back in until he found the hammer.

One of the flashlights started moving away from the house.

"I changed my mind." Danny plodded back to the bikes. "I should get going. I mean, I'm bleeding. I don't want it to get infected in that old house. I think I might need a tetanus shot or something."

Reid flashed the light on Danny's back. "You're a big pussy. You're just scared. Scared of a house and a story. Admit you're scared, and you can go home and no one will say anything else or try to stop you."

Danny whipped around and cast his light on Reid's face. "I'm not scared."

"You are. Admit it. It's no big deal. Admit you're a baby, and you can go home and suck your thumb."

Laughter boomed from Clint.

"Just say, I'm afraid, and you can go," Reid said. "Or come back here and bust into this house with us. We'll look through the house, prove there's no flame or ghost or anything, and go home. Then you'll be able to tell everyone you went in the haunted house at night. Think of the girls. They'll all be wanting to rub that round belly of yours while you tell them what a badass you are."

Reid knew Danny's weakness. He was the type of kid who wouldn't be getting a ton of dates this year in high school. Not until some more of that baby fat came off him. If there was a chance that going into this house would earn him some points with the ladies, he'd take it and Reid knew it. He wasn't bad looking, though. Pretty funny, too, in a goofy way, and some girls like that. What turned them off the most was his sneezy, runny nose and that they couldn't get over his old nickname from years back. Booger Baby. He had it rough. Dumb luck or whatever gave him the allergies and sneezes, but his mom falling all over him made him a straight-up baby and no girls dig that at all.

"Well, if he doesn't want to go in," Alex's voice

cracked, "maybe we should all go home. Stick together and all."

"No, no, no!" Reid protested. "We're here. Let's go." He took the hammer, flipped it to the claw side, and walked right up to the front door. "Gimme some light."

Heather stepped up, shone the light on the boards. Reid wrenched the hammer's claw in between and began prying them off.

It was a lot easier than he'd expected. The old nails, with their tips covered in rust, were no longer firmly planted in the wood. The slightest pull had them slipping out as if they wanted to be removed.

Within a few minutes, he had the front door unblocked. The he reached for the knob and gave it a quick twist. The door swung open with a high-pitched creak. It made him think of all the scary movies he'd watched again recently—*Nightmare on Elm Street, Friday the 13th, The Shining*. He exhaled the breath he didn't even know he was holding. *I'm not scared. The whole thing is stupid.*

Reid let go of the handle and it opened all the way, smacking into the wall behind it, giving off an eerie echo. *That was easy. Like the house had been waiting, happy to finally have those boards removed.* The hair on his arms stood and a chill rolled down his spine, but he shook it off.

"Ladies first." Reid turned back to face the rest of the crew, with a wide toothy grin.

"You're all talk, why don't you go first?" Clint nudged Reid in the back, sending him lurching forward a step before he regained his balance.

"You seem to know the story and the house better than all of us," Reid said. "You should go first, Clint."

35

He wrapped his arm around Clint's shoulder and shoved him inside.

One by one, they followed, cramming just inside the door. Each ran their flashlights about the room. Five beams dancing and spilling off the walls. The dark wood of the exterior matched the walls inside exactly. The only window in the room was dark and smudged with something grimy. Reid's mind told him they were handprints, but he blocked out the thought as quickly as it came.

A tangle of spiderwebs dangled in the corners of the room, low and full of dust, sweeping across the floor. The webs looked so old that even the spiders had given up on them. They looked more like long, lazy strands of yarn the way they hung so heavy. After all this time, there were still a few pieces of furniture scattered about the room. A small wooden table lay on its side in the far left corner, next to the fireplace. A tall bench sat beside it, covered in dust. Two stools lay toppled over on the floor next to an ancient cupboard along the far wall. The faint smell of a long dead fire danced through the room and dissipated swiftly. It was overtaken by a musty smell. The smell of something old and forgotten.

A succession of sneezes from Danny cut through the silence. It seemed to Reid like they were waiting for a response. Any sound at all. When nothing came, Reid turned his attention to the cupboard, the most ornate thing in the old house.

As he stepped closer, shining his light down on it, intricately carved leaves on both doors became illuminated. He ran his hand across it, removing a heavy layer of dust. What surprised him the most was finding the key still wedged inside the lock. *Every house has a secret. What's yours?* He reached for the key, then thought better of touching it. He pulled his hand back and stuck it in his pants pocket.

Someone pushed at Reid.

Heather brushed by him. "Wow, that's gotta be wicked old."

Her fingers were on the key, turning it. A clicking sound released the lock and Heather stepped back, bumping into Reid.

"Lemme see that." Reid reached forward and swung the cupboard open.

He squatted, flashed his light and peered inside. Nothing.

A puff of something came out at him.

"So much dust!" he choked out, as he waved at the air. "Do you guys smell smoke or something?"

Heather stuck her face inside the cupboard and sniffed.

She came back with her nose scrunched up. "Like an old fire."

Alex tugged her away from it. "Don't!"

"Don't what?" she asked.

"I don't know. Just don't." Alex held his grip on his sister's arm. "This whole thing is getting too weird."

Reid could feel the others crowding around behind him. *Bunch of babies, always hiding behind me.*

"How'd you do that?" Clint whispered in his ear.

When Reid didn't answer, he asked again, "How'd you make the smoke? Matches? Lighter? I didn't see anything in your hand."

Reid jabbed an elbow back without looking and caught Clint in the stomach. "I didn't *do* anything."

"Guys?" Danny said, in a small voice. "Guys. We should go now. The smoke. It's…it's getting bigger."

Reid turned to face Danny, who looked like he was about to cry. The corners of his mouth were tugging down and his eyes were cartoon-wide. He had one hand out, index finger pointing up, shaking. Everyone else turned to see as well.

Reid could see now that his first thought of dust was wrong. It was darker than dust and hung in the air unnaturally before floating to the ceiling and lingering there. It was smoke.

"What the—"

The puff of smoke by the ceiling grew and spread out, like some strange creature taking shape.

"This isn't good, guys," Danny said. "I don't like it. Call me a baby, but I'm leaving." He swung his light and his body to face the way they'd come in.

Maybe we shouldn't be here. The thought crawled through Reid's mind like a spider. He tried to move, but his feet felt like they were tangled in that imaginary spider's webs. *Trapped inside.*

It wouldn't have mattered if he could've gotten his feet to move anyway. There was nowhere to go. The door they'd entered through was gone.

Chapter 5

C lint stared at the wall, trying to understand what he wasn't seeing. The door had been there. Now it wasn't. *How could it just disappear?*

"What in the—" Alex dropped his flashlight.

It hit the floor and spun around and around, casting shadows off the wall.

The sound of small wings fluttering tickled the air. As the light slowed its spinning, Clint thought he saw shadows of deformed little birds dancing along the walls. Another turn and he decided they were bats. After another spin he was sure there was nothing there at all. Never had been. Yet he couldn't shake the feeling something had been there, watching them.

"Where's the door?" Danny whimpered.

"What's happening? Guys…" Clint ran his fingers across the wall where the door had been. "Nothing." Just a stark wooden wall.

He couldn't keep his cool. The anxiety welled up inside him. He started taking shorter breaths, feeling like something was squeezing his lungs. The muscles in his neck and shoulders tightened as he fought to keep from hyperventilating. He pulled his glasses off and dropped his head, closing his eyes, and counted to ten. His mom had taught him that. *When the world begins to close down on you, shut the world out. Start small. Breathe. And then return to the world.*

At ten, he lifted his head. The world looked fuzzy. His peripheral vision was limited, like those blinders they put on horses. He put his glasses back on, but that still didn't seem to help. *Not ready to see.*

Clint knew the panic was irrational, but in the moment it was more real than anything else. He felt closed down, trapped. A scream welled up inside his throat, but he fought to swallow it back down.

What came out instead was, "Let us out!" Clint flung himself forward and banged on the wall. He blinked hard, trying to focus. "If this is some kind of joke, good one." He found his way over to the window and ran his light across it. A few more deeps breaths and his vision began to clear. "This isn't right." Rubbing his hands over the glass, he tried to remove the dark smudges. When that didn't work, he spit on it and tried again. "The window isn't even a window, I don't think." He rapped against it a few times with his knuckle. "It's not even glass."

Heather moved to the wall where the door had previously been. She tilted her head as if studying it. Clint stared at the back of her head, concentrating on her dark curls. *Focus on something small.*

The sound of Heather's hands on the wall pulled his attention. She slowly ran them over each wood panel.

Inside

"What are you doing?" he asked. His voice came out breathy.

"Looking for a hidden latch or something. Some proof of the door." Methodically, she moved inch by inch over every part of the wall.

How can she be so calm? How can she stay so rational?

Fighting to not break down into full panic mode, he sucked in a deep breath. What he couldn't afford right now was to ball up in the corner, wrapping his arms around his legs and rocking back and forth. *Do not shut down. Do not panic.*

Clint's short breaths grew longer, deeper, and he pulled himself out of the anxiety attack.

He cringed and felt his heart jump when Alex screamed too close to his ear.

"There's no goddamned door!"

Clint turned to watch Alex's face morph into a terror-stricken expression. Alex took one deliberate step back at a time, away from Clint, away from the wall, away from a door that was no longer there. He backed right into Reid, who was facing the other way.

"Guys, look," Reid said, feebly. "Here."

Clint looked past Reid to where he was staring—the old fireplace.

Though he knew the answer, Clint asked anyway, "Wh-who lit the fire? Hey."

Inside the fireplace, a flame flickered, swaying back and forth. The cobwebs in the corners swayed, too, as if dancing to the beat of the same song or a breeze that didn't exist. A whistle of wind crept through the room, yet came from nowhere. No breeze, no door, no window.

Clint turned back to Reid.

41

"Nobody," Reid said. "It lit all by itself." His eyes were unblinking, seemingly hypnotized by the flames.

Danny started shaking his head, whining, "It can't be, it can't be. No, no, no, no, no. We're all trapped. It's haunted. I knew it. I knew it. We're screwed!"

Heather slapped Danny across his cheek. "Knock it off, you big baby. Can't you see? It's a prank. Reid got us here to scare us, and you're falling right into his plan." She turned to Reid. "Nicely done. Don't know how you got the fire to start or make the door disappear, but you've outdone yourself. Totally awesome." She curtsied and bowed her head. "You win, Reid."

Clint didn't buy it. No way could a kid make a door disappear. He fought back a wave of nausea as the anxiety tried to seize him again. The whole thing was unreasonable, impractical. Unnatural.

He moved around the others and got up in Reid's face. When Reid didn't acknowledge him, Clint poked a finger into his chest. Reid finally looked down the six inches he had over Clint. He seemed surprised to find Clint there, as if he hadn't been with him all along.

"You got us here. Great. Well played, man. And now this." Clint spread a hand out, palm up, gesturing across the room. "I don't know how, but okay, you win. You faked us out. You got us all shitting our pants." He looked to the others, who nodded, then back to Reid. "You don't even need to tell us how you did it, just get us out of here, okay?"

Reid blinked in quick succession, like he was coming out of a trance. "When did you get here, Clint?"

Alex pushed Clint aside and looked at Reid. He waved a hand in front of Reid's eyes.

"Yoo-hoo. Earth to Reid!" Inches from Reid's face, he snapped his fingers.

Nothing.

The fireplace crackled and popped, and everyone jumped except for Reid. It simply broke him from his stupor.

"Why are you guys looking at me like that?"

"You're kidding, right?" Clint said. "Your brain just took a vacation there." He looked on, exasperated, eyes bulging.

Danny's voice came out small like a child's. "Guys, can we argue later? I really wanna go home. This isn't fun and it's not funny."

"Okay, guys, let's focus," Heather commanded the room. "What do we do? The door we came in is, uh, gone. So what are our options? Think. There has to be a way out."

"Right," Alex said. "The wall sort of ate up the door. So that's out. The window's not really a window. Where can we go from here? We need a plan."

There wasn't much to the room, though. Clint thought the odds of finding an alternative weren't good. And the fire was growing larger. The shadow of a mouse or rat scurrying away from the fire pulled his attention.

"Eep!" Danny squeaked. "Rat!"

"Never mind the rat," Reid said. "Look at the fire!" He took a brazen step toward it, palms up as if to feel the heat coming off it.

As the flames grew, the glow spread farther across the room, illuminating all the cobwebs and years of layers of dust and dirt. Clint caught a glint of the flame reflected in Reid's eyes—those wild eyes he knew well.

When the glow was strong enough to hit the farthest corner, off to their right, Danny let out a high-pitched scream.

Clint recoiled. "Not another rat, is it?"

He was just starting to calm himself, to feel a less scared and anxious, when he looked to where Danny was pointing.

The light betrayed a dark figure forming, hunching in the corner. As the fireplace swelled, its shape became more and more clear. The figure seemed more like smoke than a solid mass, and it floated and swayed from side to side just like the flame, just like the webs. It sat on its haunches, hunching over, with abnormally long arms draping along the sides of its legs and spilling onto the floor. Palms faced up, with fingers that were too long and jagged to be fingers at all. The shadowy figure's head leaned forward, toward the ground, if it was a head at all.

Clint grabbed Danny's arm and yanked him back to where Alex and Heather and Reid were now standing.

"What...is that?" Alex whispered.

Heather grabbed Alex's shoulders from behind and shook him. "It's the ghost. The creature. I thought it was a joke, just a—"

"Guys, I didn't do this," Reid whispered, as if afraid the figure would hear him. "Gotta get outta here. But the door...what do we do?"

Clint looked back to where the door had been and gasped. Unthinking, he lunged for the door which now stood where the original one had been.

"Come on!"

No one hesitated.

Clint whipped the door open and charged through,

the rest following tightly behind, fighting not to be the last out of that room, the last left alone with that thing. Grunts and groans issued from them all as they tried to force their bodies in front of their friends'. Every man for himself.

On the other side of the door, Clint had expected night and outdoors and escape. Instead, he ended up inside another room.

Chapter 6

Nothing in Danny's thirteen years of life had prepared him for this. He was crying, shaking.

All he could think about was how much he wanted his mother. She always fawned over him, but he loved every moment of it. He whimpered as he glanced about the room.

"I wanna go home. I want my mom," he kept mumbling. At this point, he didn't care who heard him or what they'd call him if they heard. "I'm scared and I wanna go home."

He jumped at Heather's voice. "Whoa! Look at this." She took a few steps forward, shining her light at the far wall.

As the room became illuminated by her flashlight, the darkness shifted. Slowly, but the room was growing brighter. He rubbed at his eyes as if it were just a trick, yet the room grew brighter still.

"Does anyone else notice that?" he asked. "The room? The light?"

An audible breath came from Clint. He took off his glasses and wiped the lenses with his shirt, then slowly put them back on and nudged them up over the bridge of his nose.

"Yep, the room got lighter," he said. "Like sunlight. But no window for it to come in through."

Danny drew back as Heather took a few steps forward.

"Look, over there," she said, enthused. "It's a crib."

It freaked Danny out. She crept forward, the only brave one of the bunch it seemed to Danny, until she was standing over the crib. She reached into it, an act of courage Danny would've never done, and pulled something out.

Cringing, he averted his eyes.

"It's a doll!" she said. "Looks brand new."

Danny peered at it with one eye still closed. If he hadn't just seen what he'd seen in the previous room, he might not have been scared. But he knew what he'd seen. It was a demon, the creature that haunted the house. He knew they'd been fools to come. Everyone knew the house was off limits. He wasn't sure how anyone knew, though. It was just common knowledge, something passed down through generations and widely accepted without asking any questions. Questions they should've asked before coming. Why is it haunted? What's it haunted by? What'll happen if we go inside?

Heather distracted Danny's thoughts as she spun around to face the boys, with the doll. She shook it back and forth, and the doll's head lolled from side to side, its eyes rolling open and shut.

Alex swatted it out of her hand. "Don't touch anything!"

The doll landed on the floor next to the crib. It lay on its back, eyes staring blankly at the ceiling.

"Anyone notice anything weird about this?" Alex asked. Even with the room illuminated by fake sunlight, he ran his flashlight back and forth from one end of the crib to the other. "Anyone? Anyone? Bueller?"

Heather leaned forward, peering inside it. She swept one of her dark curls out of her eye. "It's not old. Like, not like the house old."

Reid stepped forward and ran a hand along the crib. "No dust. And this cloth lining the crib, it's new. And clean."

"How did we get into a room like this?" Alex scratched his head. "This shouldn't even be in this house."

Danny whispered, "Haunted houses don't make sense. Maybe we walked through that door and went back in time or something."

Reid punched him in the arm.

"What was that for?" Danny rubbed his aching arm.

He experienced a fleeting feeling of déjà vu. Like he'd been in this room before. As he continued to rub his arm, he pictured himself at what must've been just over a year old, clumsily scrambling down the hall and entering a room he'd never been in. A room that was always closed off. Inside it was a crib that wasn't his.

"If you say dumb shit, I'm gonna punch you," Reid said. "It's that simple."

Danny scowled. "It's not that dumb. I mean, this

room doesn't belong in this house, like Alex said. It doesn't fit. I feel like, like I should know this room."

Danny glanced around at the cream-colored walls that looked so familiar and a painting of a family. A man with his arm around his wife and her arms wrapped around a baby. He found himself moving closer without meaning to, until he was face to face with the painting. As he studied the man, he could make out his father's details—the strong brow, the dark brown eyes, the straight line of a mouth that looked like it never smiled. And the woman could've been his mother, the more he thought about it. It was almost as if the painting was shifting, molding to his thoughts, memories. But that couldn't be. The hair that he moments ago swore was dark, almost black, was now blond, falling just past her shoulders. Lips peeled back into that smile that lit up Danny's world. But the more he stared at the picture, the more it changed. He tried to see his mother's eyes, but all he saw were dark holes where eyes should be. He took a step back and tripped. Hands struggled to catch him but failed, and he slipped to the floor.

"What's wrong with you?" Clint pushed his face in front of Danny. "Hey."

And just like that, Danny's feeling of déjà vu faded into nothingness. This wasn't his house.

"I mean, I don't think I know this place, after all," he said.

Yet something niggled at the back of his mind. Some memory, some *thing*.

"Maybe they lived here." Clint backed away from Danny and pointed to the painting.

Danny sat on the floor, struggling to understand

what he'd just seen. He looked back up at the painting, and the man he saw, clearly wasn't his father. He had dark eyes, thick furrowed brows, and much thicker lips than his father. And the woman in the painting had wavy raven-black hair that fell past her shoulders, soft doe-eyes, and a cute button nose.

"Did anyone else see that?" Danny asked. "The painting. It changed."

Clint reached out a hand to help him up. "Maybe you hit your head when you fell, huh?"

"No. It was my mom and dad, then it wasn't. Like their faces melted and changed. As soon as I saw their eyes, they changed. Same thing with their mouths and stuff."

"I saw it, too," Alex said. "I didn't believe my eyes at first. I thought it was a trick of light or something."

"What did you see?" Heather asked, excited.

Alex looked to Danny, and Danny nodded for him to tell them.

"I thought the lady had curly hair, like Heather," Alex said. "And then she didn't. When I first looked at the man, he didn't have eyes. Wait, no, that's not right. He had negative eyes. Like two dark holes where his eyes should've been. It was like seeing nothing, in the shape of eyes. I don't know how to explain it." He looked down at the floor.

Danny got excited. "Yeah, like that. I saw it, too."

"That doesn't make any sense," Heather said.

Clint poked his glasses higher on his nose and got all history-scholar. "It's the family that lived here way back then."

"You don't know that," Reid said. "That's not part of the story. You're just making shit up now."

"A man lived here with his family, a wife and baby," Clint said. "But no one knows what happened to the wife and baby. When King Philip and his men came to burn the house down, there was only one man. Only one person here."

"Liar," Reid said.

Clint straightened his posture, sticking his chin out. "You should know more than any of us. I heard that your dad's family has Indian blood, King Philip's blood. Maybe that's why your dad can't handle his alcohol."

Danny's mouth dropped open, and he thought his jaw would hit the floor. The room got so silent he could swear he heard Reid's blood boiling. Danny took a step away from Clint, like he was contagious and if he got too close he'd catch whatever it was. Reid's face turned bright red, and for a second Danny thought of those cartoon characters that got so hot under the collar, so pissed off that their heads popped off. He wondered if Reid's head was gonna pop.

Reid balled his right hand into a fist and charged at Clint. The whole thing happened in slow motion. Danny watched, his jaw still on the floor as Reid pulled his fist back. Knuckles white and shaking, he let it go. It was lined up perfectly with Clint's face. Danny almost couldn't watch, and then time sped up again just as Alex leaned in and shoved Clint out of the way. Reid's punch went wide, and he fell forward and caught himself on the wall.

A muffled sound came from nowhere and everywhere at once. Everyone hushed. Danny strained to hear better.

It grew louder and more distinct until he could

clearly hear a baby crying. The crying escalated into wailing.

"Maybe they still do live here." Danny's voice sounded rough and unfamiliar to his own ears, like it had scraped against sandpaper on the way out of his throat. "You hear that, right?" The crackle in his voice reminded him of the snap of the fire, and it unnerved him even more. *Did I say that?*

"A baby crying." Heather backed away from the crib.

"I told you not to touch anything," Alex said to her.

"Like me touching the doll did that. Whatever."

A soft, doleful melody wafted over the child's cries. A woman's voice singing, cooing to the child, though no one could be seen. At first, it seemed to come from one corner of the room, then another, then it filled the whole room as if it were coming from speakers lining the walls.

At the sound of the lullaby, chills danced up Danny's back and neck until he was left squirming as if trying to shake off creepy, crawly bugs.

The baby stopped crying and the lullaby faded into silence. The room grew quiet once more. If the sounds he'd just heard weren't scary enough, the silence became more frightening. It pushed unnaturally at Danny's eardrums.

"Can you hear that?" Clint asked.

No one moved or said anything.

Danny listened closer, afraid to breathe.

"No, I don't hear anything." Reid tilted his head from side to side.

"Exactly," Clint said. "No sound at all. The air in here feels weird. Like it's pushing on my ears. I can hear my own heartbeat. Dag, my own breathing, even. Like too much pressure."

Heather leaned her head forward, stretching her neck out. "I hear that, too. But what if…what if that's not our own heartbeat we're hearing, but, like, the baby's or something. Or the creature's? Or the lady's, even?" Heather cupped her hands over her ears, creating a suction, and pulled them away. She did this a few times.

"We just have to figure it out. Like a puzzle or a maze maybe." Clint stroked his chin. A pose he used when deep in thought, working on a scheme.

Danny had seen it a million times when they were up to no good. He sighed, hoping his clever friend might be able to work this one out.

Clint spun about, taking in the room. "Okay, so this room looks about the same size as the other one, except this one looks new and the other was old. What's possible? Did we end up in a secret room? Another world? I don't believe we can think logically here."

"Okay, Mr. Spock," Reid said. "Logic wouldn't have a door in a wall one moment and then disappear the next." He massaged his knuckles and finished with a crack.

Danny hoped he wouldn't haul off and try to punch Clint again.

"Yeah, like that's the weirdest thing so far." Heather snorted, shaking her head. "Boys. Logic. This could take a while." She moved back to the crib, leaned over and looked inside. Nothing. "Hey, la-deee. Creepy sing-ing la-deee," she mocked. "I think I see your baby in the crib. Yeah, right here. Pretty little baby!"

Danny cringed at her mocking. Always had to be the tough girl.

Alex scurried to her side and peered in the crib. "What're you doing? You crazy? There's no baby in there. And don't do that!"

"Don't do what?" She tiptoed her fingertips along the rail of the crib.

"Taunt the ghosts." Danny's voice cracked.

Heather lowered her voice. "But if the lady comes into the room, maybe she'll use a door." Her eyes grew wide and she wagged her eyebrows.

"And maybe she'll just appear or float through the wall," Danny said. "You don't know anything about ghosts, do you?" He wrinkled his eyes, fighting back tears. His mouth turned down, tugging at the corners of his lips. He wanted to scream at her, curse her for being so calm, so jokey in a situation like this.

"Pretty baby!" Heather continued in a baby coo-like voice. "Where's a pretty baby?"

Reid shoved her, and she landed on her ass, next to the crib.

"Ow, jerk!" she cried.

"Stop being so stupid." Reid crossed his arms.

"You're just scared. Big scared bully Reid. Ha!" Heather leaned forward onto her hands and knees. She stopped. "Hey, guys, look here."

It was a crack in the wooden floor that wasn't just a crack.

Reid was on the ground beside her first, running his hands over the floor. "It's a door." His fingers played over a little catch in between the floorboards.

"So open it." Clint sank to his knees and got a better look.

"But guys," Danny said, "maybe the next room will be worse than this one. This one wasn't really that bad, after all. Crying invisible ghost baby and momma. What if...if...if that thing comes back," he whispered. "You know, the dark smoky creature."

"I think our best bet is to keep moving," Alex said. "There's obviously no going back, so we have to keep trying to move forward." He kneeled, pried his hands in between the floorboard and the wooden hatch, and gave it a tug.

No wonder they'd missed it at first. Although it was entirely possible that it wasn't there until it was. The house seemed to have a way of doing that to them.

A small two-by-two hatch was visible in the floor, only slightly darker than the boards. Rusted metal hinges held it at the corner. The wood was withered and weak, and made Danny think of cockroaches and termites. *Creepy crawly critters*. He shivered.

The floorboards creaked but wouldn't give.

"Since when did you become the boss?" Heather put her foot over the door in the floor. "What makes you think we should all just blindly get in there? What if it's a box full of rats? What if it's, like, a tomb of some sort and we get sealed in there forever?"

Danny hadn't thought of either of those possibilities. "She's right. We should just stay put. There are worse things than this."

Alex called to Reid, "Give me a hand." He pushed at Heather's foot until she finally stepped off.

Just before Reid could wedge his fingers in between the cracks, footsteps sounded but no one was moving. Alex was next to Reid. Heather behind her brother, next to Clint. Danny was leaning over them all. He glanced around the room, half-expecting to see someone coming at them, and half-hoping he wouldn't see anything.

"Who moved?" Heather whipped her head around.

"Nobody," Clint said. "I mean, none of us did."

When sight failed, Danny froze, trying desperately to hear any little sound. He held his breath until he thought he'd pass out.

And then it started again. Heavy, shuffling footfalls moving across the room, toward them. The boards creaked and bent under the invisible weight.

"Let's not wait to find out what it is!" Alex yelled at Reid. "Get this thing open. Pull, on three. One... two...three!"

They both yanked and the door in the floor finally budged, spilling them backwards to the floor. It smacked all the way open, cracking down into the floor with a reverberating thud.

The footsteps were now just feet away.

"Go, go, go!" Alex yelled.

Everyone hustled to climb down into the doorway in the floor. Clint first, then Heather, but Danny remained frozen. He knew he should be moving, but he couldn't.

He slipped into that déjà vu moment again, back when he was a baby in that off-limits room, and footsteps were coming down the hall. Moments later, his mother peeked her head around the corner, a worried look on her face. She hurried toward her little boy, Danny, her arms outstretched. He could almost feel her hands on him, so warm.

"Move!" Reid shouted.

But Danny stood still. Stuck in between a memory and the moment.

He wished he could be that little baby being discovered by his mother instead of being in this awful house with this awful creature and no way out.

"Alex, get in. I'll grab him."

Reid's voiced wafted through the memory, tickling Danny's ears, yet he couldn't let it go.

He watched with a faraway stare as Reid jumped to his feet, grabbed him by the scruff of his shirt and dragged him to the doorway. Danny thought he felt his mom's hot hand on his arm. She always had such warm hands.

Reid jumped down inside and pulled Danny in beside him.

The footsteps seemed to stop just short of the door. The floorboards creaked as if someone was waiting, shifting their weight in that spot.

Then the door slammed shut.

Chapter 7

"My arm! My shoulder!" Danny jumped about like he'd been lit on fire, waving his arms up and down. "Make it stop!"

"What's wrong with you?" Clint said. "Quit flapping around like a damn bird." He grabbed him by the shoulders to still him.

It didn't work.

"It hurts. It burns!" Danny squirmed in Clint's grasp.

Clint held him and shook him. "Snap out of it. Hey!" He pulled Danny close and looked into his eyes. "Settle down!"

"What's wrong with you?" Heather asked. "Danny, what is it?"

"My arm's tingling. And my shoulder, it burns. Like somebody held an iron up against it." He yanked himself free of Clint and pulled at the top of his shirt, exposing his shoulder. His eyes grew wide. A burn, in the shape of a hand print. "Look here. My skin is burned." Speaking faster now, his words a jumble. "When we were up in the other room, I couldn't move. It was there in my house, I think. No, the creature, it was everywhere. The footsteps, my mom, the creature, and then I tried to get in through the door in the floor, but it grabbed me by the shoulder. And then you pulled me through, Reid." He took a deep breath, catching up to himself.

"It touched him, and it burned him. Whoa." Clint took a few steps backward, away from Danny, his gaze on him the whole time. He rubbed his hands on his jeans like he was trying to scrape off some unseen cooties.

Danny watched as his best friend shied away from him.

"What was it, though?" Alex asked. "I didn't see anything. Anyone." He surveyed Danny's burned shoulder from afar. "You think it was the creature? That smoky thing that did this?"

Danny was crying now, slumped to the floor in defeat. "What if that's, you know, a mark, by the creature? And now it's gonna come for me first." His body racked with sobs, his chest heaving and falling with each one. "I wanna go home, I wanna go home, I wanna go home." Like a mantra, he kept repeating it to himself until his crying lessened.

Snot was dripping down his face, to his lips, so he pulled his shirt bottom up, exposing his belly, and wiped at it. He gave off a combination of a snort and a sniffle, sucking the rest back in.

"Maybe you're imagining the whole thing," Clint said. "Your arm burning and all that."

Spit came flying out of Danny's mouth. "Maybe the

picture didn't change right in front of our eyes. Maybe an invisible ghost didn't chase us down here. Maybe we never saw a smoky demon-thing, either! None of that happened, right? Oh, yeah, it did. So shut up!"

"Maybe the demon's inside you already." A grin lit up Reid's face. "That's why you're foaming at the mouth right now."

"Stop!" Alex yelled. "Everybody, just stop. Fighting each other is not helping."

He stepped in between Reid and Danny, but Danny noticed how much distance Alex was keeping between him.

Danny finally calmed himself and looked around the room. A basement. The entire floor was made of cement. The walls were made of that same cold material, a dark gray finish. *How the hell did we make it through the door in the floor and fall to a cement floor without getting hurt? I don't even remember hitting the floor.* He scratched his head.

Light was spilling in through a small rectangular window at the top of the basement wall. *No flashlights needed here.* He breathed a sigh of relief. Things were less scary in a room with some light. It made him think of his own house. His basement had looked a lot like this before his little sister Rebecca was born. Sad and cold. Once Rebecca was born, everything lightened up. Dad took the deadbolt off the basement door and started a project to turn it into a livable space.

But before that, Danny remembered venturing down those stairs to his basement, unnoticed, one morning. The air around him had grown colder as he descended, sending a chill through his pajamas. Barefoot, he could feel the cold cement on his tiny feet. At the bottom, he flipped on a light and the basement came to life.

He'd immediately grabbed at the first thing he saw —a tarp. He peeled it back to reveal a crib. The same crib he'd seen when he was younger. The crib that never once contained a baby. It was wrapped tight in something that looked like cellophane, preserving it forever as new. As he journeyed further, taking tarps off everything he saw, he had discovered a world of baby things he'd never seen before. They hadn't been his.

A flipping feeling in his tummy forced him back to the present with his friends in the old haunted house.

"Guys, I don't feel right," he said. "I feel dizzy. Is it hot in here? It's hot. I'm hot." When he spoke, his breath came out in visible puffs in front of his face.

"You're sweating like a pig," Reid said. "But it's freezing down here." His words left trails of hot air wafting through the cold basement as well.

"You don't look so good." Heather reached out with the back of her hand, toward Danny's forehead.

Before she could make contact, Alex swatted her hand away.

"What'd ya do that for?" Heather crinkled up her nose. "Stop hitting my hands."

"Just don't...don't touch him." Alex diverted his eyes from Danny.

Danny couldn't believe what was happening. They were afraid of him. Afraid of what he might have. Contagion. Death. A whimper escaped him. He slapped his hand over his mouth.

"I was just gonna check if he has a fever."

She reached her hand out again, but Alex caught it and pushed it down to her side, once again.

"See, even you think that thing got to me." Danny's mouth pulled downward as he fought back a cry.

"It's not that." Alex met Danny's eyes this time. "Don't be so dramatic. Maybe you got a flu-bug or something. Mom will kill me if I bring Heather home sick." He shrugged.

"Besides," Clint's deep storyteller voice came out, "there's nothing in the history of this house to suggest that touching is a problem."

"Right," Heather said. "So that should make you feel a little better?"

"But…" Clint said, "we are in uncharted territory. I've never heard of someone being inside this house. No one's ever set foot within these four walls and walked out to tell a story of what happened, what they saw—"

"You're not helping!" Danny yelled. He wavered on his feet. "The room is spinning. I smell smoke. And I think…" He sank down to his knees and leaned over, clutching his stomach. "Gonna puke." He coughed and dry heaved. Wheezing, he whipped his head back, trying for air.

"Calm down. You're panicking." Alex kept his distance.

Danny didn't care anymore. Not that his friends were afraid of him, the looks they gave him, or how they wouldn't touch him. All he could care about was the fever brewing, stirring up a storm of nausea.

"It burns." Danny's voice came out hoarse. "Like a fire in my stomach and throat." He rubbed at his neck, scrunching his face.

"Dag, man," Clint said. "It's just stomach acid, that's all." He didn't sound convincing.

"No, something's wrong." Danny laboriously

climbed to his feet and leaned against the cement wall. It felt soothing to his hot body. He pressed his cheek into the wall. "Gotta cool down."

Sweat dripped down his temples in rivulets and trickled down his neck, into his shirt. His lungs burned and ached from deep inside. Each breath felt more labored, more strained. And sounded that way, too.

"Maybe it's your allergies." Reid crossed his arms and stepped back. "Dude, maybe you have asthma."

Danny opened his mouth to speak but shook his head instead. He bucked again, back down to his knees. Everyone took a step back. A brownish stream of vomit spewed from between his lips. Everyone jumped back further. Danny choked and gagged, fighting it the whole time. When he was finished, he flung his head back, eyes to the ceiling, and took in a raspy constricted breath.

Chapter 8

Heather couldn't just watch Danny go through all that alone, so she moved closer, batting away Alex's attempt to grab her again. Reaching out, she drew nearer to Danny, then froze a few feet from him. She grabbed the closest thing to her while staring at Danny. It was a tarp. She pulled it off, revealing a crib wrapped in cellophane. She reached it forward to wipe the vomit off Danny's mouth, but the closer she got, the more she hesitated. Maybe it wasn't such a good idea to get too close or touch him.

His eyes were all wrong. The whites were streaked with red. Fiery zigzag lines crept and swam out from the corners and grew, getting lost in the brown of his irises. Like something was alive in there, spreading its sickness through him.

Heather dropped her arms and stumbled back a few steps. She regained her balance and locked her fingers together behind her back.

"We should quit talking and get outta here. I mean,

we're wasting time." Concern for Danny had been squashed by what she'd seen in his eyes.

Her words were met by a series of nods from the rest of the group, while Danny sat hunched on his knees.

"The window," Reid said. "We'll all squeeze through." He dropped his backpack to the floor and began rummaging through it. He pulled out the hammer.

"No offense," Clint said, "but I don't know if we can all fit through there." He shot Danny a sideways glance.

"We're wasting time," Heather repeated. "He doesn't look so good," she whispered.

She cast her worried gaze on Danny, who shimmied up against the wall for support.

Hammer in hand, Reid moved to the wall with the window. He strained onto the tips of his toes, trying to reach the bottom of the pane but falling short. He groaned.

"I got this," Clint said to Reid. "Outta the way."

Reid turned, scowling.

"Anyone give me a freaking' hand?" Clint bent over the wrapped crib and started to yank it toward the window.

Relief crept into Heather's heart as Clint's plan unfolded. She hurried to help him, along with Alex. They lined the crib up under the window.

"Nice." She patted Clint on the back.

"Wait." Alex took a step back from the crib. "What if we shouldn't touch anything. Heather touched the doll in the crib, and then the footsteps came."

Heather rolled her eyes. "Don't be a dumbass. The

doll didn't make anything happen. This whole house is wicked fucking haunted, no matter what we do."

"I got it from here," Reid said. "Stand back and hold the crib still." He climbed into the wrapped crib, then pulled off his shirt and draped it over the glass. "Look out." He grabbed the hammer, raised it above his head and took a good swing.

Glass shattered, but luckily most of it was shielded by his shirt. A few pieces rained down on Reid, who dipped his head and waited. Heather stood by, twirling her hair and watching as he took swing after swing until all that was left were a few jagged edges.

"Okay, Heather, you gotta get the rest. I'll boost you up." Reid pointed to his shoulders.

A trail of blood trickled down his temple, and a few shards still rested on his shoulders.

With the back of her hand, she gently dusted the glass off his bare skin. She climbed into the crib, then wobbled up onto his shoulders, grabbed the hammer, and began tapping out all the remaining shards.

"Okay, we're good," she called down.

The crib shook and creaked under their combined weight.

"This thing isn't gonna hold long," she said.

Reid turned his head and shook his shirt out before handing it to Heather. "Put this over the bottom of the window, just in case."

As she lined the window with his shirt, she could hear Reid's breath as he struggled to keep her on his shoulders while standing in the unbalanced crib.

"Now climb through." Reid tapped her on the leg. "Then Alex, Clint. And then you guys can help pull me and Danny through."

"Wait," Alex said. "Not Heather first. What if—"

Heather was already working her way out. Her head and upper body disappeared though the window.

She called back, "Guys, it's a hallway."

With that, she pushed off and was through in an instant, slithering through like a wily snake.

There was a long silence when Heather got to the other side as she shifted and turned herself around. After contemplating the urge to inspect her new surroundings, she resisted, knowing forward was better than where they were. Had to keep moving.

She finally poked her head back through the window, gazing down on their expectant faces. "Come on, ass-wipes."

Alex was the next through, getting a push from Reid and a pull from his sister. The crib protested under their weight, and Reid lost his balance and fell over.

Heather popped her head back through. "You okay?"

"Yeah, yeah." He waved. "C'mon, Clint."

Clint had no problems either. Then came Danny.

Heather sighed in frustration, realizing everyone was still afraid to touch him. "Seriously, guys, we're all in this house together. Grab Danny, already!"

Halfway through, Danny's stomach rubbed from the tight squeeze and he let out a yip.

"What's wrong?" Reid pushed at the bottom of Danny's feet. "Keep going!" He slapped the side of Danny's foot. "Go!" he grunted.

"Glass cut my side."

"Sorry," Heather said. "Thought I got it all." She softened her voice. "But you're almost there. Come on."

"But what if there's more glass?" Danny froze.

Reid sighed. "On three."

In unison, Reid and Alex counted, "One... two...three!"

On the three, Reid pushed and Alex and Heather pulled Danny into the hallway. As Danny made it through, Heather heard a crash from back inside the room. After poking her head through, she saw Reid in a heap on the broken crib.

She was about to ask if Reid was okay, when he looked up at her and said, "Don't you dare ask. Just don't."

Heather bit her tongue and watched Reid get to his feet.

"Can you guys reach down a bit? Pull me through if I jump?"

Alex poked his head through, beside his sister. "Shit, you crushed that thing." He leaned down and reached for Reid.

Heather matched her brother.

REID CLIMBED out and shoved the crib aside, then lined up under the window. "Ready? Here I come!" He jumped up, reaching for his friends.

Heather missed. Alex

caught Reid, but the weight was too much. Reid started slipping out the window, the shirt sliding from underneath him.

"Whoa!" Alex yelled. "Help! Grab my feet!"

Heather pulled herself back through, and she and Clint grabbed Alex's feet and pulled with everything they had, their own feet digging into the ground.

"Pull!" Alex shouted.

Heather moaned, exerting all her strength, and then finally got him through. She reached for Reid as he, too, was pulled inside. Just through, he made an Indiana Jones-type move and reached back to grab his shirt before it fell back into the room. Once everyone was tucked through the window, they collapsed to the floor.

"That sucked," Heather said.

She rolled over to see Danny trying to get to his feet. He wavered, and there was nothing she could do to catch him in time. His legs buckled and he crumbled to the floor. His eyes rolled back in his head and then he was still.

Chapter 9

Danny finally woke up. Slow and confused, he lay on his back on a hard surface. Voices echoed in his ears, but he couldn't make out any words. Couldn't make out anything over his heartbeat pounding away on his eardrums. Light played in beams across the ceiling he stared at. That little bit of light burned his eyes and he squeezed them shut as they watered from the pain. He tried to open them, but they wouldn't see. If he could look into a mirror just then, he wondered if his eyes would be all red, like that one time Reid got hit so hard by his dad that it gave him a subjunctive hemorrhage. For over a week, Danny was afraid to look at Reid. His mind had conjured all sorts or terrible things—a spider had crawled into Reid's ear and laid eggs behind his eye and now they were hatching, or that Reid had been possessed by the devil and his true colors were finally coming out. Out of his eye.

Danny squeezed his aching, burning eyes tighter shut, and then he swore he felt his heart beating through them as well. Like a battle drum slamming down, the feeling beat through his whole body.

A whimper escaped him. His arm fell away as he heard the voices getting closer. As he peeled his eyes open, he began to see shadows, strange blobulous human-like shapes leaning over him.

"Get away!" He tried to scramble backward, using all fours until he hit the wall. "Guys! Where are you? The smoke, the creature, it's coming for me!"

The shadows leaned in closer still, and Danny shrieked, "Get away, demon!"

And then his eyes saw a little bit more. One of the figures had dark curly hair. It fell over the figure's shoulder as it leaned closer. Sound was coming from this curly-haired shadow, different from the others.

"Heather, is that you?" he cried.

"It's me, Danny. Can't you see me?"

Heather's voice brought him more to his senses.

He couldn't make out the other voices in the background, a mixed hush of mumbles.

He blinked his eyes open and shut several times. The last time, he opened them wide, staring at the blob with curly hair. Her face began to form and he could see her brow furrowed.

"Wh-what's wrong?" he said.

"I'm just worried. We gotta get you outta here. You got a bad fever, Danny. You blacked out."

"No, I'm totally fine." He inched his way up the wall, to a standing position.

The hallway lurched to the side, spilling Danny back to the floor.

He laughed, nervously. "Shit, maybe I'm not good." He sat still, waiting for any other movement. "Like when I get motion sick." His stomach churned with acid at the thought. "Like I'm on a boat."

Reid shouted, "What the hell?"

"Did you guys feel that?" Alex asked.

The hallway moved again, and this time Danny was pretty sure it wasn't just in his head or his stomach. On the floor, Danny rolled over to his right, like the house was tipping over down a hill. After lifting his head, he could see the rest of his friends struggling against the same gravitational problem.

"Earthquake?" Clint yipped, as he struggled to grab onto something while sliding down across the floor.

"The house is tilting!" Alex screamed.

He grabbed onto Heather and the two of them slid on their butts, toward the far right wall, heading down that invisible slope.

Danny lifted his arm and shielded his face from the inevitable impact of smacking into the wall. And then the moving stopped. He moved his arm away from his face and looked around. The house wasn't at an angle at all. Moments earlier, he and his friends were sliding across the floor. But now they all sat still, on the floor.

Danny flitted his eyes up and down, side to side, inspecting the room, but everything appeared back to the way it was. "Did any of that really just happen, or did I dream it?"

Heather untangled from her brother. "It happened. The house just shook us up." She rubbed her shoulder. "This is starting to freak me out."

Clint yelled, "Let's get outta this hall before something else happens." His voice quavered. "What are you guys waiting for? I knew this house was haunted for real." His eyes were large and crazy.

That look on his friend's face made Danny want to cry. Right after he vomited. The feeling in his stomach grew—burning acid churning like an angry sea.

"After you, ass-wipe." Reid motioned to the hallway. "You know the way?"

"Why ya always gotta be such a dick?" Clint poked Reid in the chest.

Reid smirked. "At least I have a dick." He moved in closer to Clint and bumped his chest. "You wanna do this?"

Alex forced his arms between the two. "Stop being such pussies, both of you!"

Alex's body bucked forward as Heather pushed him from behind.

"You're all a bunch of losers!" she said.

Rage seemed to course through every one of them except Danny. He was too dizzy, and he couldn't understand how they could be fighting at a time like this.

Clint grabbed a fistful of Heather's curls and yanked her head to face down the hallway. "If it's so easy, why don't you get us out? So smart! Which door?"

Alex twisted Clint away from Heather and punched him square in the face. "Don't touch my sister like that!"

"Stop, guys, please," Danny said.

But no one even looked in his direction. As he strained his eyes to see better, he realized all his friends had shadows. But they didn't make sense. Although his friends all faced different directions, each one's shadow stood directly behind them. And the shadows weren't right. They weren't mimicking his friends' movements. Instead, the shadows acted as if they were locked inside an invisible box, trapped. The shadows threw their hands up and wildly banged against the invisible walls to get out, to get back inside their own bodies. They kicked and threw themselves against that supernatural barrier, but it wouldn't budge. It was like something was controlling his friends' bodies, making them fight and argue.

"There are six doors," Alex said. "How will we know which is right?"

"Your sister knows everything," Reid said. "She's wicked smart. She can do it."

Alex pointed a finger in Reid's face, dangerously close to his eye. "She's a hell of a lot smarter than you, that's for sure."

Clint stepped in between and shouted in Alex's face, "You and your sister think you're so much better than everyone else. So smart. So tough. So perfect!"

As he watched them argue, Danny felt like they were getting farther and farther away from him. No one moved, but the hallway seemed to elongate, stretching them down, down, down an ever-growing hall while he remained. Felt as if the atmosphere was laced with anger. It danced and crept along his skin like some invisible insect. It crawled in his ears and mouth and up his nose when he breathed in, as if the house, the energy, pushed them, goaded them into fighting each other. And pulled their attention away from Danny. He wondered if they'd forget all about him while lost in their anger.

Farther and farther away they got until their angry voices were just murmurs.

To Danny's left, in the hall, he noticed the first door, which didn't look welcoming. It was a dark, smoky aged wooden door standing about five feet. Its hinges and doorknob were rusted and flaking. He shuddered. Past that one was a bright green door, the color of sweet summer grass, like the door to his father's shed. He knew all his dad's tools were off-limits in that shed, so he mindlessly looked past it. He couldn't make out the two doors at the end of the overgrowing hall, but to his right, there were two more. One was metallic silver, like the door of a cooler in a restaurant. The idea of going through that door made him shiver. Just past it was a door that looked like it belonged in a dollhouse. Soft lilac with pink trim and a pink door handle.

He shook his head. None of those doors looked right. None of them *felt* right. He was certain he'd have known which door to go through, but doubt had taken over. He dropped his head to the floor until a warm breeze from down the hallway brought a familiar voice whispering in his ear.

"Danny..."

He drew his head back up to look down the hall once again. Such a long hallway and he was so tired. He could make out the outline of his friends still bickering in the hallway, but he focused on another shadow, one he hadn't seen until then, standing at the other end of the hall. He forced his eyes to adjust, and noticed the shadow waved at him. He stared at the hand until he could make out the rest of the figure, a woman's figure. He saw blond hair which fell straight to her shoulders. Glasses sat high on her delicate nose, and her mouth pulled back into a full-lipped smile. He knew that smile.

"Mom," he whispered.

The shadow called out, "Danny, come lay down in your bed. You look terrible. Let Mommy take care of you." She waved her hand again, beckoning him closer. "Mommy's little boy, come here." Her smile broadened.

Danny didn't hesitate. He trudged down the long hallway, past his arguing friends, and stopped just short of the door, gaping at his mother in disbelief.

His mother stepped to the side of the door. "Go in. I'll be right there, sweetheart."

Danny nodded, then wrapped his hand around the doorknob and began to turn it. The figure of his mother melted into nothingness out of the corner of his eye, but he continued forward anyway. It was his door, after all. How did he not notice that earlier? It was the door to his bedroom.

"Danny, wait!" Alex yelled. "Don't open that door!"

Even though Danny heard him, he wasn't going to let anything or anyone keep him from his mom. So he flung the door open and crossed the threshold.

Heather's voice sounded like a faraway dream. "We can't let him go in there alone. It's settled, he picked the door. Let's go."

He didn't understand what she was talking about. All he wanted was his mom, his bed, and to sleep for a long time.

Chapter 10

When Reid first led them into the room, Danny was nowhere to be found. Flashlights searched the room until Reid's stopped on a figure lying on a rundown bed. The frame rusted, the mattress tattered and dingy and appeared to have been chewed up by rats. The room reeked of mold and decay.

There was a dilapidated dresser straight across from the bed against the wall. The wood was rotted and had strange holes that resembled smolder marks. Atop it stood a four-foot mirror. Although intact, it was covered in a sooty smear.

"Danny?" Reid approached the bed, apprehensively, placing one foot fully flat before lifting the other.

The others also turned their flashlights onto Danny, lying on the bed.

Alex moved to within a few feet from the putrid mattress, and a look of disgust washed over his face.

"Hey, Danny, I know you're not feeling well, but I don't think...not that bed."

Danny opened his eyes and acknowledged his friend before him. His tired eyes softened, and he gave them all a warm smile. "Hey, guys, thanks for coming. Mom just went to get some medicine."

Reid looked to his friends, confused. "Huh? What the fuck is—"

Alex lifted a hand toward Reid. "Your mom? She's here?"

"She'll be right back. I asked her to open the windows, maybe bring a fan. It's so hot."

"You got a fever, remember?" Heather stepped behind her brother and leaned over his shoulder to look at Danny in the grubby bed.

Danny rubbed his arm. "Yeah, I think from those scrapes I took on the way to the house the other night. Infection." He nodded, slowly.

Clint scratched his head. "The other night? Where are we right now, Danny?"

Danny laughed, which turned into a cough. "You guys are being weird." He lifted a brow. "We're at my house. You guys came to visit me 'cause I'm sick. Duh."

Reid turned to look at his friends, wondering if they were seeing what he was seeing. They all stared at Danny, worried expressions on their faces. He started to talk but thought better of it.

Danny weakly lifted a hand to his brow and wiped off the sweat. "This must be a real doozy of a fever. My eyes...I can't see so good. All cloudy and fuzzy."

It must've indeed been difficult because Danny's eyes were no longer streaked with red. The white was completely gone, swallowed up by the flaming blood-red that had taken over, as if he'd never had any white to them at all. Reid could count on one hand all the things in his life that'd made him scared and then added this to the list.

"Just close your eyes and rest until your mom gets back." Alex frowned and looked back at Reid.

Reid pulled the others across the room, beside the dresser. He turned back to his friends, and whispered, "He doesn't even know where he is."

"We don't really even know where we are," Alex said. "This is Danny's house, but it's not. We're inside a one-roomed house, yet we've gone through a few different rooms, a basement, and a hallway."

Clint hugged his arms around himself. "It's the mark. The house, haunted. And the creature. Now... he's dying."

Heather's hand came up so fast Clint never had a chance. The sound of her palm across his cheek made a *thwack* sound.

Clint's head jerked to the side.

Reid erupted with laughter and bit his tongue to hold the rest back. "Sorry."

"Enough!" Heather snapped. "Don't you say any—"

A blood-bubbling scream bellowed from Danny. "It burns! Make it stop! It's burning me!"

Heather leaned forward, but Alex held her back. She didn't fight his hold this time.

"What is?" she asked. "What burns?"

"Everything! Inside!" Danny convulsed and lurched forward, holding his stomach. Coughing and heaving, he clawed at his skin as if trying to release the fire. "Get it out! Make it stop!"

Sweat beaded and pooled all over his body, his clothing sticking to him. His skin turned flush-red as if he was sunburned.

Reid watched, paralyzed by fear.

Then with one painful sounding gasp of air, Danny flung back down to a laying position. For a long moment, he appeared to not breathe at all.

Reid could hear his own heartbeat as everyone in the room seemed to hold their breath, anxious to hear the faintest sound, the slightest evidence that Danny was still alive.

The air grew heavy and warm. The feeling of a sleepy night around a campfire rushed in and tried to lull Reid's body into false sleepiness. He panicked.

His voice came out fragile, almost inaudible. "Does anyone else feel tired?"

"And hot," Alex said.

They all nodded.

Clint scratched at his chin. "Something terrible's about to happen."

Danny flung his eyes wide open and stared at his friends. "You found Mom." He smiled.

"Mom?" Heather said. "Where?"

"Just beside you." Danny pointed at the dresser—the mirror.

Chapter 11

Clint didn't see Danny's mother. *No one here but us.* And then he doubted that thought.

He glimpsed something in the mirror, dark and dirty and smudged by some smoky quality, but he was sure he could see a figure. Some*thing* without a defined shape cast a dark reflection across the mirror. It was as if the smudges on the mirror came to life and moved and mixed together to form something large and amorphous. It swayed ever so gently. Clint wasn't sure if it was his own imagination that was moving it or if it was all real.

He felt the others' bodies all come together, pressing against him. They pushed themselves into a mass in the corner of the room.

The heat and heaviness enveloped them, pulling them to the floor with invisible hands, into a heap of tired bodies. Clint clung to his friends and they to him as they sunk to the floor. They lay helpless in the corner, and Clint could feel someone's fingers gripping him so tight he was sure he'd bruise. But he didn't care. The proximity to his friends was the only safety raft in the sinking ship. A heavy feeling, like cement bricks tied around his ankles, pulled at his consciousness and he was sure he would pass out. A taste ran across his tongue, acrid and bitter, and he thought it must be what fear tasted like.

Clint fought the heaviness as he watched Danny reach out to greet a shadow as if it were someone familiar. It moved toward him, peeling from within the mirror. Claws materialized first, working across the wooden frame. They scratched along the wood before they finally found purchase and sunk in. As the form pulled forward, its head inchoate, black and opaque as it pressed through, followed by a long, smoky trail which coalesced into a torso and body. Clint wavered, his mind not able to comprehend what was unloading in front of him, what was making its way toward his best friend. His bowels tightened and clenched, and he hoped he wouldn't lose their contents. Nothing he'd ever seen in his short life had prepared him for this, to understand this horror, this evil thing before them. Even through all the stories about this house, they were always just that. Stories. But *this* was real.

Sounds of tiny wings began to flutter. First, one or two sets, then what seemed like hundreds. Clint couldn't see what was making that sound, but he knew it was probably better that way.

"Mom," Danny said, as the thing moved closer to him.

Clint wanted to call out to warn him, to get to his feet and save him, or run away and hide from what was about to happen, but his body wouldn't obey the simplest commands. He felt like he was trapped in one of those nightmares where he needed to scream but no sound would come, in which he needed to run but his feet were glued in place.

Petrified still, by fear, the oppressive heat, by the evil of the room, Clint and the rest of them could only watch in dread.

As Danny reached out, the smoky figure pulled up over the foot of the bed, with hands first, if they were hands at all, and then dragged the rest of its vague form over the dingy mattress. It slithered onto Danny's chest, like a serpent, and crouched there, now more like an ape. It reached its smoky tendrils down, clasped the sides of his head and leaned forward, its wispy shape bending and folding unnaturally until its head was over his.

Danny tensed his feet and shot straight up off the bed as he bellowed, the rest of his body pinned down. From his position, Clint couldn't see what was happening to Danny. All he could see was the black cloudy back of the creature.

The cries didn't last, though, as the figure shifted and bent further over Danny's body until their foreheads seemed to be touching. Danny's agonizing howl shriveled and tightened as if he were choking on something.

The darkness oozed forward. With each touch, Danny's body sizzled, and smoke billowed out of his pores.

It's burning him alive.

Clint swallowed down a scream, not wanting to draw any attention from the creature. He looked away, to his friends next to him.

Reid's eyes bulged from their sockets.

Tears streamed down Heather's face as she watched, frozen.

Alex slammed his eyes shut.

AND THEN THE heat and heaviness of the air finally won and pulled them all down. Clint fought to stay awake, struggling to force his eyes to stay open. He watched each of his friends give over to it, their bodies going limp as they drifted into unconsciousness. He bit down hard on his lip, hoping the pain would keep him awake. Blood trickled down his chin, and for a moment he thought he might make it. But he lost the battle.

Chapter 12

Alex woke up, fuzzy-headed. He couldn't think or see clearly and his thoughts were a muddled mess. *When did I fall asleep? Why? Where the hell am I?* There was an arm across his face. It wasn't his.

He moaned while pushing at the dead weight, and the arm finally fell off him. Reid's arm. When poking at him got no response, Alex twisted to the side and saw Clint staring back at him.

Clint blinked a few times, his eyes a groggy mess.

He licked his lips. "Did we all fall asleep, Alex? It was so hot, so heavy, and then—" His eyes grew wide as he looked past Alex, into the room.

"You okay?" Alex rolled over too quickly and got to his knees.

The world swam. It felt like that one time he rode the Thunderbolt rollercoaster at the park. When his eyes stopped floating, he saw what Clint was looking at.

Heather was on her knees, by the bed, head in her hands. Sobbing.

"Heather?" Alex made it to his feet, with Clint's help, and approached the bed.

Grunts and groans issued from Reid behind as he began to wake up.

Before they'd passed out, the room had been dark, only lit by flashlights. Now the room was bright, as sunlight poured in from the window by the bed. But there were no window in this room when they'd first followed Danny in, Alex was sure of it. There it stood, in all its glory, beckoning to him as if safety lay on the other side. *Could it be that easy?*

Something was scraping at the window from the outside. Alex's mind raced, drawing a picture of that smoky creature running its nails along the glass. One deliberate footstep after another, he moved closer to the window. But it wasn't the creature, it was a tree branch swaying in the wind, tapping.

Heather's sobs pulled Alex's focus from the window. At first, he barely noticed the bed or what was on it. He placed a hand on Heather's shoulder. She jumped. Her eyes were full of tears as she looked at him, her face a mask of sadness and defeat.

Through sobs and short breaths, she said, "Danny...it got him." She pointed a shaky hand to the bed.

The bed looked the same as it had before—dingy, worn, tattered. But what lay on top of it was something else.

Sometimes, when you see something so horrible, so awful, your mind blocks out all comprehension, trying to save you from it. Alex had heard that before but never really understood it until just then.

Where Danny had been lying was now only a charred ruin. Blackened, burned flesh, features marred and unrecognizable. No hair stood on his head. It looked like a marshmallow that'd been held over the campfire for too long. Crispy, black. Alex looked down at Danny's hands. They were balled up into claws. All that remained of him were his clothes, perfectly intact. Not a burn or scorch mark anywhere on them. It was like when everyone else had fallen asleep, someone switched out Danny's body for this crispy shell and dressed it in his perfect clothes.

And then it all came crashing down on Alex. The realization smacked him. Danny. Dead.

He turned his head and puked. When he was finished, he puked again. The hacking and coughing continued after he'd stopped gagging. It was Clint this time. On hands and knees, he heaved and ralphed.

Heather's small hand grazed the top of Alex's head, and he reached up and pulled her down to him. He hugged his sister like he never had before. He couldn't let go. Her sobs continued in his ear, her warm tears spilling down his neck.

"Is that...?" Reid said. "Wait—what? Not...Danny?"

Clint grabbed Reid by the shoulders and spun him away. "Don't look. Just turn around. Please don't look."

For once in his life, Reid didn't fight. He turned his back on what used to be Danny.

He seemed to be holding back the tears, but then he lost his shit. "It's all my fault. My fault. I made us come. He's dead. Why?"

Clint rubbed Reid's back in the only moment of actual tenderness Alex had ever witnessed between the two. It squeezed at Alex's heart to see them like that. He would've given anything to trade this Reid for the snarky bully he knew. He would've given anything to go back in time and stand up to that bully and say no. Say they weren't going to blindly follow Reid to this house. To tell him the whole thing was a stupid idea.

Those thoughts turned Alex's sadness to anger.

"It is your fault!" he yelled. "You *made* us come! And now he's dead!" Alex shook his head.

Heather pushed her fingers over his mouth. "Shh, shh, shh…"

As Alex eyed Reid with disgust, he thought he caught a movement out the corner of his eye. So slight, he wasn't sure he saw anything at all. That was when the laughter started, but it wasn't coming from any of the group. It was coming from the mirror. A wisp of smoke, a shadow of nothing, darted across it.

The laughter grew from soft and playful like a child, to a thunderous and deafening roar. The room quavered.

Alex grabbed his sister's arm and pushed her toward the window. "Go! Get out! Everyone out!"

"Where? How?" Reid's face screwed up into a mix of fear and confusion. "The door's gone! Where do we go?"

THE LIGHT, sweet glow of freedom beckoned him. "The window!" Alex feared that was exactly what the creature wanted, that they were playing right into its trap. *But where else can we go?*

Reid smashed his flashlight through the glass. It dropped from his hand and he finished the glass off with his fist, without hesitation. Blood trickled from his knuckles, down his arm. He jumped through first and called out to Heather. Alex gave her a boost and Reid pulled her through. She reached back for Alex, panic brewing in her eyes.

She whimpered, "Hurry. Shadow."

Alex threw himself through and landed on his wrist. A bolt of pain shot through it. Screams from Heather and Reid forced him to forget the pain and scurry to his feet. Both of them had wide eyes as they turned back to the window and reached for Clint. Alex swallowed down his racing heartbeat when he saw it. Behind Clint. Reaching for him with those smoky curling wispy fingers. Clint waved his hands, trying to get his friends out of the way as he dove through the window.

He made it.

Alex reached to pull Clint to his feet, but his wrist stung with pain. He winced and pulled it back. He glanced back to the window and it melted away until it was gone. Nothing but a wall. Once again, the house had tricked them. *Where's the tree? Where are we now?*

"Where's your other shoe, Clint?" Heather asked.

Everyone looked down at Clint's feet. His left sneaker was missing.

Chapter 13

The glares of Clint's friends bored holes through him, their unvoiced accusations ringing in his ears, as they kept their distance from him.

Clint rolled his eyes and kicked with his shoe-less foot at nothing on the floor. "Dudes, when I jumped through the window, I hit my shoe on the pane and it got knocked off. So stop looking at me like that, jack-offs!"

His words were met by steely stares and quiet.

He walked past them, seeing them take nervous steps backward to avoid him. He pretended to stumble, and fell forward, his hands reaching out in Reid's direction. Reid dodged to the side to avoid contact. But that action didn't solidify Clint's worries about his friends' fears. Reid was a dick and would've done that just for fun to see if Clint would fall or not. No, it was the fear that flashed in his eyes. And then it was gone. *Can I blame them, really?*

Trying to block out his friends' unease toward him, he marched forward. They were in a short hallway, perhaps ten feet long, at most. At the far end of it was a door. But not a normal door. It was only four feet tall, and instead of a doorknob it had a metal latched handle. The walls were covered in old dark blue wallpaper which appeared to be peeling away in some parts. It looked familiar, but Clint couldn't place it. He'd been here before, hadn't he? The floor was covered in a thin, cheap pale-gray carpet with well-worn footprints beaten into it. The fabric stained and worn to the floor in some places.

"This looks like that weird hatch to your attic, Reid." Clint pointed. "And your floor?"

"Yeah, it does." Reid crossed his arms and his body stiffened. "I don't think we should go in there."

"What other choice do we have?" Heather stepped forward, reaching for the handle.

Alex stepped in front of her and put a hand up. "Wait. Think about it, guys. In every single room, it seems like we've done exactly what this house wanted us to do, played right into its plan. Maybe we shouldn't go through that door."

"What other option do we have?" Clint said, the rift between them growing more evident by the second, as all his friends stood as one, opposite him.

ALEX SHRUGGED. "Let's stay right here and not go through that door. At least until we think of a better option."

They all sat down where they'd stood, Alex with his

back to the little door, his sister in front of him, Reid to her side, and Clint a few paces from the rest.

"Your hand is pretty cut up," Heather said to Reid. "You need to wrap it. Alex, help me. Tear off some of my shirtsleeve."

Alex pulled and yanked at her shirt. It was a lot easier in the movies. He struggled, then finally got it to rip and handed the shred to his sister.

"Gimme your hand," Heather said.

She took Reid's bloodied hand and gently wrapped her shirt-shreds around and around, covering all the nicks and cuts as Reid winced and grunted. Once satisfied, she tucked the end of it under and looked at her handiwork.

"I think that should do it."

A nod was all the thanks Reid gave her.

Everyone grew silent. Worry and indecision hung heavy in the air.

Heather's voice was gentler than normal. "I know it sounds a bit silly, but I keep hearing Mom's voice in my head. She'd want us to pray. 'Pray keeps the devil at bay', she'd say. Can we try?"

Clint had never prayed a day in his life. He didn't believe in any of it. He believed in the God called money, to which his father was a slave, but not some guy in the sky, all-knowing, all-seeing being. No way. As far as he and his father were concerned, money was what made the world go round and made people do what they did, not some invisible man up above. But he wasn't about to alienate himself from the group even more.

Small nods were issued forth in agreement. Heather scooted to the side of her brother and reached for Alex and Reid's hands. They took hers, but stopped before grabbing Clint's.

With his hands reached out to his friends, Clint's eyes grew large as they did not reach back. "Guys, I'm not infected! My shoe fell off when I came through the window. That thing didn't touch me!"

Reid shook his head. "It's not that. I just don't wanna hold another guy's hand. It's sorta gay." He looked to Alex. "Do you?"

"Nah, me neither," Alex said.

Heather let out a huff and shook both their hands away. "Never mind, then. It was a stupid idea anyway." She crossed her arms. "Jerks."

It *was* a stupid idea. Clint was both relieved he didn't have to fake pray and disheartened that his friends were keeping their distance. Absentmindedly, he began touching his shoe-less foot. He stopped when he realized Reid was staring at him.

"What?" He pulled his sock up higher.

Reid squinted and tilted his head. "What, what?"

"I dunno." Clint shrugged. Then he reached down and yanked off his other shoe. "Feels weird to just wear one." He flung it at the wall where the window had been.

The wall shuddered and momentarily gave in where the shoe had hit. Then it was normal again.

"You see that shit?" Clint asked. "That just happened, right?"

The hair on his arms stood up. Goosebumps ran wild over his body, pricking from the back of his neck to his calves. He shivered.

Everyone was on their feet now, staring at the spot the shoe had hit the wall.

"It bent and moved," Heather whispered. "Like a funhouse," her voice grew smaller, "except not fun."

The shoe lay motionless on the floor, about six inches from the wall.

Everyone was still.

And then something else happened. The wall bent out forward, like something or someone, or a mass of bodies reached out from the other side. Hands of all shapes and sizes pushed out towards them and then stopped. Tiny fingers, long fingers, palms splayed out, knuckles kneading at the malleable wall, moving it forward. Soon, the shoe rested against the wall which was now much closer than before.

"It's just trying to scare us to make us go through that little hatch door," Alex said. "Just stay still."

He stood firm, and the others followed suit. Clint was shocked to see Alex remain so calm. *Hands just reached out from inside the wall, for Christ's sake.*

Clint rubbed at his eyes and waited for something to happen. He began to wonder if what he'd seen had really happened at all. Then the wall reached out again, even closer this time. Fingernails—or were those claws —pushed and threatened to break through. When it stopped, only the toe part of the shoe was still in sight. The rest had been swallowed up.

"I dunno. I'm wicked scared." Heather reached out for her brother's hand.

He grabbed it and squeezed.

Once again, the wall moved closer, eliminating another half-foot of space and shrinking the already small hallway. The sound of wings beat from some-where inside the wall with all those hands and fingers.

Flap, flap. Scratch, scratch.

Clint imagined an awful scene from that famous movie where the birds went crazy and tried to shred people alive. Clint shivered. *I don't think those are birds.*

The wall moved closer. And closer still. *Nowhere to go.*

A clicking sound came from behind, and they all swung around to see. The hatch door sat open a few inches, where it had been closed only moments before.

"Keep an eye on that door!" Reid shouted.

"WHAT ABOUT THE WALL?" Clint asked. His breathing was getting shallower. He blinked furiously as his peripheral vision shut down. *Not now, not here.* He panted.

"Alex and Heather, you watch that door," Reid said, "and Clint and I will watch the wall."

Clint turned to Reid and nodded.

"Stay with me, man. Don't freak out. I need your help." Reid looked Clint in the eyes and nodded slowly. "You got this."

Reid's focus and determination pulled Clint out of the panic attack. He swallowed his fear and stared down the wall, feeling a renewed sense of bravery.

Clint turned to face the wall, and gasped, losing all his newly achieved boldness. While he'd been focused on staying calm, the hallway behind them had closed in. Only four feet of hallway stood between wall and door. He backed up and bumped into Alex, who jumped back, brushing off the invisible cooties Clint had left on him. Heather stared at her brother, wide-eyed, fearful. Clint tried not to let it get to him. Not now. Hopefully there'd be time for him to criticize them later. He wanted to hold it all back, but it welled up inside. Pissed him the fuck off.

He reached out and touched Heather with one hand and Reid with the other. "There! Now you've all touched me. I told you I didn't get infected by that thing, but none of you believed me and you're acting like a bunch of bitches. Believe me or not, but we're all in it together now."

"It's not like you're big on telling the truth," Heather said. "You're the biggest liar of the bunch."

"Yes, I am. But I'm not lying now. I swear."

Reid's lip pursed in anger. "If you just infected us—"

Clint groaned. "Then we're all dead. Dag, man, get over it. We've got bigger shit to deal with right now." He pointed to the wall. "Who even knows what this infection is or how we get it? The creature touched Danny and then he got sick. That doesn't mean we can't touch each other without getting it, too. And for the last fucking time, I'm not infected!" *Dumb shits.* He shifted his gaze from them to the wall.

The window was back. Broken, the way they'd come through it. The wall wasn't moving any longer, either. Everything remained as normal as it could, like it had never moved at all.

Reid stepped closer to the window and peered inside the room they'd left behind. He shrunk back. "It's either the window or that door. We won't have any hallway left soon."

Clint could only imagine what Reid had seen. Danny's ashy, crisp body lying there, waiting for them. He closed his eyes at the thought of it, but that only made the images clearer in his mind. Reid's suggestion terrified him. The last thing he wanted was to see his best friend, or what remained of him, in that state again. He wanted to remember Danny the way he was in life. *In life. Danny's dead.* Clint choked down the beginnings of a sob.

"I don't wanna…" Heather shook her head. "I can't go back in there…see him or that thing."

Alex dropped his head. "Then we move forward again."

"Through the hatch?" Reid said. "I don't think we should."

Clint panicked at the idea of seeing Danny's body again. "We can't. We can't. I won't go back in there. He's in there. Dead."

He bent forward, tucking his head as far down as he could go. *Catch my breath.* His knees shook with each uneven breath.

"Okay, we won't," Reid said. "We can't. You're right, Clint. Calm down."

Then a voice came from the room they'd left behind. It was Danny's voice, Clint was sure of it, but knew it couldn't be.

"Mom? Mom? Where are you? I can't see anything."

Impossible.

Clint's heart leapt, and he darted to the window and leaned his head through. "Danny? Danny, is that you?"

He looked about, but saw no movement. No proof of Danny but the burned ruin still on the bed. He stared at in horror, waiting for it to move. He pictured Danny's crispy lips opening and moving, calling out to his mother. He imagined his burned claw of a hand, reaching out for someone to hold it. Someone to help him. Someone like his best friend. *I let my best friend burn.*

Clint stared, unblinking, trying to focus to see. But the body didn't move. Not the lips or any other part of him. Danny was dead.

Danny is dead.

But his voice still floated through the room. "Mom? Mom, I'm scared." Light sobs trailed behind his words.

Clint pulled his head back through the window and clutched his ears to block out the sound. "We can't go back. We can't go back in there. God, make it stop." Tears fell from Clint's eyes.

For the first time in his life, he hoped there was a God, someone to comfort poor Danny, to take him from this awful place and help him and his remaining friends out of this horror. He hoped and said a silent prayer to that invisible man in the sky, but deep inside, he knew they were all alone.

He moved forward to the little door and flung it open with his foot, keeping his hands over his ears. He never turned to see if the others were following as he ducked through.

Chapter 14

Alex watched Clint disappear through the hatch as the wall pressed in again.

"Looks like we're moving forward." Defeat washed over Alex.

Once again, the house had pushed them in the direction it wanted the group to go. Were there any choices?

On the other side of the door, the girl Alex had always seen as his bratty pain-in-the-ass little sister, softened and ran to Clint's side. He was sitting on the floor, Indian style, mumbling and shaking his head, with his hands still clasped over his ears and eyes shut tight.

In that moment, Heather reminded Alex of their mom as she gently pulled Clint's hands away from his ears and held them in hers.

She whispered, "It's okay. You don't have to see it anymore. We're in a different room. Look."

How many times had their mom used that tone on them when they were hurt or scared or upset? Like magic, it always worked, and it was no different this time with Heather. She channeled their mom's soothing ways. A sense of pride washed over Alex as his sister cooed to Clint.

Clint slowly lifted his head, opened his eyes, and looked straight at Heather. She smiled and nodded, releasing his hands. As Clint climbed to his feet, his face was twisted in agony and his eyes were still full of tears.

"Did you guys hear him?" he asked. "Couldn't you? He was calling out. I thought maybe…maybe he might still be alive. Didn't you hear him?" His mouth drooped. "He was calling out."

Heather pulled him in for a hug. "He wasn't. It was the house. It's messing with you." She rubbed his back. "I'm sorry, we didn't hear it. None of us did. Did we?" She turned back to the others.

Alex shook his head. "It was just you, man."

Reid nodded. "I didn't hear it either." He stepped forward and put a hand on Clint's shoulder. "The house, the creature, was messing with you. Messing with us. I dunno, maybe trying to get us to separate. Get you back in the room and leave us in the hallway. But Danny's gone." Reid choked on the last words. He wiped at his nose and stepped back, stiffening.

"I don't blame you guys," Clint said. "I woulda been scared, too. Like, shitting-my-pants scared."

Heather's tone remained cool, soothing. "What do you mean?"

"When I came through the window and my shoe was off, and that creature was so close. I think it pulled my shoe off. At first, I thought it had me. Had my foot. That maybe it touched me, marked me, and I was a goner. And then you all looked at me like that. Like I was some dead man walking. You wouldn't come near me or touch me in case I was infected."

Clint was right and Alex knew it. They were afraid. At least, he was. The guilt hit him and he looked away.

Clint's words came out soft like a shy child. "But I wasn't. I told you."

Alex still couldn't look at him. His eyes stayed glued to the floor. That old wooden floor. It looked familiar. Alex lifted his head to see that they were inside the same four walls as that first room they'd walked into. Same fireplace. Yet different.

As if in response to his thoughts, the fireplace came to life, a flicker blooming into a flame.

"Hey, guys," Alex said. "We're back to where we started. Kinda." He pointed to the walls, where there were now no cobwebs, no dust bunnies lying in the corner. The table wasn't on its side, but upright. The stools were righted and placed alongside the table. Everything looked clean. Warm and inviting, even. A soft glow from the fireplace lit up the room.

"Whoa, it's like we went back in time or something," Reid said.

Heather took a deep breath. "Does anyone else smell that?"

"Smells like...food." Reid clutched his belly.

Alex's stomach growled. *How long have we been in here, anyway?*

Wonderful images of a pot boiling over the fire jumped into Alex's head. Meat and vegetables, perhaps celery, carrots, onions and potatoes all simmered. Food.

"What's going on in here?" Reid walked closer to the fire. "I swear somebody's making dinner. This is super fucked."

Alex moved up beside him, stealing a glance into the fireplace, but there was nothing there. Just the fire. No pot. No dinner.

As strange as it all was, this was the least afraid he'd been since entering the house. The room, the fire, the tempting scents of stew wrapped around him like a soft blanket. For a moment, he could relax and take a deep breath instead of fearing when and from where that creature might come next.

He sighed.

And then the voices and shadows started.

First, it was a voice, low and muffled. A man. "He is not well. And he's not getting any better…"

And then a woman's voice. "He's fine, he's fine. You worry too much." She coughed.

While searching the room for a sign, Alex's eyes failed him.

He looked to Clint, whose eyes grew wide as he muttered, "But you do hear that, right?" He clutched his ears again. "No more. Please."

Heather put a shaky hand on his shoulder and brought her other hand up to her lips in a shushing gesture. She got his attention and nodded.

Clint wasn't crazy. They'd all heard it. But why were they hearing it? Perhaps these ghosts were trapped here forever, after their deaths. Alex shuddered.

The man said, "He's not fine. And now you're ill as well."

Alex kept searching for where the voices were coming from.

The woman's voice sounded raw, like she had a sore throat. "The doctor said it shall pass."

A flash of light, like a momentary reflection of

sunlight off a window, drew the group's attention to the same spot—the bench by the fire. A translucent figure of a woman appeared. Soft, light, and hazy. She wore a long pale gown, her hair pulled back in a bun. She looked like the woman they'd seen in the picture, when they heard the baby crying.

In her arms, a blurry shape of a body appeared. A baby. She cradled it against her chest.

The man's shape also began to appear. His form was darker and more solid. His eyes were like two lumps of coal, dark and empty. "The doctor doesn't know. I saw the way he looked at you. He lied. He was afraid."

"Of what, dear husband?" She bent forward and placed a kiss on the baby's forehead.

"To catch his death from you both."

"Nonsense." She turned her head and coughed, a painful, wet sound. "Just stir the stew. We need a little warm food." She hugged the baby closer to her chest.

"You haven't kept anything down. Nor the baby." The figure of the man stepped closer, walking right by the kids, oblivious to their presence. His footsteps creaked upon the floorboards.

"My fever is much improved already." She lifted her head to him and smiled.

Alex could tell she'd lied. Felt it like pinpricks racing across his skin. Her sickness, even as a ghostly vision, was palpable.

The man reached out a hand and touched her cheek. "I fear death is looming, hovering over this house, you and the child. Watching, waiting—"

"Shush. No more. Death comes for us all, some time. Though, I feel this is not our time. But when it does comes, I will meet it." Her eyes looked exhausted.

Behind her, the fire burned brightly, casting shadows across the walls. Alex hoped his eyes were playing tricks on him as he watched shrouded wispy shapes dancing, turning and twisting around each other in the shadows.

The man's voice boomed, growing louder with each word and shook the floor. "I cannot abide. I will not." He scowled and stormed away, each footstep rattling Alex's teeth. And then the man disappeared.

The woman turned toward the group and her appearance shifted. She no longer held the baby. Her hair was disheveled and fell around her shoulders in sections, while some of it was still pinned into the bun. Her dress was too big. It hung from her body, making her appear to be made of skin and bones. She slowly raised herself up to a standing position. She took a few steps toward the group, looking them over one by one.

Alex was sure he should've been afraid of her, some sort of ghost looking straight back at him, but he wasn't. He felt sorry for her. She had a soft, motherly air, with concern and kindness in those tired eyes.

The closer she got, the more her outline disappeared. Her dress, her hands, her hair and face still there but losing form.

She lifted one hand out to Alex. "Death comes for us all, some time."

The woman faded away into nothing, but the weight of her words remained long after.

Chapter 15

A gust of icy air howled through the room and the fire went out, leaving everyone in a chilly darkness.

Clint felt like a bubble blown from a wad of Big League Chewing gum, about to pop. He couldn't think straight and now he couldn't see. He wanted to scream, but the sound got stuck in his throat. He wanted to run, but where could he go? So he slouched on the floor, in the dark.

Images of Danny's burned body flicked through his mind. Danny crying out played over in his ears even though he tried to block it out. It was no use. All of it was in his head. The tiny pieces of fear and doubt tunneled through his brain like termites eating away at a house's foundation.

"Make it stop, make it stop, make it stop!" he screamed.

"Hey, guys," Reid said.

Clint jumped.

"Remember when we had that wicked snowstorm last year and lost power for three days? Just pretend it's like that. It's no big deal. We'll just hang here for a minute." He sounded unsure.

Heather still had her hand on Clint's shoulder. Was it her hand? It felt wiggly and squishy, like worms.

"Worms!" Clint screamed. "There are worms on me!"

They spread from his shoulder down his arm, slithering, oozing down to his hand.

"Get 'em off me! Help!" He ripped his hands from his ears and flung Heather's hand from his shoulder.

No more worms. No more anything. He sighed.

"That was just my hand, dickwad! I was trying to help you." Heather's voice hit him like a slap in the face.

He cringed.

"No, it was worms. They were everywhere. Everywhere!"

"WHO STILL HAS A FLASHLIGHT? ANYONE?" Alex asked.

"I do!" Heather fumbled around, and then a light flickered to life. "Holy hell, I forgot all about it." The light dimmed and came back full again. "Batteries might be dying though."

The light went out and Clint screamed.

Heather tapped the side of the flashlight a couple times and it came back on. "You gotta calm down. You're not helping." She shone the light in Clint's face.

He batted the light toward the ceiling. "Get it outta my face!"

"Sorry, sorry. I was just trying to see you. Oh, my God!"

Something moved. A long figure, too long to be a man. Its hands were splayed in front of the body. The shadow crept across the ceiling, through the light, and disappeared.

"Did you guys see that?" she asked.

"Y-yeah," Alex whispered. "We're not alone."

The light flickered off.

Heather tapped it once again. "Come on, you little fucker. Light, light, we need light here." Her voice raised a whole octave.

"Get that light back on!" Reid yelled. "We can't just sit here in the dark like this."

Clint felt the pressure again. The unmistakable feeling that he couldn't take anymore. He needed to run, hide, scream for days and days until his voice ran out and his throat bled raw.

"Stay close to each other," Reid said. "We can't get separated. Alex, I'm gonna put my hand on your shoulder, okay?"

Clint tried to see Reid reaching for Alex, but it was too dark and all his mind's eye would conjure up was the shadow lurking, waiting to strike.

"Alex, grab Clint. Clint, you grab hold of Heather. And nobody let go."

Clint whimpered, "I can't move, I can't. Too scared."

The idea of finding something other than Heather when he reached out kept him frozen. It became hard for him to breathe. Too much movement might give him away, alert his location to that thing in the room. *Be still, be still.*

"Clint, get your shit together!" Reid shouted. "I'm telling you right now, if you don't do what I say, I'm gonna beat the shit out of you!"

Clint reached out and found Heather's shoulder. "I got her."

"I'm reaching for you now, Clint. Don't freak out." Alex found Clint's shoulder. "It's me. My hand. Relax."

Clint tensed under Alex's hand. He remembered the way it'd felt when he thought the worms were on him. He tried to block it out and think of anything else. He remembered he and Danny watching MTV the night before they came to the house, arguing over the words to a song. *Kyrie Eleison...*

His fingers clamped into Heather's shoulder. "Lord, have mercy," Clint whispered.

How fitting. He was smart enough to know what that song meant and it had nothing to do with lasers, like Danny had sworn. He'd totally take a laser right then, though.

"Stop digging your nails into me!" Heather jerked, but he held on.

"Sorry," he said. "It's just so dark."

Whispers floated through the darkness, sounding like they were everywhere and nowhere all at once.

Heather tapped the flashlight again and it came back on.

Another frigid breeze blew through the room. Clint, Heather, and Alex shivered. Reid most likely did, too.

"I'm gonna lead us to the front door," Heather said. "We're gonna try it and see if we can get through. Follow me, don't let go. I don't know if this light will last."

After a few short steps, it flickered again. But before it went out, the shadow reappeared.

"It's here again," Clint said. "The shadow. That thing. Here in the room. Get out. Everyone run!" He let go of Heather and shook Alex's hand away.

It was as if the darkness itself was a thing. It closed in around him. He couldn't catch a breath. It pressed in on all sides, squeezing his lungs. He gasped. Ran forward blindly and tripped over something. He hit the floor with a hard thud, smacking his face on the wood.

He could hear the others, voices muffled as if they were far away in another room, another world.

"Clint—"

"Stay still…"

"Come back…"

But in his mind, he was alone. They were gone. The darkness pressed in closer. He touched his aching nose and felt wetness. Wiped it on his shirt.

"Carry a laser through the darkness of the night," a voice sang.

He knew that voice.

And then realization crept over him. He'd tripped over something. What was it?

The same voice tickled his ears, this time much closer. He could the feel breath on his neck. Cold, dead breath. Cold, dead words.

"Clint, I wanna go home." Danny's voice was in his ear. "I'm scared. That thing, that creature is everywhere."

Heather's flashlight flickered on once again.

In the light, Clint could see Danny, charred and blackened, reaching for him. Clint couldn't think clearly. All he knew was that his friend needed him. So he reached out and touched Danny's fingers. Crispy, cold.

They crumbled, ash falling to the floor.

The cold turned to a searing hot pain. Clint shook his hand to put out the burn on his fingertips.

Chapter 16

When Heather's flashlight flicked on again, Reid could see Clint on the other side of the room, reaching out to the Shadow. He saw the creature's tendrils, long and spindly, about to touch Clint's hand. But he was so far away.

"Clint! No!" Heather screamed.

"It's the creature, don't touch it!" Alex cried.

Reid grabbed them to keep them from running to Clint. "It's too late."

They watched the creature reach out to touch Clint's hand.

Heather yanked free from Reid and threw the flashlight at the creature, beam first. A perfect spiral, like Joe Montana throwing a Hail Mary. It was a perfect shot, and had the creature not been made of smoke, it would've hit it in the back of the head. But it went straight through and hit Clint instead.

A scream pealed through the room.

The shadow disappeared.

The flashlight hit the floor with a thud. Flickering on and off, it spun around and around, until it finally stopped. It made Reid think of earlier that summer when he and Alex had played spin the bottle for the first time, with his crush Stacy Keene and a couple of the other football cheerleaders. Reid had given it a good go and it spun several times before stopping just past Stacy. He couldn't have planned it any better if he'd tried. She was blond, had those blue eyes that made you think of summer skies at the beach, and the pom-poms on that girl made her an early bloomer for sure. Reid's heart had thudded. Everyone had been watching, so he'd made it quick. Too quick. She leaned forward, on the floor, pursing her lips. His hands began to sweat, like springs had arisen from all his pores. He wiped them on his jeans and leaned in. Licked his lips—

The flashlight flickered out.

"Danny!" Clint wailed. "Where'd you go? Danny?" He started sobbing. "I don't think that was really Danny. Guys...guys, where are you?"

Reid squeezed his eyes shut, hoping that when he opened them this would all have been a bad dream and he'd see Stacy's lips in front of him. This time, he'd take his time with the kiss. If only a kiss were his biggest concern. If only Stacy's lips were the scariest things around. He peeled his eyes open and saw nothing. A dark room. And Clint was sobbing.

Reid gulped down a growing rock in his throat. "Clint. Hey, we're here."

He wanted to say more, but he couldn't. It was like he was struck stupid. What could he say to him now? He'd seen that creature touch Clint, and had a pretty good idea that it meant he was done for, just like Danny.

And it was all Reid's fault. None of them had wanted to come here. It was all his stupid idea. He'd forced them into this house and now they were trapped and dying.

WHY'D he have to be such a dick? Was it even a choice for him? He was a bad seed, after all.

None of them wanted to come here. It was all his stupid idea. He forced them into this house and now here they were, trapped and dying.

"Reid." Alex sounded distant.

Reid tuned it out. He wanted to suffer, stew in knowing it was all his fault.

He felt a hand on his shoulder.

"Hey, Reid."

"Yeah, yeah. I'm here." He shook Alex's hand away.

"We gotta get outta here, somehow. We can't just sit." Alex fumbled around, his feet shuffling. "Heather?"

She didn't answer. And then Reid heard muffled voices. Two of them. Slowly, he moved toward the sound. His foot kicked something and he tripped but caught himself. It was the flashlight and it flickered back on, illuminating Heather squatting over Clint.

Reid and Alex yelled, "Don't touch him!"

She shot them a wicked glare. "You're both fucking kidding me, right? We've been through all this." She turned back to Clint, put her hand on his shoulder and rubbed it.

"It wasn't Danny, was it?" he asked her. "My finger's burning. I don't think that was Danny."

She didn't answer, just shook her head.

"My hand feels all tingly and warm, too." He shook it out.

The tender sight of it made Reid's chest squeeze. He forced a deep breath and moved to them. Reached out to help Clint up.

"What're you doing?" Alex asked. "If he's infected—"

"Heather's right," Reid said. "I don't think touching him is the problem. Not us touching him, anyway."

Clint took Reid's hand and got to his feet. "Thanks," he said.

What had just happened to Clint sunk in for Reid. Clint seemed too calm.

Alex stared at Reid with that crazy bug-eyed look he got when something was too wild to comprehend.

REID SHOOK his head and hoped he'd sound convincing. "We gotta get outta here. That's the only way any of us will make it. And soon. If we get out, I think we'll be okay, infected or whatever. We have to try."

They all stared at him in puzzlement.

"We can sit around here like a bunch of fucking babies and cry, or we can get the fuck out."

Heather grimaced. "Yup, you're still a dick."

Reid swallowed another rock in his throat. "That's right." He shrugged.

Whatever they needed to believe to get them going.

The front door called to Reid like Stacy's bright cherry lips. But just like then, even though he wanted what was in front of him, he was afraid. There wasn't any choice. They had to keep moving, keep trying to get out. The next door could be the one.

He marched up to it, hands clammy and shaking, and flung it open. He wasn't surprised when it didn't lead outside.

Chapter 17

I t was a hallway, though not like the previous one. Reid reached out and touched the wall, finding it hard and cold, like stone. He stepped one foot inside the hallway, and the worn wooden floor creaked in protest beneath it. At least they'd be able to see in this hallway, thanks to the torches that hung every ten feet. A small flame burned inside each one. The hall was long and only wide enough for them to move in a single file. Reid led the way, with Heather, Clint in between, and Alex bringing up the rear. Each footstep they took was slow and cautious, and the floor groaned, filling the hall with an eerie sound, with every move they made.

"I can't see the end of the hallway," Reid called back over his shoulder. "It's like it just goes on and on."

"We gotta keep going," Alex called back. "Keep moving."

The last word bounced off the walls and kept reverberating down the hallway ahead of them.

Reid picked up the pace. A couple minutes passed

and nothing changed. The hall still went on with no end in sight.

"I'm getting tired," Clint said in a breathy voice. "And hot." He braced his arm on the wall and leaned in.

"Reid, stop," Heather called ahead. "He needs a break."

Reid turned back to his friends and saw Clint's face was red like a tomato. He was leaning against the wall, his breathing audible.

"Sorry." Clint gulped. "So hot."

"We've got to get out of the hallway," Alex said. "I don't wanna scare you guys. It's just a feeling, but... someone's following us."

Reid could feel it, too. Something he couldn't put into words, but he feared it just the same. Something was behind them, just out of view, following.

"Heather, lean back against the wall," Reid said. "Clint, walk past Heather, come to me."

"I can't. I'm so tired. Just need to wait here a bit longer."

That's when
the tiny voices started. Piercing whispers.

"Watching..."

"Waiting..."

"Watching..."

"Waiting..."

It sounded like the voices came from behind and danced across the walls, up the ceiling, past everyone. And now they were circling back.

"Now!" Reid shouted at Clint.

Clint pushed himself off the wall and rushed past Heather.

Reid scooped Clint over his shoulder, in a fireman's carry, and hurried on down the hallway. Pure adrenaline gave him the strength and will. He grunted as he tried to keep his breathing steady.

"*Watching...*"

"*Waiting...*"

"You hear those whispers?" Heather called out. "Where are they coming from?"

"Keep moving!" Alex yelled.

And still the hallway didn't let up. Reid steeled himself, trying not to think about his legs or his lungs, both burning like motherfuckers. He thought about Stacy and her lips and how if he could just get out of this thing, he'd plant a real kiss on her. The hallway began to turn to the right and slope downward, as if to challenge him further, but Reid didn't falter. He kept going, his legs turning into jelly, one painful step after another. For another five minutes, the hallway went on, sloping and turning. He never looked back to make sure the rest were following. He couldn't. He had to focus. He never took a moment to ask Clint if he was okay. He couldn't spare the breath. *Keep moving.*

And then the hallway opened, growing to about ten feet wide, revealing a winding, ascending staircase.

Reid wanted to topple over, to drop Clint's weight, take a goddamned deep breath and relax for a moment, but he couldn't. He knew someone or something was following them. Even though he couldn't see anything, the whispers were enough.

"*Watching...*"

"*Watching...*"

"*Watching...*"

Nowhere to go but up. He took a deep breath and

lifted his foot for the first step. As he wavered, Reid felt a hand on his back.

"I got you." Alex said.

He steadied Reid enough to take another step. Then another. Reid risked a glance back to make sure his friends were following and to make sure Alex still had his back in case he fell.

He saw Heather reach back and grab one of the torches off the wall. It illuminated their path further down the hall, and they all turned to see what lay ahead. At the far end, the torches began to snuff out one by one, heading toward them. The wooden floor creaked with what sounded like tiny footsteps, shuffling quickly down the hallway.

"Watching…"

"Waiting…"

Heather spun around, trying to find the source of the voices. Everyone's eyes followed the light as it bounced off the floor, ceiling, walls. Reid's breath caught in his throat as the light cast a shadow on the walls behind them. Tiny figures with flapping wings raced up and down the wall, chasing each other, nipping at each other's heels.

They had no choice. Forward into the darkness once more.

Chapter 18

Heather was the last to reach the top of the stairs. She gasped at what lay before her. Defeat sunk in as she glanced about the large, white circular room with no doors or windows. The only exit was the stairwell they'd just come up. But that wasn't an option.

She knew where they'd come from, and her mind could only imagine what waited for them down there. She'd heard the whispers, the creepy voices trailing them through the hallway. Evil little fairies, their feet barely touching the ground as they half-ran, half-flew over the floor and walls.

Instead of the pretty Disney-esque fairies that Heather had watched in so many movies, they had dark ashy faces, long mouths with sets of jagged teeth, beady black eyes devoid of light, hunched backs, and long necks pushing out and forward.

Instead of pastel pinks and blues, they wore brown

and black, their clothing tattered and rough. Wings like bats.

As she thought these terrible things, she watched Reid finally let go of Clint, the weight too much to bear. He eased him to the floor and collapsed beside him into a heap, panting. His eyes rolled back until his lids closed.

"All that for nothing," Reid strained. "Down that hall and up those stairs, and here we are in a room with no other way out." He took a deep breath.

"Looks a lot like a hospital, all white and clean and bright." Heather glanced around the room.

Something about it was so familiar it tugged at her mind.

Clint coughed, a racking painful sound. "I think I need a hospital."

The familiarity of the room dawned on Heather. "Reminds me of when I was in the hospital, after that football game we played. Remember?"

No one replied.

"Guys?" she said. "Douchefaces!" She turned to Reid. "You must remember that, Reid, don't you? My wrist? That was some kind of sack." The last words rolled off her tongue rather snarkily, and she wished she could take that tone back.

Reid avoided her glare.

"Even smells like a hospital," she said. "All medicine-y."

She waited, but no one said anything, so she let it go. She was talking just to make noise, anyway.

Heather turned back to Clint and put the back of her hand across his forehead. She pulled away quickly, shaking it out.

"Wicked hot! He's burning up, for real."

His skin was bright red, almost glowing. It made her think of Rudolph the Red Nosed Reindeer and she almost giggled. Except this was her friend Clint. The burning body boy. She could feel the heat coming off him when she kneeled over him. It pulsed in time with his heartbeat. Sweat glistened all over his face. Big droplets pushed out of his pores, trying in vain to cool his burning. His head rolled to the side as if his neck couldn't support the weight of it any longer. His eyes also rolled back before the lids slammed shut. He let out a long, shaky breath.

As Heather reached out to him, she felt a hand on her own, drawing it back. It was Alex. Her eyes shot him the question.

"Let him rest," he said. "Just give him a sec."

She nodded and attended to Reid instead. "Wicked impressive feat of strength." She stared at the heap of Reid on the floor. "Never thought you had it in ya. Reid the Hero."

He shook his head. "No hero. Just wanted to get the hell up those stairs. Figured if I was carrying the sick kid, you guys would let me go first." He took a deep, even breath. "Those things. Those whispers and footsteps…" he shivered. "I wasn't gonna wait around."

She shot him a sideways glance and bit her lip. "Nice, ass-wipe. That's the Reid we all know."

"Dick," Alex said.

Reid's gaze shifted to the side and he shrugged. "What can I say?"

When he looked back, his eyes widened. Heather followed his gaze and turned around. Clint, who only moments before was nearly passed out, now moved toward a hospital curtain at the other side of the room.

"Where's he going?" she asked.

Clint pushed aside the curtain. There was a gaping hole in the wall, like a doorway. A dark one.

"Hell no," she said.

A large, white wooden door formed within that dark hole in the wall. The only thing that made it stand out from the rest of the white room was the chipped, peeling paint, well-worn and beaten from years of facing the harsh New England winters.

Heather gasped. "Isn't that the door to Clint's basement?"

Alex nodded. They both turned to Reid, who seemed like he was shaking off an invisible chill.

"You're wrong," he said. "It's the hatch to my attic. Again."

"No, it's not," Heather said. "I don't know what you think you see, but it's clearly the worn-out white door to Clint's basement. Duh." She rolled her eyes.

Heather worried as Reid shakily got to his feet. She thought about reaching out to help and then thought better of it. That douche-face would only slap her away. *Macho dick.*

She was pretty sure that was the door to Clint's basement. But what was Reid seeing, then? Didn't he know what his own attic door looked like?

"Seriously, Reid?" Alex scoffed. "It's the basement door. How can you mistake that for the hatch to your attic?"

"It's a goddamned hatch," Reid snapped. "My attic, dipshit!" He paused as if contemplating something huge, scratching his head. "Maybe we're all seeing different things. Like the house is showing us something that applies to each of us?"

"But how?" Alex asked.

"Danny?" Clint said.

He moved to the hatch, reached out and grabbed the handle.

"Clint, don't!" Heather shouted.

He wrapped his other hand around the handle and gave it a yank. It fell open and he lost his balance. When he regained it, he shuffled forward like a zombie and disappeared inside, leaving the door wide open.

Heather watched, dumbfounded as Reid made a beeline for the door. He reached for Clint's shirtsleeve but missed.

He turned and gave her a smirk and a nod. "Time to split up, it seems."

Then he ducked through the hatch, after Clint, and yanked it shut behind him.

Heather thought her jaw would hit the floor when she realized she and Alex were alone.

She shook her head. "He left us. He left us here. That fucking bastard!"

"I don't think it was like that." Alex stepped in front of her. "I think he was trying to help Clint and protect us in the meantime."

"He's a selfish prick, Alex. When are you gonna see that? He wasn't looking out for us at all, just—"

A noise from the stairwell caught their attention. Small scratching sounds. Heather hoped it was only rats, but she knew better. If only it were rats.

She watched the fear creep across Alex's face as he too realized what was happening. The evil fairies. The ones that'd followed them down the corridor. They were coming up the stairs. Coming to get them.

"You hear that, Alex?"

Sounded like thousands of tiny footsteps shuffling up the steps. Shrill giggles pierced Heather's eardrums. She tried not to imagine them, picture their feet, all claws, scraping up the steps, searching for something to shred.

Before Alex could answer, the whispers came again.

"Watching..."

"Waiting..."

Heather turned from the stairs, grabbing Alex's hand. She gave him a sharp tug when she saw the hatch still there. It was indeed the hatch to Reid's attic. How had she been so mistaken before? How could she and Alex have thought they saw the door to Clint's basement?

"Watching..."

But she couldn't stop to care what kind of door it had been before. She had every hope that once inside, they'd find Reid and Clint. But even if they didn't, she'd be able to put some distance between them and the little creatures giving chase.

Hand in hand, Alex and Heather scrambled through the hatch.

Chapter 19

"Reid, where are you?"

Silence. Blackness.

"You little no-good son of a bitch. Reid!"

The voice shot daggers through Reid's heart. He held his breath. It couldn't be. Not here.

"I know you're in there. I saw you. Come out, now!"

Reid told himself this wasn't real. His father was back at home, probably drunk, stumbling around the house, or maybe passed out on the floor.

No matter how many times he tried to convince himself otherwise, Reid knew where he was. He'd been in this space a million times since his mother died almost four years ago. He knew every inch of this darkness. It had become part of him. It wasn't his fault his mother had died. He knew that, somewhere deep inside himself. In the darkness, in this attic, he had faced that.

But there was another monster that chased him, haunted his every waking hour. His father. Banging on the door.

"Come out, you worthless piece of shit!"

Reid sank back against the door and lost himself in his memories. The door rattled behind him from his father's pounding fists. He had more demons to face than those that lay within this nightmarish house. He squeezed his eyes shut and wrapped his arms around his knees, drawing them into his chest. As he took a deep breath, a familiar smell perked his nostrils. Mothballs. They were tucked inside the chest along the far wall. The chest which held some of his favorite things of his mother's. The red dress she'd worn on her last Christmas, the jeans and tattered hat she wore while gardening. He could almost see the sun reaching down over her shoulder, making her golden hair glimmer in its rays. He imagined the few sprinkles of freckles that danced across the bridge of her nose. That was the reason she started wearing the hat, after all. Said it protected her delicate skin.

Reid shook the thought away as the faint scent of her perfume wafted through the air. He knew his mother was long gone. And the memories hurt him too much. Too agonizing to think about.

But this room, it had always been the one place he could remember his mother and escape his father's punishments.

That first night after she passed was when it had all begun. The end of a life, of a child's innocence, and the start of something else entirely.

The house was especially cold and quiet that night as Reid lay in bed staring at the ceiling, silently mourning his mother's death. He was all cried out. The tears would no longer flow, his eyes too tired, too dry for any more. His throat felt raw like the time he had strep throat, though he knew this sickness would take longer to heal.

After huddling deeper inside the blankets, he still couldn't shake the chill, the emptiness. She was gone. His mother was dead, and he'd witnessed the whole thing. No, he had more than witnessed it.

And in the still of the night, he'd heard the strangest sound.

After creeping down the hall, following those sounds, he came upon the kitchen and stopped just outside the doorway. The noises which had led him there made sense, but still terrified him. Sobs. Pitiful moans and whimpers from his father, who sat at the table, with his head lying flat on its surface. A bottle of whiskey tipped on its side next to his head spilled its remaining contents to the floor.

NEVER HAD he seen his father cry. Not one single tear. Until then, Reid would've said it wasn't possible. Yet there he sat, a mess of a man.

Reid couldn't help it, the surprise of it all seized him, and he whimpered at the sight.

That was enough to gain his father's attention. And his wrath.

In a drunken tirade, he'd raced to Reid, his eyes wide and glossy as he grabbed him by the earlobe. He yanked him down the hallway to Reid's bedroom and tossed him on the floor like a pile of dirty clothes.

He wrinkled his nose as if he'd just smelled a rotten egg. "You? Sneaking up on me! Are you proud of yourself? Watching me like that?" He raised an open hand and brought it down across Reid's cheek. "You! It's all your fault! You!" Spittle flew from his father's lips. "She's gone, and I'm stuck here with you." He slapped Reid across the cheek and then clenched his hands into fists.

Reid had curled into a ball on the floor, taking one punch after another until his father finally gave up from exhaustion and booze, and passed out on the floor next to him. Reid lay there, petrified, crying silently, trying to breathe through the pain.

When he was finally able, he got to his feet, clutching his aching ribs, and snuck out of his room, up the stairs, to the attic.

At least there his father couldn't find him. Touch him. There, he'd be safe at least for a little while.

Reid kept his eyes squeezed shut as the fists still pounded away at the other side of the door, forcing him to relive his nightmares in the darkness of the awful house. He reminded himself that it was his fault he'd brought his friends here. None of them wanted to come —he'd forced them. He was rotten and he knew it.

Reid cringed and flung his eyes open, but it was no use. It was too dark. He made himself smaller, sinking down as much as he could against the door, hoping that if he could just be still and small and quiet enough, his dad wouldn't find him here.

"Reid, get up." This was a different voice. A voice he hadn't heard in so long. Unmistakable. But it couldn't be.

Tears welled up in his closed eyes. A childish whisper escaped his lips. "Mom?"

"Reid, get up. Don't give up. Your friends need you. Get up now."

"Mom?" He called out, but there was no reply.

The voices were gone. Had they even been there in the first place, or had he imagined them? He waited longer, hoping to hear her voice. While straining his ears, he thought he heard the distant sound of beating drums. *Thrum-thrum-thrum…*

He kept his eyes closed and held his breath, trying to hear more, to feel something. He waited. Wasn't sure what he was waiting for, but he knew it was important. Like a word that remains on the tip of your tongue. So close you know you should know it, but it's just out of your grasp.

Nothingness.

And then Reid had an idea. He shuffled to the far side of the attic and finally found his goal. He sparked to life a lantern sitting on a small wooden table beside his mother's chest of belongings.

"We *are* in my attic," he said. *I know this room.*

Lantern in hand, he turned to see a figure out of the corner of his eye. It was Clint, lying on the floor in the fetal position, shaking. He seemed to be in a fevered state, dreaming, far, far away.

Chapter 20

Like a fly on the wall, Clint watched the scene play out in his dream. Adult Clint and Danny sat on a floor, in front of a huge TV. The biggest one Clint had ever seen. Both held Atari controllers, their eyes glued to the screen. Danny glanced away, reaching for an opened can of beer on the coffee table. Beside it were two six-packs, one already emptied and one still to go. A pizza box lay open with half the pizza gone. Danny tipped the beer back and drained it all in a few gulps. He slammed the can down and let out a long burp, then wiped away the dribbles down his chin, with his sleeve.

Clint shook his head. "What are you doing, Danny? Dude, you just got burned. You're dead."

Danny looked back to the TV, where his avatar lay, burned and crispy.

"You're outta the game." Clint leaned forward and focused.

Danny grabbed another beer. "Looks like it. Guess

it's you now. I'll just drink another beer and sit back and watch." He leaned back against the coffee table.

The table slid across the wooden floor a few inches, making a screeching sound. Danny shifted his weight and leaned back further.

Clint scowled at Danny's nonchalant attitude towards getting offed. He fidgeted.

"Does it feel hot in here to you?" Clint asked. "Could you open the window or something? I'm sweating." He turned back to the game and tapped away at the controller, trying to navigate his way into a new room, through a long dark hallway. "Smells funny, too. Like smoke."

Danny didn't answer.

The smell of smoke grew heavier, until Clint had to wave away a cloud forming in front of him.

"What the hell? Open a window or some—"

The floor under Clint was scorching hot. His ass felt like it was going to melt there on the spot. After glancing at Danny, he saw why.

Danny still sat with his back against the coffee table, holding a beer. The table's legs were on fire, and the floor beneath it had turned to ash. Danny didn't even seem to notice the heat or the fire.

His clothes looked fine, but his skin was burned. Like someone had left a hot dog on the grill for too long.

"Burned, man," Clint whispered, way too casual about the whole thing.

Real-Clint tried to wake himself up. Nothing.

Dream-Clint turned away from burned Danny and back to the game. The long hallway he'd been exploring in the game was gone, and he found himself in a little room. An attic.

He tapped away at the controller and it began to feel funny under his fingers. It melted, turning to liquid and ran through his fingers as he tried to hold on. He shook out his hands.

It felt like someone was shaking real-Clint, grasping his arms.

He couldn't see Danny anymore, nor the TV or the living room. It all faded to black. And then he flung his eyes open to see Reid leaning over him, shaking him by his shoulders. He could hear Reid's voice clearly.

"Wake up. Get up."

After sitting up, Clint began ranting. "I was just dreaming. Me and Danny were old, like twenty-two or something. We were hanging out in this living room, playing Atari on this freaking ginormous TV. It was my game. I created it. It was called *Burning Man*. In the game, you have to go inside this house, see. Inside, everything changes. Like some kind of maze. The rooms move, doors disappear, and there's this wicked creature made of smoke chasing you. If you get caught by him, you'll burn right there on the screen. Poof. Burned to a crisp. But if you can figure out the maze, you can get out. The game just got released on the market, so we were celebrating with beer and pizza. But then—"

"We'll get you outta here" Reid said. "We'll figure it out, so you can make that game for real and we can all sit around and drink beers and stuff."

Clint felt hopeful. "You really think so?"

Reid nodded unconvincingly, but Clint didn't care.

He wrapped his sweaty hands around Reid's forearms and pulled him close. "I don't think I'm gonna beat the game. I think I lost this one. But you guys shouldn't. Maybe to beat the game, you gotta sacrifice. Or leave the weakest behind or something. I dunno." He hacked. "You guys gotta figure it out quick. I'm too hot and tired." He closed his eyes. "Remember that time we all went to the quarry together?" He let out a painful laugh. "Heather followed us that time, too. There was that rope tied to a tree. You made us all jump from it into the water. That was awesome, man." He took a deep, shaky breath. "And Danny panicked of course and let go of the rope at the wrong time. He did that crazy belly flop, and he started flailing all around in the water like he was drowning. But you jumped in and pulled him out. Remember?"

Reid smiled. "Yeah, his stomach was all red and splotchy from hitting the water so hard." His smile faded. Swallowing audibly, he stared back at Clint. "What are you getting at?"

"Reid, you pushed us into some dumb shit, but you almost always made sure we got out okay, too. You're not a bad dude. You just got a bum deal." He pulled Reid closer, so close he could smell the sweat coming off him. "You're gonna have to pull them out of this jam, too. Too late for me. But Heather and Alex, get them outta here, okay?"

Sweat trickled down Clint's forehead. With each labored breath, he winced. The pain in his lungs was so hot, so heavy. He wondered if a person could drown in fire.

Reid didn't speak.

"You know it wasn't your fault, right?" Clint said, his voice softer, no matter how he strained to be heard.

"It is," Reid said. "I made you guys come."

"Not that." Clint waved his hand and licked his lips.

"No, I mean your mom. She didn't get sick and die because of you. It wasn't fair. Your dad shouldn't have blamed you for her cancer. And he shouldn't have beat you. He just couldn't let her go. He screwed up. Not you."

"You don't know what you're talking about. It was my fault."

"It was not. She asked—"

"What…how…don't." Reid averted his eyes from Clint.

Feeling as if it weighed five tons, Clint lifted his hand to Reid's mouth. "Shh. You're not bad. She wanted to…"

Clint could see through blurry eyes what he thought were tears streaming down Reid's face. He tried to focus his own eyes, but it didn't work. They were giving up on him just like his lungs, just like everything else. His heartbeat pounded on his eardrums, and it wasn't a steady *thump-thump, thump-thump*. He had a moment of fevered delirium that made him laugh out loud. *My heart just did that bad-ass drum break in Phil Collins's In the Air Tonight.*

Two things stopped his laughter—the fear in Reid's eyes and the internal pain he felt from laughing. It burned. *Wicked fucking hot.* He wheezed and finally caught a breath. Pulled his arms back and clenched them over his chest. Shook his head at Reid.

"Now I gotta lay down. Not doing so good. Go find Alex and Heather." Clint shifted down sideways and curled back up into the fetal position. Then his body began shaking. "So hot, but so cold. Doesn't make sense." He closed his eyes. "There's a fire inside."

He felt cold hands on him and sprung his eyes open. "No!" He went into a fit of coughs. It felt like hot lava racing up from his belly to his throat and out of his mouth. When he turned his head to the side, he saw the lava for real. But it wasn't lava. It was blood. He was throwing up blood. "That's...not...good."

He looked back to Reid, who was staring at him in horror, shaking his head.

"Hang on, buddy," Reid whispered. He wiped Clint's face as if he didn't notice there was blood-vomit there.

"We've never been buddies, you and me. Like circumstantial comrades, we were." Clint forced a smile. "Nah, I gotta go. Gotta find...Danny. I'm burning, man."

Shuffling sounds came from the hatch door, but it didn't open. Footsteps. As if someone was inside with them. Clint watched hazily as Reid lifted the lantern toward the door. He saw a brief shadow slip past the light and dip down into a dark corner.

"Watching.."

"Waiting..."

"It's here." Clint panted. "Get out. Now."

One eye closed, the other locked on Reid as he spun around and around with the lantern, trying to catch up with the shadow. But it was always one step ahead of him.

"Go."

By the time Reid flashed the light back on him it was too late. Clint saw the devastation on Reid's face before he realized what was happening. Weighed down

by an impossible feeling on his chest, like a damn pterodactyl was sitting on him, he wondered how he'd gotten
onto his back. His gaze flew to a shadow above him.
Maybe it was a pterodactyl. It had wings, didn't it? Or
were those long arms? An unusual darkness blotted out
the beam of the lantern. He wondered how a shadow
could weigh so much. Trying to take in a breath, he
found it was no use. Too heavy. No matter, breathing
hurt too much anyway. The fire was already inside.

He locked eyes with the creature pinning him down.
If they were eyes at all. Deep and empty, dark like charcoal. He felt as if he was falling inside them, into the
abyss. There was nowhere to go but down, into the
darkness.

He closed his eyes one last time and yelled with all
his might, "Reid, run!"

And then he felt his mouth opening against his will,
jaws plied back by inconceivable strength. The pressure,
the force on his temples felt like it was going to pop him.
He heard his jaws creak and wondered how much it was
going to hurt. Wondered if his friend would take his
advice and get out before it was too late. He wondered
if—hoped there really was a big man in the sky, God or
whatever, who would look out for them all. But most of
all, he hoped it would end soon.

Chapter 21

Heather's hopes were dashed once she and Alex made it through the door. She hadn't expected it to be easy to find a way out or their friends, but she didn't expect this. A spiraling staircase leading up. She watched in awe as the stairs formed and wound around and around. The movement made her sway as she fought to keep her focus on the ever-growing stairs. The same staircase they'd just climbed. Where would it take them this time?

"Oh, no! No more goddamned stairs!" She turned back to the hatch door, but it was locked.

She yanked it with all her strength until her hands grew weak. Her fingers slipped off the handle and she fell on her ass.

"I can't do this anymore, Alex." Her mouth turned downward, about to betray a frown, risking not being the tough little sister anymore. She whimpered, "Why did I have to follow you guys? Why didn't I just stay home and play with dolls or something?"

Tears streamed down her cheeks. "Why can't I just be a girly girl?" She choked on her sob. "Why-did-I-come?"

"Hey, you're the toughest person I know," Alex cooed to her. "You were the last one to panic about all this. You were the one who tried to help Clint, while we were all too scared."

"I figured—" She snorted the snot that was running down her face. "I figured we'd all get out by now. I tried to think like it was all a game, a trick or whatever. That we'd find a way out."

"We will. Keep thinking that way."

"I tried to believe it wasn't really happening. Like it was just a bad dream or a stupid hokey haunted house. But then the fairies—"

Alex scrunched his eyebrows. "Fairies?"

"The evil fairies that chased us in the hall and the staircase." She grabbed a curl and twirled it around her finger.

She hated doing that, the one girly thing she couldn't stop.

"Watching and waiting," Alex said.

She stopped, finger in mid-twirl. "Yeah, that. I wasn't sure…I mean…well, for a while I thought I was the only one seeing and hearing it. But they are real?"

"Seems so. The voices and the little creatures and the dark smoky monster thing. Check. All real."

A whisper came out so soft, she wasn't sure if she said it out loud or only in her head, "And Danny. Really gone?"

When Alex didn't respond, tears threatened to spill from her eyes again.

He nodded. "Remember last summer when we were

all playing football in the backyard together and you broke your wrist?"

"Yeah, the wrist thing again. Football with Reid. So—"

"You were scared and really hurt, but you didn't cry. And you didn't want to stop playing either. You wanted to finish the game."

"Cause we were winning." She let the curl go and absently touched the wrist she'd broken and began massaging it. "Reid was such a jerk."

"But you didn't quit. We all made you go, but you didn't cry the whole time. Not when you broke it, not at the hospital, not ever."

Alex seemed to be looking past Heather and at the memory. He chuckled.

"Why are you laughing?"

"Cause I just remembered what else you did in that hospital room. You didn't cry, but you made that orderly cry for sure."

"Oh, yeah. He was a moron. He deserved it."

"Nobody deserves a kick in the nuts."

"He totally did. The way he grabbed my wrist shot a damn lightning bolt of pain through my whole arm. Besides, it was an automatic reaction. Couldn't be helped." She could feel a smile creeping up, but forced it away.

She tilted her head, gazing at her brother through squinted eyes. "So…"

"So you're not a quitter." Alex reached out to her. "You weren't then, and you're not now. Get up." He shoved his hand out farther until she grabbed on.

After rising to her feet, she felt hopeful, and dried the remaining tears from her eyes.

"Thanks, Alex." She squeezed his arm.

She was sure Alex was just as scared as she was, but she knew he'd pushed aside his fears for her. And she wouldn't forget it.

"No prob. Now let's go. Nowhere to go but up." He gave her a playful wink.

Heather laced her fingers through her brother's, and together they climbed the stairs.

When they reached the last step, she said, "You didn't have to say all that, but thanks."

Alex shrugged. "I meant it."

Once again, she felt like an unstoppable force. The tough girl who didn't give a shit. She sighed in relief and gave way to a smile.

But it was short-lived.

Once they reached the top of the steps, they saw a platform about two feet long, leading to stairs going down. Nothing else.

The smile dropped off her face. "Enough! No more."

From the direction they'd come, Heather could hear the tiny footsteps climbing the stairs. Shrill chirpy giggles flew up, raking at her eardrums.

"They're coming," she said. "The evil fairies are coming."

She reached deep inside herself and grabbed every ounce of courage she could find. Squeezed Alex's and led them down the stairs, cautiously at first. But the whispers and giggles were getting closer, pushing them to move faster. Closing the gap behind them. *Don't turn around.*

She didn't turn back to look, she pressed on, faster, galloping down the steps. She lost her footing a few times, but wouldn't let go of Alex as if he was her anchor. As long as he believed in her, she might be able to believe in herself and not lose herself. Or lose her shit.

But the stairs wouldn't end. And those nasty little critters seemed to be gaining on them. As much of an athlete as she was, fatigue was setting in. Her calves flexed as she stepped down, down. Thighs burned and tightened as the stairs went on and on.

They were getting shorter, smaller, making it harder for them to keep their footing. What once were foot-long steps, were now about six inches. Heather stumbled again, skipping a step. Alex held her up. She righted herself and they flung themselves down the staircase.

A whoosh of air flew past them, and it was enough to shake their footing. They stumbled down the last few steps and fell into a twisted heap.

Panting, she pulled herself off of Alex. "You OK?"

Alex got to his knees. "I think so."

"Listen." Heather brought her index finger to her lips.

There was no sound. No footsteps, no laughter. Nothing.

SHE PULLED her brother to his feet. As she surveyed their surroundings, a sense of hopelessness crept up her back like the shiver of a chill. She shook it off. They stood on another small landing, with the stairs they'd just fallen down behind them, and another set of stairs going up looming in front.

Alex's eyes widened. "What the f—"

The wind howled again, stealing the words from his mouth.

A savage sound that made Heather think a pack of wild coyotes had crept into the room. It came at them from the stairwell before them. The frigid air wrapped around her, making her shudder.

"It just got wicked cold in here, didn't it?"

Her words turned to steam as they left her lips.

"We shouldn't stay. Gotta move. It's too cold." Alex wrapped his arms around himself.

"Hell no. That's what the house wants us to do. It wants us to climb those stairs." Heather planted her feet.

"Or it wants us to be afraid of the cold and go back the way we came."

"So what do we do, then?"

Alex's teeth chattered. "Maybe we should go back. It's getting colder."

"Or maybe we should go forward. Like a challenge to see if we can get past the cold." Heather crept closer and huddled against her brother. "I don't know which way to go, Alex."

"Me neither."

Alex leaned in closer to his sister. "We have to agree. We've got to do this together. Let's weigh our options—"

Another howl of wind blew past them, sending Heather's curls up around her face.

Alex pulled her closer. "We need to decide quick."

From the way they'd come, another challenge urged them to decide. Voices.

"Watching…"

And then from the staircase ahead, floating down on

the chilly air, as if in response, voices whispered, *"Waiting…"*

"Either way is awful, Alex. What do we do?"

Gusts of wind raced at them, stinging Heather's eyes and momentarily blinding her. Her hair flung across her face. At first, it came from the front, then it headed back at them from behind, as if the wind were a thinking entity. The force pushed them, urging them to move forward. It was so strong that Heather could lean back into it and not fall over. Her toes began to cramp from fighting its strength.

"What do we do, Alex?"

Her words were muted in the wind.

"Watching…"

"Waiting…"

Wind whipped and howled, swirling up, around, and over them. Leaning back, then forward with the ever-changing flow, Heather couldn't keep up, pushing and pulling at her brother to stay upright. Her legs were exhausted and she just wanted to sit.

And then the floor beneath them disappeared.

Heather's arms flapped helplessly as she fell through the air. She tried in vain to grab a hold of Alex. His face was contorted in fear as they plummeted into the unknown. Visibility grew worse as blackness closed in more the further they descended. It seemed to be consuming them. No longer able to see her brother or her hand in front of her face, she released the scream that'd been building since they'd first ended up in the hallway. Out of her mouth it went flying up the hole they were falling from. Then it changed direction and hit her like someone was screaming with their mouth pressed to her ear. She shook her head, covered her face and kicked her legs out, frantically.

Somehow the scream pushed past her, down the tenebrous chasm, echoing out, bouncing off the walls, waiting for her.

Before Heather could wonder if they would ever stop their descent, her body slammed into something. She heard Alex thud nearby, with a grunt. It sounded like something wooden had broken his fall, but she couldn't be sure. All she could make out was the faint outline of his figure on the floor, to her right.

Lucky or not, she'd landed on her bottom. Besides the initial shock that raced up her tailbone, there was no pain. She rolled to her side and felt nothing. Maybe an achy butt tomorrow, but for now—

There was a crunchy, crumbly feeling under her hand. She scooped a handful of whatever it was up to her face, but it was too dark to make out what it was. She opened her hand and felt the stuff run through her fingers, like sand. The smell of smoke teased her nostrils and she sneezed. She shook her hand out but couldn't help that feeling of the heebie-jeebies crawling under her skin.

"Alex?" she whispered. "You okay?"

Alex groaned. "I thought you'd never stop screaming. You okay?"

Heather felt around blindly but only came up with more of the sandy stuff. "It wasn't me. I mean, it was, but it kept going. Like my scream was alive. It was everywhere."

"I know. It was like you were yelling right in my ear, but I couldn't feel you near me even when I reached out."

Heather sneezed again. "What was that sound when you landed? Like you broke something."

"I think a chair broke my fall." Alex moaned. "My leg aches, but I'm all right."

"Something broke my fall, too, but I can't see what it is. Feels like a pile of sand or something. It's all over me."

Chapter 22

Reid had been faced with an impossible decision—watch his friend be consumed by the creature, or heed Clint's last heroic plea and run for his life. As helpless as he was, it still seemed cowardly to run and leave Clint to his death. But what could he have done? Could he have stopped it? He could no more have stopped this evil than the one that had crept though his mother's body. Still, he felt responsible.

His father's words echoed through his mind. *It's all your fault, you worthless piece of shit. She's gone, and what am I left with? A rotten, good-for-nothing waste of space.*

For a moment, Reid cowered on the other side of the hatch door, shaking at the memories, waiting to feel his father's fist. But it didn't come. In the end, he'd followed his friend's instructions and ran for his own life. He'd made it back to the hatch door and slammed it shut behind him, then collapsed in a heap of despair, back against the door, hearing the muffled cries of Clint as he burned. Like the boy who had just sat there and taken blow after blow from his father, he sat helpless and petrified, hearing wail after wail from his friend.

That had all been some time ago. Everything around him now was silent. Perhaps it was better to think about his father beating him than what Clint had gone through.

His friend's voice in his head pushed all thoughts of his father out. *Heather and Alex, get them outta here, okay?*

Reid forced himself to open his eyes and check his surroundings. He held the lantern out. The hatch door behind him was gone, but he didn't care, nor was he surprised. *Time to move forward. Time to get Heather and Alex the fuck out of here.* He was back in the first room they'd entered when they came into the house. When had that been, anyway? For all he knew it could've been days, weeks even. Or had it been mere hours? This house made him lose all his senses. Thirst raked at his throat. The pungent smell of dried sweat came off his body in waves. It made him sure he'd been in this house for longer than he'd originally suspected.

The crackle of the fireplace drew his attention. A log collapsed, sending sparks and ash forward. Reid sighed. Lost in a maze. He felt like a rat, running round and round, never finding the way out. Of course, the front door wasn't there, nor was the window, for all the good they'd done in the past.

The view of the fireplace became obstructed, like he was looking through a murky window. He squinted, and then the fireplace disappeared as the shape of a man came to be, huddled on the floor in front of it. Reid had seen this man before. It was the same man they'd all seen, except this time he was alone. No baby, no wife.

The man's figure bucked and heaved, no sound at first, only the jerking motions. And then, as if someone turned the volume dial on the radio up, Reid heard sobs. Chills climbed his spine. Men weren't supposed to cry, Reid knew that. When they did, it meant they were either weak or something awful was happening. Like when his mother died and he came upon his father sobbing.

He shook the thought from his mind. Cautiously he rose to his feet, hoping to get a better view through the dreamlike haze but not draw any attention. The cloudiness of the scene in front of him dissolved, getting clearer the closer he got.

The man continued crying, seemingly unaware of Reid's presence. As Reid came up behind him, from the side, he could see him covering his face with his hands, his sobs muffled.

Through his hands, the man muttered, "They're dying. Both of them. And there's nothing I can do. Why does God punish me so?"

The scene sucked Reid in, and he needed to test the reality of it. He reached out to touch the man's shoulder, but it went right through. Frostbite stung his fingertips and he gasped, clutching his hand to his chest.

In the fireplace, the flame cracked and shot up, lighting the room. Reid flung back to the wall. It was as if the fire was alive, and even more disconcerting, the flame spoke. It had an inhuman voice, neither male nor female, and was garbled and scratchy. The volume faded in and out with the quivering blaze.

"It doesn't have to be this way. They can stay. They can stay."

The man pulled his hands away from his face and

gazed into the fire. He drew in a deep breath and halted his sobbing.

Reid, too, held his breath, waiting for what might come next, afraid to be noticed by anyone or anything in the room.

But there was silence.

He began to doubt if he'd ever heard anything in the fire at all. He exhaled. Just the mind playing tricks, of course.

The man also seemed to give up on having heard anything, and lowered his head again.

After gaining courage from the stillness of the scene, Reid stepped forward again, just off to the side of the man.

"Hey. Hey, Mister. Can you hear me, Mister?"

The man didn't move.

"Hey, buddy! How the hell do I get out of this house? Is this your house? What did you do?" Reid felt like he was going to burst from everything he'd seen and done since he led his friends into this place. "Hey, fuck-face! Cocksucker."

The man still didn't budge.

"Dip shit. Douche-nozzle. Penis-breath! How do I get out of this hellhole?"

The fire spit forward, a flame licking toward the man, whose head shot up, and Reid bolted backwards.

"Fire consumes. Fire cleanses. Fire renews."

The man shook his head, covering his ears. He mumbled, "Madness. I must be ill as well."

"The fire consumes sickness." The voice sounded like the hiss of a snake, and slithered across Reid's skin like a living thing.

As Reid stared into the fire, he thought the flame

appeared to have a serpentine quality, a tail curling in on itself, wrapping around and around. But it was gone as quickly as it had appeared. No snake, only a flame.

"I know a way they can stay," the fire whispered.

The man leaned forward, sucked in by temptation.

The fire licked out again and this time touched the man's face like a lover's tender hand, stroking his cheek. When the man didn't draw back, another flame came out to his other cheek and caressed as it whispered,

"Lean closer. I'll show you what you must do."

The man moved to hands and knees and crawled forward, his face just inches from the fireplace. The flames still held his cheeks, coaxing him closer.

Reid struggled to hear as the voice's volume rose and fell. He couldn't make out much of what was said, but he had a feeling he was missing something unseen. As if the fire showed the man what must be done. The flames drew back like a vacuum had sucked them into the fireplace, leaving the man's cheeks scorched.

"To burn, to burn, as you must, too."

And then the fire went out.

Reid risked turning the lantern back on, hoping that whatever had been in the room was now gone. Part of him knew it was a memory playing out in front of him. A memory imprinted on the room, the house.

He looked back to where he'd entered the room and found the hatch door there once again. He

jerked the door open and climbed through.

Frightened voices reached out from the darkness, to him.

The first one said, "Someone just opened a door."

A female voice said, "I can't see past the light. I'm scared, Alex."

Reid breathed in a sigh of relief. "It's me. It's Reid."

He stepped further into the room, shining the lantern light toward Alex, who sat on the ground, beside Reid's mother's rocking chair. Or at least, what remained of it. It was snapped, broken, pieces of it strewn around Alex.

REID HESITATED. "Alex, is that really you?"

"Who else would I be?"

Reid held the lantern as close to Alex as he could without stepping forward any farther, and studied the face of the boy who sat before him. Alex's brown eyes twinkled back at him. The glare made Alex cringe, and Reid couldn't help but stare at his best friend's almost-unibrow. If it hadn't been such a dire time, he would've laughed. Leaning closer, he noted the soft, uneven scruff of a mustache that'd been coming in for the past six months. He'd been bugging Alex to shave it for some time. He unconsciously brought a hand to his own chin and stroked it to see if his stubble had yet begun to grow in since he'd last shaved. Wondering how long they'd been in the house.

Finally convinced the person in front of him was Alex, he then turned the light to Heather, who was standing and brushing her hands on her pants.

"Heather?"

Her eyes grew wide and she raised her eyebrows as she fumed at him. "Did you hit your head or something, jag-off? You're acting wicked dumb."

"Yup, that's you." Reid reached out and helped Alex to his feet.

"Where's Clint?" Heather asked. "You find him?"

Reid took a step toward her and then froze, real-izing what she was covered in. He'd been in this room not too long ago with Clint.

"Stop. Stop, stay still."

Heather ran a hand across her face, leaving an ashy smudge above her lip and across her cheek. "I fell in something. Like sand or—"

"Stop that right now!" Reid yelled.

"Whoa, whoa, chill." Alex put a hand on Reid's chest.

Reid dropped his head toward the ground. "Yeah, I found Clint, but…it was too late."

He scanned the room, then spotted the chest in the corner and moved to it. Flung it open and pulled out one of his mother's scarves. Strode to Heather and brushed the scarf over her face, trying to remove the smudge. He wondered how best to break the news, to tell Heather what was right in front of his face, and all over hers.

"The ash on you. That's Clint."

Chapter 23

A lex could hear the words, but he couldn't comprehend what they meant. Or maybe he just didn't want to get it.

Clint's dead.

His ashes.

all over my sister.

Before that moment, Alex had never heard his sister scream like this. Yes, he'd heard her howl, yell, growl, groan, swear, and all the rest. But that blood curdling, pierce your earhole, melt your face off horror movie scream--- never. Until just then.

"St-st-stop. Don't sc-scream."

He stumbled backwards.

The meaning of Reid's words struck him dumb. His mouth dropped open, hair stood on end, heart skipped a beat, breath caught in his throat. And then he felt the tiny needles scraping under his skin, making his body shake and shiver.

At first, he thought it was the house. That the evil

was creeping inside him, infecting him. But as he stood there, paralyzed, watching Heather scream at the top of her lungs and frantically rub her cheeks to remove the remains of Clint, Alex realized that no ghost, no demon could frighten him as much as that sight. His fearless little sister, in hysterics. The little girl he'd always wished she would be was now in front of him, and all he could think was that he wanted the tomboy back. Wanted to be in the backyard playing stupid games with his friends, most of whom were now dead.

And still he couldn't move.

And Heather kept screaming.

Reid pulled her hands away from her face and held them down at her sides. He whispered words to her that Alex couldn't hear, and gently wiped away the smudges. It worked for a moment, but then she was swatting at his hands and wailing.

Alex tried to move, to go to her, but he was stuck, helpless.

Clint's ashy smudges now mixed with splotchy red spots on Heather's face from screaming so hard. Her eyes were wide, too wide, and darting in every direction. She opened her mouth to scream again, but Reid covered it with his hand. But just like slapping a Band-Aid over a gushing artery, it made no difference.

It came out misshapen and muffled, but it was a scream just the same. Alex stood by, horrified as her face contorted into something he'd never seen before. Her eyes grew smaller, her brows so furrowed they could've been cartoons. Her head began to vibrate like a volcano about to erupt.

And then she did.

She clawed at Reid's hand and ripped it away from her face. She seethed through gritted teeth.

"You did it. You killed him! You went with him and left us behind. You were supposed to help him, but you didn't. Now he's dead. Now he's ash. This is all your fault!"

Reid stumbled backwards as if he'd been punched in the gut. And still, Alex could only look on.

No longer blotchy red, Heather's face was now red all over. She growled at Reid like a wild animal.

"Clint's dead. Because of you! You!" She bent her hands into not fists, but claws and lunged at Reid's face.

Another first. Heather was a champ at throwing punches, maybe even elbows, but she'd never scratched like a girl. Or a rabid beast. *But that's what she is—a beast.*

Reid threw his arms up to his face, but she kept coming, scratching at his arms.

"Get a hold of your sister, Alex. She's crazy!"

Reid moved his arm too late, and one of her nails caught him on the cheek, drawing blood.

Reid's calm approach dissolved and he drew one open hand back and slapped her across the face.

"Stop it! Stop it now!" he yelled.

That was another first. Reid was a bully, and he wasn't afraid to give any one of them a punch, jab, swat, or push—except for Heather. That snapped Alex out of his stupor. And Heather slammed her mouth shut. Her eyes grew wide.

She squeezed her hands into fists and hauled off, throwing a right jab, then a left hook to Reid's chest.

He let out a surprised puff of air and stumbled backwards.

Alex stepped between them. "Whoa, whoa. Let's just all take a step back."

"He hit me!" Tears spilled down Heather's cheeks. Her voice was high and piercing.

Reid tensed his shoulders and put his hands up in front of him. "You were going crazy there. I just needed to snap you out of it."

"*Slap* me out of it, you mean, douche-face." She took in a breath that caught in her throat.

Alex laid a hand on their shoulders. Heather pushed against him, trying to beat his hand off, whirling and raging like a Tasmanian devil. He let go of Reid and focused his energy on his sister. No one could ever keep that girl down, and Alex was no exception.

He kept a firm grip on her shoulder to keep her at bay. But she balled her fists up and began swinging like a windmill. He shifted his hand from her shoulder to her forehead. Her curls bounced off her face and swept across her eyes, blinding the reckless tornado of a sister.

Yet Alex planted his feet and held firm.

"Stop it," he said. "He was trying to help you. You were screaming like a crazy lady."

"I really was just trying to help," Reid said. "I'd never hurt you. You know that, c'mon."

And just like that, the sides of Heather's mouth tugged downward. "I'm so tired. And scared." She sniffled. "I can't do this." She shook her head, and her curls swept back and forth across her face, making her seem younger than she was. "First Danny, now Clint. Who... who's next?"

Alex let his hands slide off her, hoping the threat had passed. When she didn't try to fight, he pulled her in for a hug.

"No one," he whispered. "We'll figure this out.
We're gonna get outta here. No one else has to—"
She wriggled out of his arms.

Wrapped her fingers in her hair and started twirling.
"You're not a complete douche-face," she said to
Reid. "Sorry, I didn't mean it."

Alex let out a sigh of relief.

"I thought you'd left us, Reid." The tears started
up again and she brushed them away. "I thought you
were being a dick, leaving us behind and taking off,
trying to get yourself outta here. Nevermind us. Part
of me hoped you'd figure it out and Clint would be
okay."

Reid shook his head. "I wouldn't do that. I know
you all thought I was just a jerk, but I wouldn't let you
guys down." He shrugged. "You guys are my friends.
I'm not gonna leave you. We're all getting outta here
together, okay?"

"Okay," Heather and Alex said.

Alex remembered who Reid was, why they were
friends. Behind all the teasing, bullying, and goading,
was the real person. In that moment, Alex was jealous
of Reid. Here he was being the strong one, some type
of a hero-in-the-making, and every time Alex wanted to
be brave, he froze in the face of challenge. A coward.
And cowards didn't escape haunted houses. Everyone
knew that.

"Hey, Alex, where are you?" Reid waved in front of
Alex's face.

"I...I was just thinking." Alex turned his attention to
Reid.

"While I was away," Reid said, "I saw the man
again. That ghost guy. This time he didn't have his kid

and wife, though. He was alone, with the fire." Reid bit his lip. "And it was talking to him."

As he recounted the tale, Heather and Alex were silent, hoping to find an answer somewhere inside the story. A way to finally get out. But in the end, Alex was left with more questions.

"So what should we do now?" Alex mentally slapped himself for asking Reid to take the lead, and for continuing to play the coward.

Heather yawned and rubbed her swollen eyes. "I'm spent. I feel so heavy."

"Maybe we just need a second to catch our breath?" Alex said.

"This place hasn't given us any breaks yet," Reid said. "Why would it now?"

"You two get some rest," Alex said. "A quick shut-eye. I'll stay awake."

He finally took in the surroundings. Up until that point, he hadn't been able to see past his sister and Clint's ashes.

"Reid, how'd we get in your attic? How is your attic even in this house?"

"I'm beginning to think that this house is inside us, not the other way around. Does that even make sense?" Reid shook his head. "Of course it doesn't make sense. I guess I am tired."

But the words resonated with Alex. Danny's basement and bedroom. Reid's attic. Thoughts swirled in Alex's head, too fast for him to make sense of any of them. And the more he thought about Reid's words, the more afraid he became.

"Just rest," Alex said.

Reid was about to protest, but Alex stopped him.

"No. I'll rest later. Do it."

It didn't take long for Heather to curl up in the corner, with her back against the wall, and her head bobbed as she drifted off. Reid sat down beside her and gave Alex one last questioning look before shutting his eyes, too.

Absolute quiet.

Until Alex heard the voices.

Inhuman voices, alternating.

The first, a guttural vibrating bass. *"All in this house…"*

And then shrill whispers. *"Will be…will be…forever…"*

"Neither living or dead. No such constraints."

"Bound to this place…"

By the hatchway, the tall ghost of a man appeared. His intense eyes stared right through Alex, sending chills through his body. The man nodded as if in agreement with the words.

"Bound to you," the shrill whispers continued.

Tiny shadows danced across the walls behind the man, like charcoal living flames. They flickered out as quickly as they'd appeared, and Alex saw something flash in the man's eyes. Fire.

The bass voice quavered. *"You cannot lose them. They cannot leave you."*

"Will never lose again…"

Like a puff of smoke, the man disappeared.

Chapter 24

A chanting tribal song worked through the sleeping Reid. Drumbeats thrummed, softly at first, then became louder as Reid shook himself awake, rubbing at his heavy lids to clear the sleepiness and confusion. The last he remembered was that he and Heather were drifting off to sleep while Alex stood guard. Heather was a few feet away, but where was Alex?

The drums and song faded to nothing.

The room was shrouded in darkness, like a heavy cloud sat upon it, and Reid struggled to make out the outline of Alex's body curled up on the floor.

An abnormal pulsing pushed at Reid's skin. The room was vibrating with an energy that seemed tangible. Reid held his hand out and his fingertips vibrated. He could see it happening. At first it was a gentle lull in the darkness. Soon, it became harsh, like someone slapping his skin over and over. But he could take it. He'd taken worse before.

As the intensity grew, so did the light in the room—a soft gleam building with each moment as if someone had lit his lantern. Except it was coming from all directions. Light from no source. The flicker grew bright enough to fill the room. Reid looked back to Heather and saw fear in her wide eyes. She flung her hands up to her throat as she tried to scream, but nothing came out.

"What's wrong?" he asked. "What is it?"

She didn't respond. All that came out was a sick gurgling sound. She struggled with her neck, trying to pry off invisible hands. Her panic overwhelmed Reid. He charged forward, but when he reached her, he felt nothing. No one.

He pulled back, and screamed, "Stop! Heather, no one's there!"

But as the words left his lips, he saw that he was wrong. He could see the indentation of her skin, where hands would be wrapped around her frail throat. Invisible fingers pressed down, cutting off her air. How could he pry those untouchable hands off her?

The house shook and it rolled through his body. It tossed him backwards.

After righting himself, he watched Heather stare up into a face that wasn't there. She cowered with nowhere to run or hide.

Reid pushed forward, feeling like he was wading through thick mud. He only had a few feet to go, but he couldn't get to her. He swung his arms and slogged through the unseen muck. The closer he got, the more he picked up a smell. Ash, smoke, and something bitter he couldn't identify. That last smell came off Heather in waves—salty, sweaty, sour.

An image popped into his mind, and suddenly he

could picture the house, its evil, standing like a dark blob, a black hole sucking in all of Heather's fear. Reid squeezed his eyes shut, then flung them open and pushed forward, shaking the image away.

"Heather, calm down. There's nothing there." He hoped that was true. He pulled her hands away from her throat. "See?"

She swallowed audibly and sucked in air, finally able to breathe.

Her words came out strained. "There was." She swallowed again. "Someone was trying to choke me."

She bent forward, trying to regain her breath. He rubbed her back until her breathing became steady.

The room went black. Reid could no longer see Heather. The picture of the evil blob sucking in all Heather's fear popped back into his head. He reeled at the thought of being stuck inside not only the house, but also the dark evil mass as it slowly drained them.

Heather clasped his arm and he jumped.

Her breath tickled his neck as she whispered, "What happened? Where are we?"

He placed a hand over hers.

"Where's Alex?" she asked. "I can't see anything."

The darkness gave way and revealed the frame of the strange man, swaying in the center of the room, shoulders hunched, head hung low, his form becoming more solid by the minute.

Reid squeezed Heather's hand. The light began to spread and illuminate the room. They were back in the original room.

In front of the man, a fire suddenly began to burn in the fireplace. Not there a moment ago, yet it appeared to have been burning for hours. The warmth pushed out at Reid as if reaching for him, beckoning him. The flames licked at the wood. The tinder crackled as it gave over to the heat.

The hypnotizing warmth pulled Reid in and made him sway in rhythm with the man, in rhythm with the flames.

He glanced to the side and saw Heather's face frozen in fear. She gripped him tighter. As he was about to look back at the fire, he noticed Alex walking up behind Heather. *Where did he come from?*

He watched Alex stopped just behind Heather and they, too, were swaying. Like a strange dance to an unheard song, swelling out from the fire. The house began to palpitate again. The floor pulsed with a heartbeat that pounded though his shoes and danced up his spine. The hairs on the back of his neck stood at attention, and he had a moment to wonder how he could feel so cold in the middle of such a warm room.

The crackling of the fire faded into voices. Coaxing, cooing.

"It's time."

"You know…you know what you must do."

"Don't let the sickness take them."

"They belong to you."

"To us."

Then the voices grew louder, more demanding.

"The fire will grow. Envelop all. It shall consume."

"No longer ill."

"Free of the shackles. The body's constraints."

The power of those words shook Reid. Shook the room, like an earthquake, a bombastic force which compelled them to fling their hands to their ears.

Heather pulled her hand free and backed away until

she was shrouded in darkness.

"Heather, wait," he whispered into the dark.

But she was already gone.

The shaking continued, and the floor was yanked out from underneath him, the house falling deeper into the hell it likely came out of. Yet in spite of all that, his body didn't move.

It was a trick.

He looked to Alex in time to see him drop to the floor, with a thud.

"Alex," Reid called out. "You okay?"

Alex nodded as he lay on the floor. He scrambled to a sitting position, then slowly got to his feet. Just as he was about to say something, he buckled forward, holding his stomach.

He lifted his head. "Someone just punched me in the gut."

He tried to right himself and it happened again, this time knocking him back to the floor.

"It's not real," Reid said. "It's just trying to scare you."

Alex grunted. "It feels real."

The house hummed a steady thrum which bounced off the walls. Sounded like a million cicadas on the hottest summer day.

As if the humming built and shaped the man, he was brought back to life. More solid, more clear. Not just a memory of long ago, not a ghost, but a live man. He continued swaying.

"*Burn! Burn! Burn!*" voices chanted, in time with the man's sway.

"*Inside. Burn inside.*"

The man lifted his head and shoulders and revealed

what he'd been holding.

His baby.

Flames licked out to the man, lacing around his shoulders and guiding him forward.

The fireplace grew to an immeasurable height, looming above the man, surpassing the walls. The sight of it made Reid dizzy. All this time he'd thought the fireplace existed within the house, but now it seemed the house was inside the fireplace. Maybe there never was a house at all.

He racked his brain for understanding. Where was he? And the vibrations pushed harder and faster, disrupting the atmosphere, clouding everything he perceived. The man grew more solid, more real with each vibration. He looked so familiar to Reid, as if he'd known him, but that wasn't possible.

The echo of the humming stopped. The walls disappeared and only blackness stood in their place. The room had become a void.

The man seemed to willingly accept the flames.

He held the baby out toward the fire as an offering as he walked, and more flames came out to greet the child, too, wrapping wisplike tentacles around the child's arms, legs, and finally, neck. The baby screamed at the touch. So much fluid in that scream. So much sickness. Underwater. Drowning.

The man didn't flinch, didn't seem to notice or care about the baby's cries. He kept moving forward, not even looking at the baby he held. His face was blank, empty of all expression and feeling. Empty of every-thing human.

He bent forward and gave his child over to the flames.

Reid reeled from the sight of it but couldn't pull his eyes away. The helpless child, sacrificed by its own father. Casually tossed aside as if it meant nothing to him.

Like Reid meant nothing to his father.

Screams from the child grew tight and muffled as the flame crawled down its throat. Reid felt his throat tighten and burn, but he was powerless to help. Like an octopus, the fire reached out with too many greedy hands and wrapped the baby up. First cradling and rocking it, then wrapping each flaming arm tighter around the infant until it was a tiny bundle of fire. Reid rubbed his arms, horrified, imagining what it would feel like to have those rapacious hands gripping and consuming his body. He fought back the feeling, stilled his body, and tried to calm his mind.

The fiery arms withdrew back into the fireplace, taking the baby with it.

Overwhelmed by it all, Reid retched. The bile burned his empty stomach and scalded his esophagus. Yellow spittle dribbled down his chin and painted the floor.

He turned away, unable to see any more. He tried to call out to Heather, but an invisible hand struck him across the face. When he called out to Alex, his words were swallowed by the air.

In front of him, the fire burned, a live thing threatening to consume anything that got too close. Behind him, the darkness lurked, threatening to erase him, to pull him into oblivion. He could feel a cold spot on his back, a tingly sensation pushing at him more and more the farther he backed up.

The voices began again, within the fire.

"Sickness no longer. The fire cleanses."

"The fire consumes."

"The child is yours, the child is ours…"

"Forever bound."

The man nodded and turned his back to the fire. He walked away until he was shrouded in the stygian void. He kneeled, reaching into the darkness for something.

He carefully scooped it up, rose to his feet and turned back to the fire. In his arms, the man's wife hung limp and frail, barely conscious.

Her eyes rolled, as she was unable to keep them still for lack of strength. They were glazed over. She was probably completely unaware of her surroundings. Her arms drooped toward the floor. Like dead weight, he carried her, though she couldn't have weighed much at all. Her body was withered and frail as if she hadn't eaten in weeks. Cheeks sunken in, the bones protruding from under her flesh. Lips looked like they barely existed, just open lines revealing gums and teeth. The top of her chest showed through under her clavicle as her gown fell open. Each rib threatened to push through the pale skin. Her arms were skin and bone, too, blue veins pressing too close to the surface.

An odor of sweat and decay crept into the room and stung Reid's nose.

The man stepped close to the fire, close enough to catch fire himself. But the flames didn't want him. They wanted her. The flames were human-like, thinking and moving with intent.

Again, the man held out his arms to the fire, this time offering his wife. And again the fire reached out to aid him, to take the burden from him.

The flames wrapped her up and became arms of their own, holding her just like the man had. He dropped his arms to his sides and stepped back. His face showed nothing. No recognition of what he was doing. No feeling. No regret.

The flames resembled ribbons, lacing around her arms, legs, chest, and head. It could've been beautiful if it wasn't so horrible. And then they pulled back into the fireplace, taking her with them.

She never screamed. And she was gone.

The man fell to his knees as the voices started again.

"Sickness no longer. The fire cleanses."

"The fire consumes."

"The woman is yours, the woman is ours…"

"Forever bound. Forever true."

The man scrambled backwards as the flames that had just devoured his wife reached out to him, beckoning him closer. Reid didn't think the man was afraid, more surprised. Was he shocked by the realization of what he'd done, or what the fire wanted him to become?

The flames licked out to him, and thousands of shrill whispers rang out in unison, their words lost in a hectic blur. The man moved back. He lifted his face and the light of the flame gave Reid a view of a single tear falling from the man's eye. That tear ran down an otherwise emotionless face.

And then the man was gone.

Reid exhaled a long and shaky breath. He searched the growing darkness for the man but saw no one.

The flames coiled back into the fireplace and died down to ash.

The room was black.

But it didn't last.

A loud crackle and a spark flew out of the fireplace as the flames reignited. The blackness was once again lit up enough to reveal a man—*the* man—enter the room. But this time he was older, his shoulders hunched forward.

When he lifted his face again to the light of the fire, Reid could see the lines of age etched over his brow, the crow's feet at the sides of his eyes, and deep lines creased around his mouth. His lips were thinner, eyes narrower.

I wonder how many years he lived here, alone.

"I hear you," the man said. "I've always heard you. And them, too. My child. My wife. You hang them over my head, dangle them like a prize you stole from me, that you tricked out of me. But they're gone. Dead. And I can't abide this any longer."

His voice was thin and frail, and matched his appearance.

How many years did he live with what he did?

The man fell to his knees as the voices began.

"Sickness no longer. The fire cleanses."

"The fire consumes."

"The child is yours, the child is ours…"

"As we promised…we promised…"

"The woman is yours, the woman is ours…"

"Forever bound. Forever true."

"And now you shall be, too."

The man bowed his forehead to touch the floor, with his arms outstretched in petition, and chanted, "Burn, ignite, consume, devour.

Now is our time, now is the hour.

Burn, consume, devour, ignite.

Feed us more, gives us life.

Burn, devour, ignite, consume.

Shadow come, seal their doom."

The fire grew taller still, as if there never was a room that had contained it in the first place. Just darkness on all sides, pushing at Reid, Heather, and Alex, trying to force them closer to the spectacle, closer to the flames, closer to the memory playing out before them.

The man got to his feet and the fire towered ten times his height. He tilted his head back and raised his hands out to his sides, awaiting embrace.

The voices came back.

"When flesh is gone, the shackles are free."

"Inside, outside, you will be free."

"Come, let us be. Let us inside."

A single flame shot out of the fireplace, straight for the man's face. He didn't move except to open his mouth. Down, down it went, like a reverse version of that awful trick where the clown pulls the unending string of cloth out if his mouth. Forever it went on, inch after inch of the fire pouring down the man's throat. As it happened, the flames in the fireplace shrunk with each passing moment. It thrust itself into the man until the fireplace was empty. The man clamped his mouth shut and fell to the ground.

The pull of the evil within the room was now focused on Reid. The fire reached out to him, enticing him to come closer. He fought it with all he had. The darkness behind his back chilled him, but he resisted. He stepped away from the fire, away from the heat, and backed into the darkness. Embraced the shadows. Reid had spent most of the last three years hiding from his father, in the attic, in the shadows. The chill of losing his mother had sunk deep into his bones and never let go. He welcomed the cold, the darkness.

Not looking, Reid stepped backwards, deeper into the shadows as he watched the scene playing out before him.

Still on the ground, the man dropped his head forward as he rested on hands and knees, breathing raggedly.

Then he flung his body back, head to the ceiling, and let out a long, painful scream. It reminded Reid of the sounds he'd heard from his father only minutes after his mother died.

Fire flashed from within the man's eyes as if it was trapped, burning him from the inside out. Those fiery eyes were wide as he wailed in agony.

His body fell to the ground and he writhed in anguish. Reid was acutely aware now that the flame was inside the man, burning him, eating him. Becoming him. The man twitched and clawed at his clothes, chest, and face.

The house began to pulse again. The reverberation pounded off the walls like angry fists, shaking the room under Reid's feet.

The fire in the man's eyes went out and only darkness was left inside. Empty black coals in place of eyes, devoid of light. Devoid of life.

Reid now understood what this man's grief did to him. It destroyed him. And the evil in the house had guided him through it all. The house had consumed the man—his pain, his sadness, his madness—and turned him into another entity. Another evil.

The Shadow.

Chapter 25

Heather shot up from the floor.

Alex's face appeared in front of her own. "Whoa, settle down. It's me." He squeezed her hand.

She sighed and leaned back into the wall.

"I just..." She shook her head. "I had a wicked bad dream."

"About the house? And the man? And the creature?" Reid stood up and moved to the hatch. Placed a hand on it.

Alex scrambled to the door. "Whoa, what're you doing? Don't open that door."

Reid dropped his hand off the handle but didn't step back. "We gotta get outta here. And soon."

Heather cringed.

He remained facing the hatch, his back to them. "Got a better idea? I'm all ears."

"Okay, we will, but hang on." Alex stepped between

Reid and the door. "We all had the same dream, didn't we?"

The fear crawled up Heather's skin, like ants raiding a picnic.

"It wasn't a dream, was it?" She began twirling one of her curls. "Do you think…" She whispered, "Do you think Danny and Clint are here? Stuck here with them, forever?" Her voice grew frantic, and so did her hair twisting. "I know it. They are. It's bad enough they're dead, but this is worse. So much worse." The feeling of defeat washed over her and she flopped to the floor. She pulled her knees into her chest, wrapped her arms around them, and began rocking. "And who's next? Me? You?" She shook her head. "What if I'm last? I don't wanna be alone."

A stony silence followed.

The silence made her anxious. "Why did the house show us all that?" she asked. "Why did we dream all of it together? The man, the baby, the creature."

The fear gripped her and wouldn't let go. She wrapped her arms tighter around herself and tried to get it under control. Except she couldn't stop shaking and her teeth chattered.

"I-s-is-it-co-cold in here?"

Alex's gaze drifted toward the window, to her right. It had been so dark before that no one had noticed. Heather followed his gaze until she saw what he was looking at. Her fear dissipated with the discovery and her heart leapt with hope as she squinted at the brilliant daylight. It cast twinkling rays of sunshine through the frosted pane. Alex moved closer to it and set his palm against the glass, tossing a shadow across the floor.

It made Heather think of when she was very young

and her mother would play hand-shadow games with her at night. Once Heather was tucked snug as a bug in bed, her mother would put her hand in front of Heather's bedroom light and contort her fingers to shape all sorts of animals which sprung to life in the shadows.

"Look, it's a dog," her mother would say. Heather could hear her mother laugh with delight at Heather's rapt entertainment
, and she could feel her soft blanket tucked under her chin. Snug-bug.

"It's an alligator. Snap, snap, snap go the jaws." Heather's eyes always grew wide at that one, as she was tickled, yet afraid. She'd pull her blanket up higher, covering one eye and squinting the other.

"Now a bird." That always made Heather toss her blanket back and fling her hands up to clap with delight.

Heather smiled at the memory.

But her smile melted and she jumped as the bird in her memories contorted and turned into one of those evil fairies with the ratty wings.

Her mother was gone. Then the fairy was gone.

Even her memories weren't safe.

"It's cold," Alex said. "Really cold."

He moved closer to the window and exhaled onto the pane. Then he wiped it with his hand to clear the foggy smear he'd created. With his nose pressed to the glass, his words came out in puffs, clouding it back over.

"Snow. On the ground." He tilted his head, peering outside. "The trees. Every-fucking-where." He wiped his forearm over the window.

"That can't be." Heather scrambled to her feet. "It's summer."

She pushed her brother aside and pressed her face into the glass. Her mouth formed an "O" but she made no sound.

"Maybe break the window?" Alex said. "Wait. There's a breeze, a draft coming from…"

"Maybe it is winter," Reid said.

Heather jumped at the sound of his voice.

"Maybe we've been in here that long." Reid swallowed, audibly. "Who knows?"

With daggers in her eyes, Heather swung around to face him. "Don't be stupid. They'd have found us. Mom, Dad, Mike. They'd have been here by now. They'd look for *us*." She pointed to herself and then Alex. "Even if no one would come for *you*." She regretted the words as soon as they left her mouth.

"But how do you know?" Reid said. "How do you know anything? Since we got here, it's been day, it's been night. Light, dark. Basement, attic. Rooms this house doesn't even have. It could've been a goddamned year ago, or a minute since we first walked through that door. You don't know! We could already be dead."

The last words felt like a fist upside Heather's head, and fire burned inside her belly.

"I know you're a wicked jerk!" She slugged Reid in the stomach.

He took a deep breath and stepped back, his eyes wide.

"Alex, get a hold of your crazy sister. Even I have my limits."

There was no response.

He glanced around the room. "Alex?"

Heather and Reid looked around, shouting Alex's name, but there was nothing.

"Where did he go?" Heather asked. "Where could he go? He wouldn't leave me. Something bad just happened and we didn't even see it. He's gone."

"We can't sit here and panic. It's not gonna get us outta—"

Heather pointed at Reid. "We're not getting out! Don't you get it? There's no way out. We're dead. We're all dead!" She struggled to hold back the tears but lost the battle. "I want to go home. I want Mom."

"We'll get you home. I'll get—"

"Don't you understand, Reid? This is all your fault. We wouldn't be here if it wasn't for you. You're such a big bullying jerk. No one wanted to come, and now everyone's dying and it's all on you!

I WANT TO GO HOME!" She balled up her fists and pounded on his chest. "I want to go home!"

"We will. I'll get you out. First, we gotta find Alex." Reid pulled her into him and held her tight.

"He killed his wife," Heather whispered into his chest. "His little baby. What's gonna stop him from killing us? We're screwed."

"No, we're not."

Heather stopped blathering and looked up into his eyes.

"Before Clint died, he told me to get you guys out and that's what I'm gonna do. There's no other option. So stop crying right now. Pull it together and let's go."

That was what she needed to hear whether it was true or not.

She nodded. "But why is the house doing this?"

Reid let her go and shifted his weight from one foot to another. "Why does the house do anything? To scare us? Who knows?" He bit his lip. "All I know is I've had enough."

Chapter 26

Alex wasn't sure when he realized he couldn't hear Heather and Reid anymore. He was too distracted.

A draft caught his attention, so small at first, but as he took a few steps in its direction, it grew. Cold air pushed into the room, so he followed its source. After looking out the window and seeing the snow, feeling the cold against the pane, his brain took a little side trip. It seemed impossible that they'd been in the house that long.

A bee drawn to a flower, Alex followed that draft, running his fingers along the cool wall.

He turned a corner. A corner not there before, not even in Reid's real-life attic.

Alex's hand came across a divot in the wood and he froze. There was enough room to wedge his pointer and middle finger in. The air was definitely coming from in there. Or out there. Wherever *there* was. Excitement coursed through his blood and his heartbeat sped up.

Forgetting about Reid, Heather, the evil lurking around every damn corner, he pressed on. *Gotta investigate.*

He pulled his fingers out and squatted down to eye level with the hole. Cautiously moved forward until he could look through.

HE INCHED his face closer and closer. Turned his head to the left and lined up his right eye with the hole.

"Now or never," he said.

He took a deep breath and reached both hands out to either side of the hole to steady himself, and peeked.

It was so quiet he could hear his heart beat. And nothing else.

He blinked to focus his vision on the other side.

The sound came before the sight.

Muffled sobs. A woman. The woman.

Alex begged his mind to see something different. This hadn't been what he'd expected. The draft was supposed to lead him out of the house. He swallowed down a lump of disappointment.

Squeezed his eyes shut and wished her away. Wished to find an open door, leading out.

"Go away, go away," he said. "Let me out."

When he opened his eyes, he looked back through the hole. She was still there, curled up in a ball on the floor. So much white surrounded by darkness, glowing unnaturally. The starkness of it stung at his eyes and confused his mind. It was like he was staring at a painting on a charcoal black canvas, a lone white figure laying, floating in nothingness.

He gasped at the withered sight. It wasn't just her gown that was white, but her skin as well.

She must've heard Alex, because she lifted her head. Or tried to, anyway. Heartache gripped Alex as he watched her struggle. Her neck seemed too frail to hold her head up. She raised it a few inches, then sank. Again, it raised and fell. She pushed off the floor, trying to hoist herself up.

"Two steps forward, one step back," Alex's mom used to say when she was struggling to get something done but failing. He finally understood that phrase.

The woman's dark hair fell forward, shielding most of her face. But he saw her eyes looking out at him under her dark brows, her head tilted down. It was like her face was made of only those eyes. Sad, dying eyes. Rings of black hung underneath, making her face seem too small to hold such big eyes.

All Alex could do was think of Reid watching his mother waste away with cancer, right in front of him. Death was already there, staring back at him, through his mother's eyes. Inside. Watching. Waiting. Just like this woman.

Alex remembered the last time he went to Reid's house before his mother died. They were playing together, innocently enough, in Reid's room. Reid had gone downstairs to get some sodas, and left Alex alone. A soft moan floated down the hallway, and he couldn't help but be curious. He followed the sound, to his Reid's mom lying in bed. So frail, she looked less like a body and more like another blanket strewn across the bed. Her jaw was slack, lips dry and cracked. She moaned again and Alex met her gaze. It was then that he realized that death sometimes inhabited the living.

Because she wasn't alive, not really. Her eyes were dark and cloudy, sunken and pained, with black rings beneath them. It was like death was eating her from inside. That was the last time Alex visited Reid, until after his mom died. Even though he knew he should've been there for his friend, he couldn't see that look again.

But here he was, seeing that look again. This ghostly woman through the hole didn't blink, just held her head at that unnatural angle, staring at Alex.

A stalemate of stares. Neither one of them moved. Holding still, holding still.

He could only hold his eyes open for so long before the sting made him give in and blink.

She was gone.

He searched for a glimpse, blinking furiously. "Please, don't go." His voice sounded like a stranger's.

A thud hit the wall, on the other side. Then another. He still couldn't look away. He needed to see her. Each of those thuds seemed to hit on the other side of the wall corresponding to where his hands were. Still, he couldn't see a thing.

Silence.

And then breathing.

He could hear her breathing. Long, uneven rasps just unseen inches away from his face. And then it seemed as if she were trying to speak. Coughs. Angry, wet coughs. She couldn't form a word.

A lock of her hair brushed across the hole as she moved, and then it was gone.

Lips were pressed against the hole. Alex shifted and pulled his eye back a few inches. He could feel her breathing. Hear her breathing. Smell her breath.

The putrid odor hit his face, smacking it with a

memory of when he was six years old. The time he got locked inside his grandma's basement. It was the scariest thing that'd ever happened to him, until he got to this house.

Curiosity had gotten the best of him that night, and no one had been paying any attention. He wandered away from his family, who were all gathered in the living room. Their voices faded more and more with each step he took. And then he was standing in front of that door, excitement and fear coursing through his veins. The infamous basement door loomed in front of him, daring him to open it and enter.

Michael had teased him that no one who went in there made it out alive. That it was haunted by an Indian fighter from King Philip's war, Peletiah Morgan, way back in the 1670s. Michael had said that Peletiah had gotten scalped, and if you were lucky—or unlucky —you might see his scalpless ghost walking through the house at night, headed for the basement.

Alex's grandma's basement was dark and dank. Chilly air pricked at his skin. Each stair his foot stepped down on had creaked, possibly a warning to old Pele- tiah that an intruder was lurking. Alex swore he could hear his own name being whispered. Cobwebs dangled from every corner of the low cement ceiling. There was old, neglected furniture with tarps thrown over them.

Everything smelled funny, and he crinkled his nose. Age and rot and death. Only then, Alex didn't under- stand what those smells meant. He just knew they were awful, yet he kept moving forward—Peletiah be damned.

In the dim room, Alex stumbled over one of the chair legs and fell, coming face-to-face with a rotted corpse of what he guessed was a rat. Its fur was matted and fuzzy in some spots, and in others it had no fur at all. The remaining eye looked straight back at him.

Alex screamed...and screamed.

That's how his family had found him in the basement. Michael's face was the first he saw, his eyes full of concern. But when he realized Alex was in no real danger, he smiled.

Alex's mind jumped back to the present, the ghost lady's mouth pressed up to the hole. The smell of her death and decay pushed through the air. He smelled her sickness. Her rot.

And then she finally choked out, "Run!"

Those words hit Alex and he fell backwards. Scrambling to get to his feet, he watched in terror as black smoke billowed through the hole.

Chapter 27

Alex couldn't take his eyes off it. Momentary peeks ahead were all he could manage.

By the time he got to his feet, the dark mist was almost all the way out. Its smoky claws dug into the wall where his hands had just been, and wriggled the rest of the way through. A massive formless shape rolling toward him.

The woman kept screaming, begging Alex to run, but he didn't need any encouragement.

Down a long, dark corridor he ran, his head over his shoulders, one eye trained on the creature. The blackness ahead only gave out when he was six feet away, and allowed him to see the hall in front of him. Beyond that, there could've been anything, but forward was the only way to go. His legs wouldn't go fast enough. His sneakers slapped against the floor with each crazed step.

The corridor was winding too much. Every time he picked up speed, he'd have to slow down to take a turn, or risk crashing right into the wall. A blind, serpentine path. No other sound except his breathing and footfalls could be heard.

Until the voices started again.

"Watching..."

"Waiting..."

"One...two...three..."

The voices scratched at Alex's eardrums so hard he thought they'd bleed.

"No!" he screamed.

The corridor bent and wrapped around again, a writhing snake ever moving and changing, making each turn blind until the last second.

As he sprinted, visions of Clint and Danny, their bodies burned from the inside out, flashed in his mind. *My friends in ashes. My friends, dead.* He'd seen what happened when this creature touched someone, and he wasn't going to let this fucker touch him.

As his legs ached and lungs burned, he thought of Heather. *Poor little sister, getting sucked into this stupid macho boy mess. I have to protect her.* A sense of relief washed over him as he realized that if this thing was chasing him, she was safe for now. And Reid would take care of her if something happened to Alex.

The sound of panting brought Alex back to his dire situation. They were his own labored breaths.

Around each turn, he held onto the hope that the next might take him out of this stupid never-ending hallway.

"Watching..."

"Waiting..."

The shadowy little winged creatures swirled and danced on the walls as he sped along, always a step behind. He got the feeling that they weren't trying to catch him, just keep up and watch the show. Out of the corner of his eye, he saw something else move, bodiless. The Shadow.

"*Which will it be?*" the critters screeched.

"No, no, no!" Alex yelled as he fled.

The smoky creature was getting closer. No matter how hard Alex ran, it gained on him, with its long, undefined arms outstretched. The scrape of its claws along either side of the corridor sounded like nails on a chalkboard. The hallway turned sharply again and Alex lost his footing. Scrambling, he had to slow down. Had to stay upright and ahead of this thing. His sneakers squeaked as he slowed his pace enough to turn the corner without falling.

And that's when he saw her running straight at him, but it was too late.

Alex and Heather collided and fell to the ground in a heap of clumsy tangled legs.

Chapter 28

R eid grabbed a broken leg of the rocking chair that still lay in a heap, then marched up to the frosty window and repeatedly slapped it into his palm.

Heather stared at him, her gaze following his every move. The feeling of being needed, relied on by Heather, made him even more determined.

HE NODDED BACK TO HER. "I'm getting us out."

"What about Alex? We can't leave him."

"We won't." Reid tapped the wooden leg in his hand. "I'm gonna get us outta this house. Once outside, you're going for help and I'm going back inside to get Alex. But I need to make sure you're clear of this house first."

"But what if—"

"But nothing. This is the plan."

She shook her head. "We should get Alex first, then come back for the window."

Reid stopped tapping the broken leg on his palm, and faced her. "We will get Alex. I promise I'll get him out. But this chance might not come again. This room might not be here when we come back for it after finding Alex."

"But if that's true, if we turn our backs on this window, it might go away forever."

"I have to get you out. Now."

"But—"

"But nothing. Trust me." Even if it meant his own sacrifice, he was determined.

But what had he ever done to prove he was trustworthy? A bully, a jerk, a bad seed. He was the reason they were stuck in the house. The reason Danny and Clint were dead.

He swallowed down a lump of guilt. "Not now," he whispered to himself. There would be time for regrets and guilt later.

Silence passed between them.

"Okay. It's a good plan, Reid."

"Here goes everything. Good thing this attic is on the first floor and not the third like my real attic." His smile was forced and awkward.

He closed his eyes, quieting his mind. Once he opened them, he gripped the chair leg like a baseball bat and pulled it back like Carl Yastrzemski, about to smack one out of Fenway Park. He braced himself and firmed up his stance.

After saying a silent prayer, he wound up all the way and let it fly.

The leg went tearing through the glass and landed a few yards away, kicking up a cloud of snow around it.

He picked up another broken piece of wood and smacked out all the remaining shards of glass until he stared through an open window.

Cold air rushed in and assaulted his senses. The sting of it on his face never felt so good. He took a deep breath and coughed as the iciness tickled his throat. He reached out and felt flakes of snow. They quickly disappeared as they met with the heat of his hand.

He turned to Heather. "You first. That snow felt pretty soft—it'll ease your landing. Now go."

She gave him the biggest smile he'd ever seen before she went. Her eyes lit up like a Fourth of July sparkler and the sides of her mouth creased up almost to her ears. It made him feel lighter, hopeful for the first time in a long time.

She vaulted up and through the pane like a champion gymnast, springing through with ease.

Then he dove through head first, anticipating that the cold snow would envelop him.

BUT HE REALIZED it was a trick. Another illusion. There was no snow. Maybe there never had been. The chill from the cold fell away from his skin, and all he felt was defeat.

Heather slowly got to her feet. Reid's body ached from the fall, but he was okay. He stood behind Heather and they looked down a long winding corridor. It seemed like it went on forever. His shoulders slumped at the realization that getting out of this house wouldn't be so easy.

Should've known better. He dropped his head, still hoping to see snow, but they weren't outside on a New England winter day. They were trapped in a hallway that could be anywhere in this world, or some other strange world.

"You okay?" Reid asked.

"I'm not hurt. You?"

"No." He sighed. "Sorry. I thought we had it this time."

Heather didn't answer.

Reid released a string of expletives that came bursting up through him like hot lava from a volcano. "Fuck, shit, goddamn son-of-a-bitch, whore-faced—"

"Stop it."

"I fucked up."

"Be quiet."

"I'm sorry, Heather."

"Seriously, snap your yap. I hear something. Can't you?" She pointed down the corridor.

Reid lifted his head and closed his eyes. "No—well, yeah. Wait. I think I do."

"Someone's yelling."

Heather took a step forward, but Reid yanked her back. She shook him free and took another step.

"It's Alex." She took another two steps. "Alex. He needs us. Let's go."

Before Reid could try to fight her, she was sprinting down the hall. He followed.

Tried to keep pace, but she was the Tasmanian devil, racing toward her brother and disregarding any dangers ahead.

Alex's cries were getting closer, which seemed to fuel her fire even more.

Reid tried to call out to her, but she either didn't

listen or didn't hear him. So he picked up his pace to keep her in his sight.

"Slow down, Heather."

She didn't listen.

"Stop. Come back."

All of his pleas fell flat on the air around him. Useless words. He had to get to her physically. Make her listen. As he chased her, life threw out a wildcard. He realized too late what was about to happen. Alex came running around a sharp corner. Unable to do anything to stop it in time, he watched the scene unfold like a car crash in front of him.

"Get up! Get up! Go! Run!" Alex screamed. He pushed at his sister, trying to free her of the tangle. "It's coming!"

Heather lay on the floor, dazed by the collision.

Alex fumbled about, trying to get up. After finally standing, he yanked her arm.

"Up! Up!"

But Heather didn't look like she even knew where she was.

Time slowed, the milliseconds playing out like minutes for Reid, and he wondered if it was that way for Alex and Heather as well. He saw the shadows on the walls, dancing, swirling, dipping and tumbling around the corner, toward his friends. The whispers came with them.

"Watching."

"Waiting."

"Which will it be…"

The last word held too long, turning into a piercing squeal.

In Reid's ears, a rhythmic drumbeat began, slowly,

then built in intensity. His heart picked up on the rhythm and synced to it. An idea sprung into his mind and he closed his eyes and willed time to do another funny thing—shift to another place.

"Back in my attic," he whispered. "Always safe in my attic. Back in the attic. Keep them safe in the attic."

Over and over the words came, pouring over each other and running together so that he couldn't understand them anymore. As he said the words, he heard another voice, from the inside, echoing his words. *King Philip?*

A distant beat rang out, though Reid wasn't entirely sure if it was his heart or a drum.

He stole a peek at his friends, through a slit in his eye and saw Alex getting Heather to her feet. A ray of hope shot through him, and then his hopes were crushed when Heather cried out in pain.

"My ankle. I twisted my ankle!" She fell back to the floor.

And that was all the time the creature needed. It reached its shadowy claws out, inches from the curls on her head.

Reid shut his eyes tight and started his prayer once again.

"Back in the attic. Safe in my attic."

Chapter 29

Heather squeezed her eyes shut and clung to her brother like a life raft. It was all she could do. Part of her believed in the childish idea that if she couldn't see what was behind her, it couldn't see her either. *Be still. Be quiet. Don't look.*

Alex urged her to get up, shouting in her face, pulling on her, but the pain in her ankle was overwhelming.

When she'd made it to her feet, her ankle screamed out in protest and forced her to drop to the floor. She couldn't help but obey its command as the lightning bolts of pain zapped through the ankle, the foot, and up her leg. The bones felt like they were out of line, maybe even busted up.

Alex's sweaty palms were tucked under her armpits as he tried to drag her dead weight behind him, but it was no use.

Her head jerked back and Alex's forward progress came to a halt. Something was tangled in her hair. An attempt to twist her head around failed. The invisible hold was firm.

Always getting her hair snarled in something. Leaves and twigs from playing rough outside with the boys. And there was that stupid boy that sat behind her in homeroom—Nathan. He was always pulling on her hair. Her mom said it was because he liked her, but Heather thought that idea was wicked gross.

She winced, remembering the time she fell asleep chewing gum and it ended up in her hair. Mom had to cut out a chunk several inches long. She never fell asleep with gum in her mouth again.

But this was different. It felt like four bee stings on her scalp. Needle-like jabs. Or were those scratches? More like claws, not bees. But she could feel the venom coursing through her. Was it bees? Why was she so confused? And why was it getting so goddamned hot?

A scream welled up in her throat, tearing its way up until it escaped the confines of her mouth. And it wouldn't stop.

Alex was still yanking at her, but that feeling was dull compared to the burning sensation taking over her scalp.

And then everything stopped. No more tugging, pulling, raking, tearing. No more screaming.

"My hair's on fire," she moaned.

A voice crept into her ears, soft chanting. "Back in the attic. Safe in the attic."

She opened her eyes and saw Alex right in front of her, looking bewildered. Past him, she spied the source of the chants. Reid.

"Reid, how did you—"

Each word sent an echo of sharp, hot pain searing

through her teeth and into the back of her skull. After bringing her hand to the aching spot, she found no curls. Just scalp. She snapped her hand back and inspected her fingers. Something felt hot and wet. Fingertips covered in red. Her fingertips. Her…

Blood.

Her mind clouded over like a hot, hazy New England summer day. Her brain swam. So heavy. Too heavy. Her peripheral vision shrunk inch by inch until all she could do was focus on Alex's eyes just before her. He looked scared. Sad, even. She knew that, but everything else confused her.

The last thing she remembered was Alex's voice, reaching out to her through her fog. "You're safe. We're back in the attic. You're gonna be okay."

She could tell by his eyes that he lied.

~

HEATHER WAS DOWN at the old quarry with Mike. She'd just turned seven, and as a birthday present, he promised to teach her to fish. She'd never been more excited to hang out with her big brother. She thought he was the coolest thing since peanut butter and fluff.

She put the worm on the hook just like he'd showed her. It squiggled in between her fingers, trying to escape its fate, but she held on. Squishy slimy things never bothered her like they did other little girls.

The hook went through the worm and she wrapped it around and through again. A third time for good luck. That worm was only getting off the hook if she caught something and it ended up in its gullet.

She smiled at the thought of it.

Her fingers felt hot and wet.

Strange worm.

Her first try at casting was a bust. The hook got snagged in the back of her hair when she pulled too far back.

Giggling, she tried her best to stay still while Mike untangled her hair.

He finished with a nod and a warning. "Not so far back this time, kiddo."

Seriousness fell over her as she concentrated, her tongue sticking out of the corner of her mouth. After pulling the line back, she released, and this time, although wobbly, it plopped into the dark water.

Within seconds, she felt a tug on the other end of the line.

"This is a big one!" she squealed. "I know it!"

As her catch broke the surface, she realized what she had and her smile faded. Not a fish, but a snapping turtle. It was a good eight inches across, both ways.

"Careful with that," Mike said. "They can bite a finger off. Let me help you get it off."

She turned away from him. "I can do it myself."

Dizziness swept over her. "Hey, Mike, is the hook still in my hair? It hurts. Burns."

When she turned back, Mike was gone and the snapping turtle was in her hands, its jaws opening and slamming shut. Its body shook as it tried to escape.

She used a hand to clamp its mouth shut, then slowly moved her fingers even closer.

When the turtle opened its jaws again, it said, "It got her. Look, her hair is gone. It scratched her."

She giggled. Turtles don't talk. And this turtle

sounded just like Alex. After looking closer, she saw it had Alex's eyes.

"Thank God. She's waking up."

The turtle melted away and Alex stood before her. Reid was behind him. Their expressions serious.

She looked around and realized they were back in the attic.

And her head burned, like a fire had been set from the inside.

Chapter 30

R eid didn't have time to stop and wonder if his prayer had worked or if the house flipped them back into the attic by its own volition.

HE SLID up beside Alex and inspected the back of Heather's head as she lay on the floor, dazed. After Reid flipped aside a mass of curls, Alex gasped. A clump of hair was missing. Even worse, there were four long scratches across her scalp. In the confusion of her and Alex's tangled bodies, the creature had dug its nails in and marked her.

Borrowed time.

"It was coming for me. For me!" Alex slammed a hand into his chest. "It should be me!"

Reid grabbed him by the shoulder and spun him around to face him. "I should've watched her. I'm sorry, she got away from me. The whole thing is my fault. All of it." He stifled a sniffle.

Best not to cry now, or he may never stop. And real men don't cry. Everyone knew that.

Alex shrugged him off and turned back to Heather. "She's my sister. My responsibility. I wandered off. That stupid hole in the wall. Why'd I do that?"

Doubt crept over Reid like a storm cloud looming above his head. Closer and closer to him it got, until it crept inside his very pores. His dad was right. He was a loser. Only bad things happened when he was around. First, his mom got sick and died. Then he drove his father to drinking. Now his only friends were dropping like flies. He was poison. Rotten inside.

I should just crawl into a hole and give up.

"Keep it all inside. Don't let it out." He choked back the tears that welled up inside him. "Keep it all inside. Don't let it out."

"Alex, you're a turtle." Heather reached up and grabbed either side of Alex's mouth. "Snap, snap go the jaws." She laughed. "Careful, this one's a real doozy." Her laughter turned to coughing and her expression grew serious. "I got the hook stuck in my head. Can you get it out? It burns."

Alex pulled his sister's hands from his face and laid them in his own. The tenderness of it made Reid's chest tighten.

"How does your ankle feel?" Alex asked. "Can you walk on it?"

Heather appeared not to have heard him at all.

Reid's heart pounding in his chest, then his throat. He staggered and began shaking his head.

"Someone's always getting hurt around me," he said. "Just like when I broke her wrist, playing football. I didn't mean to...maybe I did mean to. I dunno." He jerked his hands through his hair and took a step back.

Heather's gaze fell upon Reid, but her focus seemed a million miles away.

Her words had an odd, unfeeling cadence when she spoke. "You meant it. You wanted to hurt me. Admit it. Bad, bad Reid." Her face held no expression either. It was like she was a puppet and the puppet-master spoke through her.

"You can't help it. You were made that way. Bad seed."

He pictured his father standing over him, drunk and swaying, with his fists ready to strike.

It seemed that Heather had crawled into the doubting part of Reid's brain, like she could see his fears, worries, and exploited them in favor of the evil around them.

"I should've stayed away," Reid said. "I should've never led us here. I keep hurting everyone. I keep hurting you. And now I've killed you."

Alex flew toward Reid and knocked him flat on his back. Within a flash, Alex had him pinned and straddled, and shook him by the shoulders. Reid's head butted against the floor.

"Shut up, shut up, shut up!" Alex howled. "Shut the fuck up! It's all your fault!"

He punched Reid, over and over. Blind fury, fists a blur. The first couple struck him in the face, and Reid shot his hands up for protection. The next few caught him in the stomach. He lay there, covering his face, but not trying to stop Alex's rage.

He deserved it, after all.

"Why?" Alex yelled. "Why did you have to bring us

here? No one wanted to come! Why do you bully every-one?" He punched Reid in the gut. "You made fun of Danny. Told him he was a baby if he didn't come. And now he's dead 'cause he listened to you. Clint's dead 'cause of you! Heather's…

"Why does your dad blame you for your mom? What did you do?"

Reid lay there and took punch after punch. Alex's fists were painful, but his words hurt so much more.

I'm bad.

Rotten, no-good son of a bitch.

He kept taking the blows until Alex tired out and flung himself to the floor beside his friend, exhausted.

THE PAIR LAY side by side, defeated, while Heather babbled, uttering streams of non-sequitur a few feet away.

"Snapping turtles bite." She crawled across the floor, and as she dragged her injured foot, the sneaker made a squeaking sound that gave Reid goosebumps.

There was something so unnerving, so un-Heather about her that it rattled him to the core. Her curls swept across the floor, picking up dust and dirt. She didn't seem to notice or care. After scrambling to her feet, she put all her weight on one leg. "Fireflies aren't really made of fire."

She hopped over to the boys, using her good leg, and hovered over them. Must've been a trick of the eye, because she was tall like an Amazon woman, casting a menacing shadow on them. *I wonder if Heather's even in there.*

She tilted her head, as if sizing them up, her voice

so adult, so serious. "You have old eyes," she said to
Alex. She frowned. "It's going to get heavy." She turned
to Reid. "Does it burn in the dark?"

Her words sent shivers through his body and hit him
harder than Alex's fists ever could.

Her words sent shivers through his body and hit him
harder than Alex's fists ever could. "Does it burn in the
dark?"

Chapter 31

Heather knew what she wanted to say—what she meant to say—but every time she opened her mouth, the words came out wrong. All nonsense, like she had all the pieces to a jigsaw puzzle but kept trying to jam them into the wrong spots.

It made her brain ache. Her mouth felt funny, too. Dry.

Need some water. Too damn hot in here.

Her body felt alien, and when she thought about moving her feet, they wouldn't listen. She tried to close her eyes, block it all out, but some force held them open, making her witness every moment. The anxiety of it made her want to twirl away at a curl, but she couldn't even pull that off. And when she said those awful things to Reid, that wasn't her at all. Those weren't her words.

Losing control.

She imagined that turtle hanging onto the end of

her fishing line, snapping, flailing. She felt like that, being reeled in by something bigger, menacing, and she wasn't sure how to fight.

The hook's already in, my friend. Sayonara, Sucker.

As she watched Reid and Alex lay on the floor after their fight, things began to look strange, like she was watching them through a looking glass. Is this what Alice in Wonderland felt like? As she stared at their figures, she knew she wasn't moving, but now they looked small and distant, as if they'd been moved far away from her. Or had she been moved? While standing over them, she couldn't feel the pain in her ankle. In fact, she couldn't feel her ankle at all. She felt all floaty-like, and something else rooted her to the floor.

What she'd wanted to say to Alex was, *Stop fighting,* but something different came out. And when she looked at Reid, things got weirder. He began to fade, though his outline remained. All his color swirled into one, getting darker and grayer. No face, no body, no hands, no hair. A void.

Her mouth opened even though she hadn't meant it to. "Does it burn in the dark?"

Heather was a prisoner in her own body, and she banged on the imaginary walls that trapped her.

She watched through the windows of her eyes as her body moved against her will. Her mouth spoke words she'd never thought of.

The more she banged on those prison walls, the more useless it felt. Her anxiety gave over to terror and she began to cry, although no tears fell from her eyes.

And the room got hotter. The air grew heavier, pushing against her from all sides. The smell of smoke permeated everything, stinging her nostrils and tickling her throat, forcing her to gag and cough.

The smoke poured in and wrapped around her like fingers caressing her skin. It weaved through her curls, and the bald spot began to throb, pulsing to the beat of a wild drum in her ears. She couldn't keep her eyes focused. They swam in their sockets, stinging from the press of the thick smoke. Her prison was growing darker, the smoke coloring her world gray.

On her knees, heavy from the heat, she could no longer pound on those cage walls. Sweat dribbled down through her mop of hair, to her brow, to the bridge of her nose, until all she could taste was salt and smoke. Sweat poured in rivulets down her neck, soaking through her clothes. She threw her hands up, one more attempt to slam into the walls, but all she could do was claw her nails down, down the walls. A couple nails flipped back and the blood begin to pour from her fingertips. The pain was too real, and the tangy metallic smell of the blood just as real.

But actually, her body stood still, beyond her control.

Her tongue felt fuzzy, coated with what she could only imagine must be the equivalent to licking her father's dirty ashtray.

As she peered out through those eyes, looking at Alex and Reid, the foreigner controlling her body spoke strange things to them, and she could see fear in their eyes. *They're finally afraid of me.* She would've laughed if she could just then. *Hey, fuckos! It's me. Heather. Get me outta here!* But her words never hit their ears.

She buckled to the floor, head in her hands, no longer able to watch the events unfold before her.

She was too tired, anyway. Too hot.

Heather woke to see Alex standing over her. She opened her mouth to speak, and it worked this time.

"So hot." She licked at her lips, then swallowed hard. "Huh, it works."

"What works?" Alex asked her.

"Talking." Her voice came out raspy.

Alex scrunched up his eyebrows.

She squeezed her eyes shut. "I was stuck. Inside. I didn't say those things." She rolled her head to the side, looking for Reid.

He appeared over Alex's shoulder, his face painted with concern.

"I didn't say those things to you, Reid."

Alex's frigid hand on her forehead made her shiver. *Why is his hand so cold?*

He pulled his hand away and whispered to Reid, "She's burning up." The corners of his mouth pulled down. "She's—"

"I'm right here!" she snapped. "I hear you."

The boys turned away from her, discussing something. *Why are they acting like that toward me?*

Chapter 32

"She's on fire," Alex pulled Reid back a few steps from her and lowered his voice. "She doesn't have any clue what's going on. She was talking all weird. It sounded like her, but I dunno…grown up."

Reid wiped his nose and came away with a smear of blood. He grimaced and his eyes started to water.

"Sorry for hitting you," Alex said.

Reid shook his head. "Nah, I deserved it. I let you down. I—"

"Nobody deserves that."

Reid nodded, looking Alex in the eye. "Do you think she said those things? Or did something talk through her?" He averted his gaze.

The thought of it gave Alex the willies. "You mean, is she possessed or something?"

"Yeah." The spot high above Alex's head became terribly interesting to Reid. "I mean, no. I dunno." He wiped his nose again. "Did you see her eyes, Alex? Did you see how red they were?"

Alex nodded.

"That thing," Reid whispered "It infected her, or marked her, or whatever the hell it does. Like Danny and Clint."

Alex glanced back at Heather, who'd passed out a few minutes ago. It sounded like she was snoring, but she never snored before. After listening closer, Alex realized she was wheezing, like when he'd had bronchitis a few winters ago. The memory of it made his chest hurt. Every breath caused a sharp pain, and coughing made him want to die. He was down and out for three weeks.

Maybe she'd gotten bronchitis, that's all.

Alex slapped himself inside, for the thought. He knew better. Reid knew better. Alex just wasn't sure what Heather was or wasn't aware of. Thinking about it made him hope she was in a peaceful bliss, riding a dream with fluffy, happy things dancing all around her. Anything but knowing what was really happening to her.

She's dying.

The desperation weighed heavy on Alex, tightening like a hand around his throat. No amount of sugar would help coat the guilt pill he was having trouble swallowing.

"I shouldn't have disappeared on you guys. I felt that draft and I couldn't help it. I followed without thinking. So far away…it took me to this hole—to a room—and the woman was inside. Through the hole where the draft came from, I saw her. She warned me to run. Before I knew it, that creature was coming after me, chasing me down this wild corridor, until I ran smack into Heather. I should've never left you. We

should've tried to get through that window, together."
Alex lowered his head and sucked in a deep breath.

"It wouldn't have mattered."

"It might have."

"Abso-fucking-lutely not. It was just another trick,
Alex. I busted that window, hell-bent on getting
Heather out, sending her for help, and coming back for
you. That's how we ended up in that hallway. We went
through the window."

Alex's heart sank.

"Do you think we'll find a way out? Do you think
it's even possible?"

Reid straightened. "Of course there's a way. We just
haven't found it yet."

Alex wasn't so sure he could believe him. Too much
had happened that was out of their control. Even when
they thought they were making choices, the house was
controlling the outcome. How do you stop something
that's unstoppable?

"We're down, but we're not out," Reid said. "Not
yet. It's fourth down, man, and the goal's in sight. We
just need one hail Mary pass, one break, and then the
game's ours. Don't give up yet."

He sounded an awful lot like their middle school
football coach, Mr. Carter. Coach had inspired them to
fight through so many games when they were down and
should've been out.

Except this wasn't a game.

Chapter 33

The boys continued to whisper. To Heather it sounded like they were speaking a foreign language.

Her brain was hot and confused. She wondered if someone's brain could turn to mush and come out of their ears. The thought of it frightened her so much she tried to touch her ears to check, but her attempt failed. Weird. Her left hand slapped over her left eye and her right hand missed her head entirely.

Concentrating, she willed her unruly arms to the right spot. No mush coming out of her ears. A relief.

The back of her head tingled, and the more she focused on it, the worse it got. Or was it the other way around?

Wiggling. Squirming. Getting hotter.

It started in her head and quickly spread down through her body, like hot worms infecting her insides. They flopped and sloshed around in her empty gut.

She lurched forward and threw up. Crumpled to her

side in the fetal position, exhausted. She shifted and focused her eyes to see what she'd just expelled, fully expecting to see worms on fire writhing on the floor. But all she saw was a puddle of bile.

Still, she grew hotter. Was it possible they were still inside her? She clawed at her stomach as ragged coughs racked her body. Her hair clung to her face in damp, disheveled curls. One curl laid across her eye, but she was too weak to do anything about it. A trail of spittle leaked from the side of her mouth, and a cold hand gently wiped it away.

"Mom?"

Chapter 34

Alex wiped the spittle away from Heather's mouth and pushed a sweat-soaked curl from her eyes. She was tearing at her stomach like she was about to claw her own insides out.

He stifled an overgrowing need to wail, and pulled her hands away from her body and held them in his.

"No, not Mom. It's me—Alex."

She didn't respond.

"Reid, she's getting worse. I don't think she can see or hear me. What do I do?"

Reid paced back and forth, muttering to himself, eyes distant. From time to time he'd stop to fling his arms over his head, toss his head back and moan. Then he'd continue wearing out a path on the floor. But what did Alex expect he could do, anyway? What could anyone do besides sit there and watch Heather die?

. . .

"SHADOW PUPPETS, MOM," Heather said. "Then I'll go to sleep." She nodded. "Why is it so hot in here?"

Giving her shadow puppets was the least he could do, right? He let her hands go, hoping wouldn't start clawing at herself again.

Curled up into a ball on the floor, she watched Alex shape his hands into figures. Except the attic didn't have enough light to create shadows.

She waited patiently, staring at his hands.

With his palms together, he hinged the heel of his hands, pried his fingers apart, then closed them.

"Alligator!" Heather choked out, then erupted in a fit of coughs.

"Easy, easy. Watch the show quietly."

He brought his thumb together with his pinkie and ring finger, and pointed his middle and pointer fingers up. He bobbed his hand up and down. Damn, he couldn't remember how their mom had done that one, but he did his best.

Heather squinted at his weak attempt, then whispered, "Bunny?" She smirked.

"That's right"

With his thumbs facing together, hands crossed over each other at the wrists, he spread both hands out to the sides, waved them back and forth, and moved his hands in a circular motion.

"A bird," she rasped.

"You got it!"

Her breathing became quicker and more shallow. She tucked herself tighter into a ball, wrapping her arms around her knees and bending her head down.

"No," she moaned.

"What's wrong, Heather?"

She shook her head, and more spittle ran from the side of her mouth as she spat, "No! No, it was a bird!"

Alex peered around, searching for what had scared her. Nothing. The whole time, his hands had never cast a shadow. It was all in her head.

But when Alex glanced over his shoulder again, he saw Reid stop dead in his tracks and the shadows of those tiny monsters dancing on the wall.

They flew up the wall, then tilted forward and nose-dived toward the floor, ratty wings tucked to their sides. At the last minute, they pulled up and twirled, like freakish ballerinas, on their clawed toes.

"Reid, we gotta go. Help me get her. Those things always bring—"

REID'S FACE dropped and he stared at Heather. Alex followed his gaze and saw a shadow fall upon his little sister. Dark and long, it seemed to come out of nowhere.

Heather's body thrust back and she was flung to the floor from the weight of the shadow creature. Her eyes stared up into the darkness looming above. Before Alex could move, it was already working its devilry. Black claws pried her mouth open, forcing it wide. Too wide. The claws dug into the side of her face, and the shadow oozed all around her.

A garbled scream escaped Heather as the creature dove inside her mouth, face first.

Alex refused to just stand there and watch.

He sprang up and reached out for the creature, but how do you grab smoke? His hands went right through.

A black claw flew up and hit him in the head and

spun him around. His vision swirled as his body did a roundabout. A sharp pain flashed across his temple, searing red-hot, momentarily blinding that eye. Then he was on his knees, facing Reid, who pulled Alex's head into his chest so tight Alex couldn't breathe. He wished he could stop breathing permanently so that he didn't have to sit there and listen.

Heather was choking while trying to scream. The sound of what Alex imagined was her feet thumping the floor as she tried to fight, filled the room. How she always loved to fight. *Thump, thump, whack, whack.* He begged his ears to stop listening, to never hear again. As Reid held him tighter, Alex's body sunk to the floor in defeat.

And then there was silence.

Chapter 35

Unlike all the others, Reid had lost his innocence when his mother died of cancer. She had been his light, his anchor, his joy. And when she passed, he had sunk into darkness.

Those last few days of her life he could only watch helplessly as his mother lay in her bed. She'd been released from the hospital on her last wish to maintain some peace and dignity and to die in her own home.

But every night, she lay alone in bed because his father was afraid to get too close and hold her tight. He watched her from the chair by the bed, never sleeping, awaiting her last breath.

During the day, Reid faithfully sat by her side, while an occasional friend or family member stopped by to see her one last time. To mourn a woman who wasn't yet gone.

Being alone with his mother was suddenly the worst thing in the world.

While holding her hand, with her frail fingers wrapped through his, he could feel every bone.

His gaze would run from her hands up her slender arm, following a trail of blue veins so close to her skin's surface. Veins that'd been poked and prodded had given up and were left to wither like the frail body that contained them.

Her chest rose and fell unevenly as she struggled to keep breathing. Her clavicle protruded out much farther than it should have, as the rest of her thin body seemed to fall away from it.

Reid's gaze would move up to her chin, lips. The rosy, full lips which always used to shower him with kisses had become so much thinner and a tired shade of blue.

The freckles he'd loved, sprinkled across her nose, now left a bitter taste in his mouth. How could something so pretty be so dead? He used to play a game with them, like staring into the clouds, finding shapes of animals in them. He'd connect the freckles until he found a lovely picture. Those cute little freckles were why she finally reached for that hat.

Too little, too late.

The cancer had spread slowly, undetected, latching onto every cell in her body as it wrapped around her lungs, liver, intestines, then took her heart last.

In those last few days it had stolen her will to survive. That's when she'd begged Reid to do one last thing for her.

She'd said it was too hard to fight. That she'd lost the battle and her body had already given up, but her mind wouldn't let go. Over those last three days, when she'd cried and no tears would come, when she'd begged Reid for that enormous favor, he would shake his head and leave the room.

But as he'd back away out of the room, he would watch her eyes and he'd see the fear, the pain, the anguish—everything a ten-year-old boy should never see in his mother's eyes.

For those three nights, he didn't sleep a wink. When he closed his eyes, all he could see were her imploring eyes.

He was the only one who could do what she'd asked. He was the only one she could ask. But he couldn't bring himself to do it.

He tossed and turned in his bed, wrestling with his thoughts, with her request. He tried to understand why she'd asked him, how she could ask that of him.

Covers on, covers off, too hot, too cold—he never could get comfortable. Too dark in the room with the lights all out, yet a night light burned his eyes like the sun.

ON THE FOURTH DAY, he sat with his mother at her bedside.

"Why?" he asked, expression blank.

"This body doesn't belong to me anymore," she whispered.

"What do you mean?"

"This body is dying, but my mind is strong and clear, so alive." She coughed and her body spasmed. She fought to sit up, but her body wouldn't obey her.

Reid grabbed another pillow and propped it under her head. "Better?"

"I'm trapped inside." She tapped over her heart. "But it only gives me pain. Holds me back."

Reid wiped at the spittle that had dribbled down her chin.

"Like a bird, I want to soar...to be free, but this body won't let me." She grasped her skinny neck with a frail hand. "Like a prisoner it keeps me. It hurts...too much."

He leaned closer, pulled her hand from her throat and held it in his. He stroked his thumb over her hand.

"I can't do it myself. I would if I could, my love." She took a moment to catch her breath. "I know it's so much to ask. And I know I have...no right to ask it of you."

"Then don't, Mom, please."

"But who else?" she cried.

"What about Dad?" Reid averted his gaze.

"No. I love your father, but he's not strong enough. He can't—it would kill him."

"But why me?" He met her eyes and searched them for a clue.

Those eyes which were once the sparkle of the sun, now looked empty, dark, sunken into her head. The rings under her eyes were even worse. Strange bags— puffy gray circles, like storm clouds brewing.

"Because you're my hero. You're stronger than your father and I put together." She took a labored breath. "I see it inside you." She reached out toward him, but her arm was too heavy.

He pulled her hand to his chest and held her palm over his heart.

"I love you, Mom."

"I love you always, no matter what." Her attempt at

a smile showed too many teeth, with her thin lips pulling back crookedly, and her eyes drifted closed.

She lay for several seconds, looking peaceful.

Reid held his breath, hoping her body had given up on its own.

But she turned and coughed, her body racking against the bed. Reid jumped. When she opened her eyes, they had lost more color, more life.

"Please," she rasped.

"Close your eyes, Mom. Think about flying."

She closed her heavy lids, clasped her hands together over her stomach, and smiled. This time the smile was beautiful, like when she was healthy and vibrant.

"Thank you," she said.

Reid slowly lowered a pillow toward her face and covered everything he loved. White-knuckled and shaking, he pushed down, down. Surprisingly, her body gave little fight. Reid had expected some drastic last minute surge of adrenaline when her body knew she was about to go out, but it didn't come. Instead, he felt the bed sink as her body gave in.

Her words echoed through his head as he held firm.

I'm trapped inside.

He pushed down harder.

This body doesn't belong to me anymore.

Tears raced down his face, but he didn't make a sound.

Like a bird.

Her voice danced through his mind.

I love you.

When he was sure it was done, when her body had finally let her go, he fell back and crumbled to the floor.

He pulled the pillow into his chest, rocking back and forth, crying silent tears.

The door to the bedroom creaked opened, and his father froze halfway through the door. The glass of water slipped from his fingers, fell to the floor and shattered, sending a spray of broken glass and water across the room.

Reid's eyes met his father's, and they stared at each other, wordless. His father seemed to be searching for some explanation of what lay before him.

Finally finding his voice, small as it came out, Reid said, "She's gone."

He couldn't be sure if his father saw the truth in his eyes or the pillow for the deadly weapon it was, but from that moment on, their relationship changed. His father never cast another loving look at him, nor spared a kind word for his son again. Instead of comforting Reid with hugs, he showered him with fists and anger. Perhaps he knew, perhaps he didn't. His father never said it out loud, but how else could he know that Reid was dark inside?

~

THE CHARRED CORPSE of Heather lay in the corner of the attic. The creature was gone—it had gotten what it wanted. For now.

Reid held Alex like that pillow, tucked into his chest. He rocked him back and forth as Alex sobbed, and wished his father would've held him like that. Wished that even a moment's love and comfort could've come from the man.

Silent tears streamed down Reid's face. Tears for his

mother, for Danny, Clint, and Heather. For Alex, too, but most of all, for himself. For all he'd lost along the way and all he'd become because of it. For the darkness that had crept inside him, the innocence he'd lost, and for what he'd have to become to save his friend.

Chapter 36

Alex's breath caught in his throat.

He pushed Reid away and sucked in a breath. Looked up into Reid's face to see tear-streaked cheeks and red eyes, though Alex had never heard him make a sound. It hurt even more to see him like that. Reid the bully. Reid the tough one.

With a heavy chest from the emotional exhaustion consuming him, Alex wanted to fall over. His heart was so broken he wanted to curl up on the floor and give up.

"Heather," Alex whispered.

Reid closed his eyes, his face twisted in agony. "She's gone, buddy. I'm sorry." He took a deep breath.

Good that one of us should keep it together, 'cause I can't.

Alex kept shaking his head. His mouth opened, but no words came out. He wanted to say so many things, but what was the point?

He stopped shaking and composed himself enough to speak. "I give up."

"No, you don't. You can't." Reid's face was a mask of seriousness. "No."

Alex flung his hands up in the air. "What does it matter anymore? She's gone! My little sister, gone."

The words felt like poison stinging his lips. He couldn't handle it, and he was losing his fucking mind.

"I let her down." He sobbed and collapsed back on his knees.

"Get up," Reid said, gently.

But Alex didn't listen.

"Get up!" Reid tucked his hands under Alex's arms and lifted him to his feet. It should have been demeaning, embarrassing, but Alex didn't care anymore. Call him a rag-doll and be done with it.

While holding Alex and bearing most of his weight, Reid glared at him. Alex couldn't stand to look into his eyes, so he averted his gaze over his shoulder and stared at the wall. The wall that not long ago was strewn with evil little dancers. *Dipping, diving, watching...*

Reid shook him. "Get over yourself! You can't quit. *We* can't quit. I let you down, I know. I failed Heather. But I promised Clint we'd get out, so I failed Heather. we have to escape for them. For Danny."

Alex shrugged out of his hold. "It doesn't matter, it's too late. I've been marked." When he ran his finger along his temple, he felt the scratch and went over it again and again, wincing in pain as he remembered his failed attempt to grab the creature and save Heather. "Don't you get it? I belong in this house now, too! Let's not pussyfoot around this whole thing. I can feel it inside already. Behind my eye, like hot little needles poking me from my temple. It's just a matter of time." He tapped at his temple, and the pain seized him.

"No, it's not! I won't let it take you!"

Alex poked Reid in the chest. "You? You can't do anything. You're as useless as me." He started to laugh hysterically. He could feel the veins in his forehead pulsing and that creepy wormy feeling behind his eye. "I thought I could be a hero. Thought someone could be a hero, like in the movies. But this isn't a movie. There's no fucking hero!"

Spit flew out of his mouth and hit Reid in the face.

He blinked a few times to clear his eye.

Alex held his breath, waiting for the rebuttal. Or a punch.

Reid ran the back of his hand over his cheek, removing the rest of the spit from his face, and stared right through Alex.

So Alex shoved him with all his strength.

Reid held his ground.

Alex pushed him again, but his feet did not falter.

"Move, damn you! Do something! Say something!" Alex pushed and shoved him, but he might as well have been trying to move a statue.

"Are you done now?"

Alex became silent. Two could play the quiet game. He raised his eyebrows.

Reid rolled his eyes. "Tantrum over? Good. Now let's get going." He grabbed Alex's arm and pulled him to the hatch.

The urge to steal a glance back at what remained of Heather came over Alex, but Reid jerked him to attention.

"No. No looking back. I'm gonna get you the fuck outta here. We've been dicking around too long."

Hatch open, he pushed Alex through first.

As he followed close behind, Alex called back, "*We're* gonna get outta here, you mean."

Reid closed the hatch door behind him and turned around to face his friend. "Yeah. Right. Well, someone's gotta be a hero, and like you said, it ain't you." He smirked but wiped it off as quickly as it came.

If Alex had blinked, he would have missed it. It looked like that snarky shithead of a friend was back, and Alex was glad for it.

On the other side of the door, they discovered that they were once again in the first room they'd all entered. Cobwebs still hung from the ceiling, floor still dusty. But unlike when they'd first entered, it was disturbed by all their footsteps. A moment's angst washed over Alex as he looked at those prints, picking out whose was whose. Heather's were easy to spot. But the rest? *Just a mess of dust.*

And after glancing around the room, Alex realized the front door was still missing.

Chapter 37

A crackling sound came from the fireplace. Alex and Reid froze. Flames began to dance and sway, a hypnotizing display. Alex could feel his eyelids grow heavy, but for some reason he couldn't blink, didn't want to. It was all so soothing.

Just a moment's rest.

And then a figure took shape, vaguely at first, deep within the fire. It gradually grew clearer until the shape morphed into something recognizable. Curls, dark and springy. They danced inside those flames. A face emerged beneath the wild curls, and Alex's heart leapt with joy. *Heather.*

As her face became clearer, it was obvious she was smiling. Her lips were moving, but Alex couldn't make out any noise.

What's she trying to say?

His joy turned to panic as her lips continued mouthing words, but without any sound. He was so sure he needed to hear her, that what she was saying was the most important thing in the world.

So he crawled like a baby, closer to the fire, closer to his little sister.

Whispers graced his eardrums, and unlike the evil little creatures, this was the sweetest sound—a voice he never thought he'd hear again.

Closer he crawled until hands were on him, holding him back. Must've been Reid, but Alex didn't look. He couldn't take his eyes from his sister. Afraid that if he did, she'd disappear forever.

Those hands couldn't keep him from hearing her. Whispers turned to words as she leaned forward from within the flames.

So happy. So peaceful. Her face looked relaxed, soft, and delicate. Alex smiled.

"It's okay," she said. "It's better now. I was wrong."

Alex tried to lean in closer, but Reid's hands still held him back. Reid was saying something, but that was blocked out by Alex's desperation to hear Heather.

"What's okay? What were you wrong about?"

Once again, Alex strained against those hands holding him back, but they wouldn't budge, wouldn't set him free.

Curls bounced around Heather's face as she shook her head and laughed. "We were all wrong, you know. It doesn't hurt anymore. It's not dark or scary." Her words slow and deliberate. She sounded so grown-up, beyond her years. "It's warm and safe. I'm not sad or scared. I'm so happy."

"How?"

"I just let go." Her face grew serious. "You should,

too. Stop fighting. It takes too much energy. And look at you, you're so tired."

She frowned and her countenance became too extreme, too sharp. Her eyes grew dark, lined with years beyond her own. Her mouth creased in a way no twelve-year-old's ever could, like someone tried to paint a picture of a young girl but failed, depicting a forty-year-old woman instead. Her forehead was wrinkled, full of concern and worry.

Alex knew, somewhere inside, that this wasn't his sister, yet he batted that knowledge away.

"I *am* tired," he said. "It hurts. This is so hard, Heather. I'm so sorry. Sorry we failed, let you—"

"Shh," she whispered through the flames.

The warmth from that one sound reached out to him, soothing him.

"Don't be sorry. Everything's okay here. Everyone's all right. Me and Danny and Clint. But I do need you. I need my big brother. Come." She waved a hand, beckoning.

He could feel its pull, her pull on him. Warmth surrounded him and confused his mind.

"What do I do?"

"Give in. Let go. Stop fighting."

The memory of her feet beating against the floor as she died popped into his head. She died fighting.

"I was wrong," she said. "I shouldn't have fought. It's easier if you don't."

"But—" *Did she just read my mind?* "I don't want to die."

"Listen, dummy, it's not like that. It's peaceful. It's good."

Her words made all the sense in the world at that

moment. *Duh. Just let go.* Fighting was too hard. Alex knew that already. All along, even.

As he tried to lean in closer, a hand came off his shoulder and struck him across the face, pulling his attention away from Heather.

"What are you doing?" Alex yelled at Reid, who now stood between him and the fiery recreation of his sister.

"Snapping you outta this shit!" He shook Alex by the shoulders. "Use your brain!"

"But Heather—"

"That's not Heather and you know it. That's the evil. The house is fucking with you because you wish you could see Heather. Don't you get it? But that's not her. Don't be stupid." He leveled his eyes to Alex's. "Trust me."

It took every ounce of will in Alex to let her go.

"Okay, you're right. I know...I know she's gone."

A piercing scream erupted from the fireplace, and Reid and Alex watched as Heather's lovely face began to melt and contort in agony as a clawed hand reached from behind her and yanked her down into the flames. Smaller and more mangled she became, howling in pain until she disappeared from view.

But before she vanished, she screamed at Alex, "It's your fault! You killed me!"

Those words hit Alex like a bullet through the heart and he dropped back to the floor, head in his hands, and sobbed.

"It wasn't her. It wasn't her," Reid said. "It was not your sister."

"I know." But he still couldn't stop crying. "You saw her, too, right? You heard her?"

"I saw what the house wanted you to see. What it wanted you to hear. But it wasn't real. Heather's gone, Alex."

Together, they sat on the floor. Reid waited for Alex to cry it out, to wring himself dry of what he'd been through.

Finally, the whimpering faded until there was nothing left, and only the sound of the crackling fire remained.

Chapter 38

Another voice reached out from the flames, this
time calling to Reid.

"Hello, my little hero..."

Hard to believe he hadn't heard that voice in four
years. Now, in death, her voice rang out to him, clear as
in life. After what he'd just watched Alex go through, he
realized it was his turn. The evil was trying to break
him, but he wouldn't give in, wouldn't crumble. His
back to the flames, he tried his hardest to ignore her, to
block out the temptation.

Alex looked up to the fire and recognition spread
across his face. "Reid, it's your mom."

Reid shook his head, still refusing to look. "No, it's
not. My mom is dead, and she didn't die here."

Her voice reached out from the fireplace. "Yes, I am
here."

He looked into his friend's eyes, his back still to the
flames. "You're not my mother."

Her voice was so soft, imploring. "Reid. Please look at me. I've come all this way. I'm here to help you."

"You're an evil trick. A devil twisted into the voice of my mother, the face of my mother. I will not look at you."

"But I've missed you. Let me look upon your sweet face, see how you've grown. How can you deny me that?"

Reid balled his hands up into fists and squeezed them until his fingernails were cutting into his skin. He embraced the pain—it was a welcomed distraction. Anything to keep him from turning around.

"I am your mother." Her voice sounded so sweet. "Please, Reid, look at me."

"I can't. I won't." He smashed his fists on the floor. "Go away!"

Her voice changed from delicate cooing to a thunderous boom. "Look at me, my little hero! What a hero you turned out to be. You got your friends into this, got them all killed."

"No!" Reid flung his hands to his ears.

But it was useless. Her voice spread through the walls, the floor, the air they breathed. He couldn't help but take it all in.

"It's no surprise, though." The booming stopped, and she sounded serene again. "After all, you did kill me."

"No!" he howled.

"You murdered your own mother."

"No-I-did-not! You lie!"

Alex's eyes widened.

Reid shook his head, wildly. "Don't listen, Alex. She lies. *It* lies!"

"Do you deny that you put a pillow over my face?"

Reid grabbed Alex's face, pulled it in close to his own. "Look at me, Alex. Don't listen to what it says."

Again, the voice thundered and the floor vibrated. "He killed me, Alex. Put a pillow over my face and killed me! Murderer!"

Reid let Alex's face go and squeezed his eyes shut. He tried to maintain his calm, tried to block it all out, but the wounds ran too deep.

"I am not a murderer!"

"Murderer! Murderer! You killed your own mother!"

The vice grip those words—the reality—had on his heart squeezed and ripped away at him. Air became trapped in his lungs as he tried to breathe deep and remind himself that this wasn't real.

"You made me do it! You asked me to do it. You begged me to do it."

Alex stepped further and further away from his friend. "Is it true? Did you kill her?"

"Yes."

Alex stepped as far back as he could, bumping into the doorless wall behind him. "How could you?"

"He's bad. He'll kill you, too. Don't trust him. He brought you here, all of you. And now they're all dead, and you're next."

Reid flung around to the fire and saw his mother's face, scrunched up, angry, her eyes squinted, mouth pursed. And he could still see those lovely little freckles.

He wailed. "You're not her!"

"Alex, he killed his own mother!"

"No, no, no!" Reid screamed.

She reached a hand out and pointed behind Alex.

"He knew what this house was. He brought you all here to kill you. Run! Go! Get away from him while you still can."

Reid turned back to Alex to see the wall behind him shift and the front door appear.

"THE DOOR! BEHIND YOU! GO!" The walls shook with her anger. The floor vibrated with her insistence.

Alex turned and reached for the knob, but Reid was faster. He sprung upon his friend and tackled him to the ground before he could open the door.

"It's a trick!" Reid sat on his friend, pinning him down.

Fear raced over Alex's face.

"I didn't murder her. I mean…the pillow, yes. But she asked me to. She was in pain, Alex. She needed me to." His eyes were wild, searching for some recognition from his friend, and his breathing was ragged.

Alex strained against Reid, trying to get him off, but his friend was too heavy.

"Let me go!" he cried. "Please don't kill me."

Reed was aghast. "I won't. I wouldn't!"

Twisting and turning beneath Reid, Alex tried to free himself. When that failed, he began wildly swinging his hands, and caught Reid in the face several times.

"Stop! Alex, stop!"

But he wouldn't, so Reid punched him in the face.

Chapter 39

"I know what you're trying to do," Reid whispered to the room. "And it's not going to work."

The fire spit back in response, but there was no other sound. Alex was still out in the corner.

Reid hadn't meant to knock him out, but he'd been so hysterical and wouldn't listen to a thing Reid said. So goddamned afraid. And Reid couldn't have that.

He paced back and forth. "You're trying to separate us."

Something tickled the top of his head and across his face. Cobwebs. He peeled them off.

"And you're trying to scare me." He blew at the remaining piece of web dangling in front of him and watched it sway.

A voice crept out of nowhere. "But it's all your fault."

Reid didn't flinch. It seemed so natural. Just another day in his life. His father had constantly said things like that for the past few years, and it had become part of him.

"You brought them here," the voice said. "You meant to kill them, didn't you? Just like your mother."

Reid stopped pacing and turned to face the voice, the fire.

He wasn't surprised to see his father there, his face lit up with an eerie glow. At first, he seemed a disembodied thing, just a head floating amidst the fire. But then his father began to grow a body, arms, legs, feet. When the fireplace could no longer contain his father's size, he stepped out—planting one foot on solid ground. Then he stepped with the other, and as he moved forward the flames seemed reluctant to release him, clinging to his torso and arms. The fire finally fell away from him and all that was left was the silhouette of flames behind him.

"You're not him. You're not my father." Reid shook his head and stood his ground.

"If only that were true," Reid's father hissed. "I wished it every single day since you killed her."

Reid tapped himself on the chest. "I know the truth. I'm no murderer." He crossed his arms.

"You make me sick." The thing that looked like his dad seethed. His mouth curled in disgust. "Rotten, no-good—"

"Yeah, I know, I know. I don't know how I ever let you scare me. Let you hit me. You're not scary. You're a wimp. A loser. A coward. That's why mom asked *me* for help. You should be ashamed of yourself. You're the disgrace."

Reid's dad trudged forward, his footsteps reverberating, leaving a trail of flames behind each one.

"I let you make me what I am." Reid shook his head again. "I believed you. But you're nothing. You don't scare me."

His father moved with blinding speed, and Reid never had a chance to stop the blow as his father's fist came down upon him.

Reid's face seared with pain and he crumbled to his knees.

The sound of his dad's laughter seemed too big for such a small room. It reached bounced off the walls, filling the room with a mad echo. The cobwebs shook and the dusty furniture rattled against the floor.

A tangy metallic taste filled Reid's mouth. He turned his head and spat.

So this thing could make him bleed. All this time, Reid was convinced that the house reached into the depths of him, of them all, and pulled out their darkest fears and memories. But he thought that was all they were—a shadow of their inner turmoil. But this ghostly figure of his father could physically harm him, not just rip away at his mind.

His dad raised his hand again and struck Reid in the face. His head whipped to the side, but he held his balance. Stars danced around his vision, but he breathed through it. He'd suffered worse before.

"I'm done with you," Reid said. "You're a waste of my time."

Laughter once again filled the room, but this time it wasn't from his father. It was those little flying pains in the ass, squealing. Reid imagined that if pigs could laugh, that's what they'd sound like. *Fucking pigs.*

. . .

OUT OF THE fire they flew, darting this way and that, filling the room with their dreadfulness.

They swept across the floor, up over the wall, and spun about the ceiling like a tornado brewing.

"You're going to die. Both of you. And it's all *your* fault." Reid's dad pointed to the corner, where Alex was just coming to.

Reid gasped. "All a distraction!"

A shadow crept out of the fire and drifted up the wall, to the ceiling. As it passed the little flying bastards, they parted to let it through and descended to the ground.

The shadow drifted further away from Reid and closer to Alex.

Reid charged toward his friend. He had to make it there first. The little demons jumped and snapped at his ankles as he pushed past. Like little fire ants, their bites stung.

He could still hear his father's laughter booming off the walls and floor like thunder. The winged demons mimicked and echoed his laughter in a shrill tone.

Reid was awestruck as the little creatures swarmed and flooded the room. They were everywhere, thousands of them.

They settled into a circle around Reid and his dad, like whirling dervishes, their dance graceful and synchronized.

The shadow spread across the room, everywhere all at once.

The little demons began to swirl faster, creating a dizzying effect. No longer in sync with each other, they spun wildly, ricocheting off each other and bouncing off the floor. Reid's eyes couldn't keep up, but his mind finally caught on. His father's laughter lashed at him as he slid across the floor, to Alex. After grabbing Alex, he flung him over his shoulder and spun around and around. If their goal was to disorient him, they were successful. He couldn't tell which way was which. Their wings blotted out the walls until it appeared as if the room was made of the little devils.

"You can't have him!" Reid shouted at the shadow creature.

It disappeared.

Where was it? Reid swirled around and around, hoping to spot the creature before it attacked.

He hauled his friend across the room, back toward the fire.

Now the little demons were back on the ceiling, clapping and looking down on them.

Best seats in the house. There they waited, like carrion crows.

Chapter 40

Alex's listening focused before his vision, and he heard a grown man's laughter. But that didn't make sense. He blinked a few times and the scene began to take shape.

He and Reid had been in the first room, that much he remembered. He hung his head in his hand, trying to think. His temple pulsed like it was on fire, hot daggers stabbing his skull. He couldn't make sense of anything. Heather had been there, yes. Except, it wasn't Heather. And then Reid's mom...

It was all coming back. Reid, the murderer.

Fear and panic shot through Alex once he realized he'd let the house get to him, fool him with tricks and lies. Breaking them down, breaking them apart. He had lost his shit and hadn't trusted Reid.

A SICKLY FEELING came over him. His stomach cramped and spasmed. Fever sunk in and took over. He swallowed it all down, but the bitter taste remained on his tongue.

He finally began to understand what he was seeing, but his brain was still lagged and fuzzy. Reid looked like he was squaring off with his dad. They were shouting at each other, but Alex couldn't make out the words. So much rage. And then Reid's father punched him in the face. Alex cringed. He'd never seen him in action before, only the bruises after, and it was worse than he ever could've imagined. *Why didn't I ever try to help, try to stop it?*

Alex started to crawl toward Reid. He knew his feet would never carry him—weakness had settled into his bones, and his skin burned like it had its own pulse. But he didn't make it very far.

The tiny creatures shot up and out of the fire, barricading Reid and his father. Every time he reached out, they'd bite at his fingertips as they spun around in a frenzied blur.

"Reid!" Alex shouted.

He didn't budge, probably couldn't even hear Alex.

"Reid," Alex yelled louder, and his throat felt like he had strep.

The damn room was too hot, but it couldn't have been from the fireplace. The fire wasn't big enough.

Fever.

Sick.

Dying.

A chill ran up his spine. Smoke billowed out of the fireplace and up to the ceiling. It became a dark cloud engulfing the room and moving toward him. *Coming to kill me.*

"Reid!" Alex screamed, at the top of his lungs, despite the fire burning in his throat.

Reid jumped and spun around to Alex, with wicked determination on his face. Putting his father behind him, Reid he walked toward his best friend.

Chapter 41

The little demons dove from the ceiling and dive-bombed Reid's head. Their wings flapped as they squealed and lashed their claws. Reid grabbed Alex and flung him over his shoulder. He turned this way and that, hopelessly trying to spot the creature through the fray, when an idea popped into his head.

Like the fire pulsing out toward him, this brainchild thrummed until he had no choice but to pay it attention. Madness, genius—the lines were blurred.

He set Alex down on the ground.

Alex looked up at him. "What are you doing?"

"I've got an idea, and it's a fucking doozy." He took a deep breath. "Sorry for knocking you out, but—"

"But nothing. I get it." Alex nervously looked around the room. "Let's do the apology stuff later. That fucker's not going to wait." He pointed to the ceiling as a track of smoke crept across it and aimed for him.

The smoke began to form arms that reached out to

the sides, aiding its glide. Wisps of smoke trailed it, shaping into long legs and clawed feet.

Reid nodded. "Time to fight fire with fire."

Fuck it all.

Nothing in life was easy. He of all people knew that. But he had a plan. A crazy, half-cocked scheme that was likely to get them both killed, but at this point, not trying was dying.

Chapter 42

Helpless as he sat on the floor, Alex could do nothing but watch Reid hustle away. Every part of him hoped that Reid's plan worked, and quick. The fire inside him was growing, taking over his body, and he wasn't sure how much time he had left. *I'm confused. So tired. So hot.*

Horrifying thoughts about the sickness raced through his mind. Would he start to see people that weren't there, like Danny and Clint? Poor Danny, thinking his mother was there in those last minutes. And Clint, reaching out for his best friend, only to get burned. And Heather, his sweet little sister—the most terrifying of all as she morphed into some strange possessed thing, unable to fight her way out.

Tears streaked down Alex's cheeks.

All of them, gone. And there he was, powerless and getting sicker by the moment. And that thing, that smoky creature was still there, floating against the ceiling.

. . .

A VOICE CREPT into Alex's head, punching his temple where he'd been marked. *You can't trust him.* His eye began to cloud over, making everything hazy and filmy. Also made him dizzy.

And the voice whispered in his mind again, *He'll kill you, too. You're doomed. Unless...unless you act first.*

Alex shook his head to get rid of the thought, but it came at a terrible price. He felt like he'd been smashed in the skull by a boulder. He squeezed his eyes shut, whipped his head to the side, and threw up. He wiped his mouth when it was done, and resisted the urge to do it all again. The dry bitterness coated his tongue. The burn of the acid raked his nostrils.

And the voice pierced his ears. *Kill him before he kills you.*

"No!" Alex cried out. "It's the fever. The demons talking. No!" He covered his ears and his temple thrummed from the touch.

From across the room, Reid paused and looked Alex's way. "What did you say?"

"Nothin'. I'm okay." Alex was trying hard to hold onto consciousness, sanity, and logic.

"Reid is my friend, Reid is my friend..." He tried to fight off the voice in his head asking him to do this terrible thing.

Reid took charge. That was the Reid Alex knew. His best friend, not the bully, the jerk he tried to be on the outside. He was the hero. *My true friend.*

The voice in Alex's head didn't like that, so once again it raked its vocals on his eardrums, battling the drum of his temple. *He's bad. He's wrong. Put him out of his misery.*

"It wasn't his fault!" Alex yelled up at the dark shape on the ceiling, then thrusted his middle finger in the air. "Leave us alone!"

I am already inside you. We are already one.

"No!"

If you do this, if you kill him, I will set you free.

Tricks. Lies. Alex's mind swam.

Chapter 43

Anger gave Reid the burst of adrenaline and strength he needed. Like a madman, he gripped the edges of the table and slammed his foot down on one of the legs. It snapped off. He flipped the table over like a wild giant and kicked the rest of the legs off.

All that remained was the table top, which he lifted and smashed into the ground repeatedly until it was broken into pieces.

"I'm not afraid of you!" he shouted into the room.

The Shadow hung on the ceiling, watching, waiting.

The little winged freaks danced on the wall, screeching and clapping.

"You can't have him! It all ends here!"

He grabbed a handful of wood pieces and threw them into the fire, then kicked at the rest.

The fire hissed and spat, finally crackling away. Heat thrummed outward as the flames kicked up higher.

Next, he demolished the two old stools, shredding them to bits. He grabbed one of the legs and poked it into the fire, coaxing it to grow. He spread it all around, first in the fireplace, and then across the old wooden floor. He then threw all but one leg inside.

At last, he went to the bench and kicked madly until it shattered into tinder. He threw those pieces into the fire as well, and it devoured them like a starved animal.

Again, he took that last leg and pushed the fire across the room. The old floor had no choice but to welcome the flames. Hesitantly at first, as if unsure. But once it had a taste, it consumed more and more, devouring everything in its path. It crept up the walls and spread all over the tiny dwelling.

The room grew hotter, brighter.

Reid dragged Alex back a few feet to keep him from getting burned. He crouched over his friend and admired his handiwork. The entire room was engulfed. He took a breath of smoke. His eyes grew wide as he laughed at the room.

"You can't hurt me! You don't scare me. Don't you know who I am? Don't you know whose blood I have inside me? King Philip! He tried and couldn't burn you out, but look at me. You'll burn for me!"

The flames shot up to the ceiling, surrounding the Shadow.

"You can't have him!" Reid shouted up at the creature. "I'll burn it all down. All of it!"

Flames licked up from the floor, pushing Reid and Alex closer together. They huddled far away from the fireplace, by the spot in the wall where the door should've been. Reid shooed Alex further away from the flames until his back was against the wall.

"Fire is our friend, Alex." Madness glinted in Reid's his eyes.

The flames shimmered and glistened, reflected in his pupils. A frightening sight, he reckoned, yet not quite as frightening as the look in Alex's eyes. The whites of his eyes were disappearing fast, as redness crept inside. The fire burned from within Alex. The fever was taking over.

"I'm gonna burn this bitch down or burn it all out!" Reid screamed at the Shadow. "One way or the other!" He remained between it and Alex.

The creature tilted its head to the side and paused before dropping in a blur to the floor, in front of Reid.

The room filled with the sound of a voice that Reid wasn't sure belonged to the Shadow or the house.

"*Marked!*" The voice was both an eardrum-ripping scream and a tremulous bass, resonating and bouncing off each other. "*Marked! No escape!*"

Reid puffed himself up, holding the wall between the evil and his friend. Flames snuck up behind Alex and pushed him off the wall, closer to Reid, closer to the Shadow.

Now on foot, the creature moved to within inches of Reid's face. Its eyes were shiny black orbs, and as Reid stared into them, he could see his own past. He watched those eyes reflect a younger version of himself, by his mother's bedside, bringing a pillow down over her face. He cringed but didn't back down.

The voice layered itself again, the high-pitched quality interlaced with the resonant bass, and wrapped around Reid's father's voice until the three became one. But the Shadow's mouth never moved.

"You didn't even flinch. You held the pillow tight."

271

The image faded and Reid watched his father's fists landing across his younger self's face and body. Blow after blow, he took it.

And still, Reid held his ground against the smoky devil.

"Because you deserved it. You're bad." The voice seemed like it was coming from the Shadow, the fireplace, the ceiling, and inside his own head.

Reid held his breath and tried to focus on the present. *Save Alex. Get the fuck out of here. This is all a trick. Don't give in.*

The tiny winged dancers clapped faster, their hands a blur. They closed in behind the creature, swirling around on the floor, their heads tipped back to the ceiling.

Reid focused on the memory of Clint's last words as he lay dying. "*I don't think I'm gonna beat the game. I think I lost this one. But you guys shouldn't. Maybe to beat the game, you gotta sacrifice.*"

SO LOUD AND clear it was as if Clint was in the room beside him.

Maybe to beat the game, you gotta sacrifice.

Chapter 44

Alex didn't know what to do. There was nowhere to go. And it seemed like Reid's plan was to kill them both. Perhaps he'd gone mad. Maybe Alex was sitting around waiting to die and it was just a question of who'd kill him first, the Shadow or the fire Reid had started.

The voice inside his head spoke again. *All you have to do is push him into the fire and I'll set you free. It will be so easy.*

Alex placed his hands on his best friend's shoulders. Just past Reid, the Shadow stood still. Maybe it knew it had time. There was nowhere to go, after all.

Do it and this will be over.

Alex dropped his head and stared at the floor. He just couldn't bring himself to look at Reid. He could feel his fingers digging deeper into Reid's shoulders as he leaned forward onto his friend for support. He was growing weaker by the second. Doubt and fear were taking over his mind, making him think terrible things. *But if the creature's telling the truth, this could all be over. I could go home.* All he had to do was give Reid one good push. He'd never know it was coming and wouldn't be able to stop it.

Those weren't Alex's thoughts, though. At least, he hoped they weren't. He couldn't do something like that. Not to his friend. He shook his head and pain gripped his skull, tearing through his temple and eye. It was useless. Alex was already marked. This thing wasn't about to let go. It hadn't let any of its victims go. Reid was Alex's only chance. For some reason, that creature treated Reid differently than the rest of them. He was standing right in front of it, but it still waited.

Everyone treated Reid differently, ever since his mom died. Everyone looked at him with sadness, pity. He was no longer Reid. He was the kid who'd lost his mom to cancer. Poor Reid.

And then he turned into a bully. He bossed kids around, shoved them, taunted them, hit them, called them names. There was this look in his eye that scared you. That I-don't-give-a-shit-about-anything look that freaked people out. Like he was just waiting for that moment, that last straw, to break. But that wasn't really Reid. Alex knew it. Maybe Heather, Clint, and Danny knew that, too. Alex hoped they did.

Reid's different. A light bulb flashed in Alex's head. *King Philip.*

Maybe King Philip could win the day, after all. He failed all those hundreds of years ago when he'd tried to burn the house down, but maybe that was because he'd tried from the outside. Maybe he needed to be *inside.*

And maybe Alex was hoping too hard, grasping for straws where there were none.

His mind grew more jumbled and confused, the fever spreading, taking over his mind and body.

Yeah, everyone else thought Reid was damaged goods and not worth the trouble. But really, Reid's like a goddamned onion. Layers and layers, all stinky. No, wait. I'm confused. The fever boils my brain. Maybe I mean he's like a rose. Yeah, gotta get past all those thorns to get to the good stuff. And most people are too scared or lazy to bother.

He's a fucking rose.

My friend.

I won't do it.

"I won't do it!" Alex yelled.

Reid glanced over his shoulder. "Won't do what?"

Alex pulled his hands off Reid's shoulders and sighed. "Get outta here, man. I got this." Alex took a few steps back, closer to the wall of flames.

"What are you doing?" Reid turned to face Alex.

"I don't think I can feel the fire. The heat of it." Alex shook his head. "It's already inside me, man."

Reid shook his head. "I told you I have a plan. Give me a second."

"No more seconds left. Me and this creature got some shit to take care of. You get the hell outta here."

Alex took another step back and Reid reached out for him.

Alex swatted his hand away, reached back and touched the burning wall. "See, I don't feel that. I'll buy you some time. Get out!"

Reid wasn't fast enough. The creature was faster. It shot past Reid so quickly it was in front of Alex's face before they knew it.

As Alex looked into its eyes, silhouettes of people crept over them. Heather. Clint. Danny. The baby. The lady. There were others, too, others he didn't know, all streaming across those dead black eyes. Trapped inside. Forever. It frightened Alex, but there was no other way. At least he'd see his sister again.

Alex held his arms to the sides and took a deep breath. "Come on inside. Let's do this."

The creature opened its mouth, and Alex watched in horror as its jaws fell open, revealing a black pit inside. Nothingness. Death. It closed its mouth and reached its clawed hands out to him.

Alex closed his eyes and searing hot fingers touched his face. He could feel the fire, after all, but he didn't fight. He just hoped Reid would use this distraction to get out once and for all.

"No!" Reid screamed.

Alex's mouth was forced open by unnatural strength. Just when he felt his head couldn't take any more, that it would split in half at the jaw, and panic was slipping its hold around him so tight he couldn't breathe, when the last urge to fight back, to try to rip his head from its claws proved futile, something happened.

As the creature closed its eyes and pushed its head toward his mouth, Reid forced his way in between. Alex was shoved to the side and fell to the floor. He gaped at his friend, who looked like he was taking part in a staring contest with the Shadow.

Reid grabbed those smoky shoulders. "Come on in, bitch!" He tossed his head back and opened his mouth.

Shadows came from nowhere and began to swirl around Reid. They started at his feet, rode up to his knees, hips, waist until Alex couldn't see much of his friend. Darkness and flames swirled together, enveloping him, and constricted like a snake around its prey.

But Reid laughed. "Is that all?"

His laughter raked at Alex's skin. Madness.

Then Reid grew quiet. His face grew serious and he nodded.

"I understand." He smiled a crazy, wild smile. "*Inside.*"

Chapter 45

After Reid forced his way past Alex in front of
the Shadow, he realized he wasn't afraid.
Something within urged him on. He heard
the distant beating drums, as if calling out to him
through another time, and he acted on instinct born
into his blood.

Words, chanted melodies, hundreds of intermingled
voices reached out to him.

Darkness pricked at his body and evil swirled
around him like a tornado, but the steady beat of the
drums kept his heart and mind calm.

The flying devil-beasts nipped at his feet, ankles,
and calves, but he couldn't feel it. Couldn't feel his body
any longer. With his eyes closed, he laughed and the
sound of it was foreign even to him.

King Philip, his great ancestor, appeared behind
those closed eyelids, dancing around a fire. His almond-
shaped eyes implored Reid, searching him out through
the fire. His prominent cheekbones set high and wide in

his strong face. Muscular arms reached up, spread wide as he pumped his moccasin-clad feet into the ground with each step. Reid kept his eyes squeezed shut, afraid that if he opened them, Philip would disappear.

The King dipped his head to the ground, baring his headdress, a single woven band topped with four feathers.

Four feathers, one for each of my friends. Chills raced through Reid's heart.

King Philip stopped his dance, looked back up at Reid and extended a hand. The more Reid reached out, the further away King Philip became. But the King's feet didn't move and neither did Reid.

Drums were still beating and voices still chanting, but the king was fading from view.

Finally, all of it stopped and the image of King Philip became clear once again as he stepped into the fire. If Philip felt the fire, he didn't show it. As the flames danced around him, enveloped him, he stood firm.

"*Inside.*" The king pounded his chest twice with a fist, pointed to Reid, then disappeared, leaving nothing but the flames.

Reid realized what he needed to do. Maybe, what he'd been born to do. He had led his friends into this house despite knowing the stories, the horrors that might lie within. Knowing what his ancestor had gone through hundreds of years ago.

He'd been childish and it had cost his friends their lives. But one friend remained, and he couldn't stand by and let that life be taken, too.

With the blood of King Philip coursing through his veins, his courage pushed him forward.

All his experiences—the darkness, the loss—had brought him to this place. This was what he was meant to do. He would be the one to stop it all. Yes, he was strong enough, brave enough. Yes, he would win.

Or so he hoped.

Reid took one step closer to the beast, tipped his head back and flung his hands to his sides as if expecting an embrace. He closed his eyes and dropped his mouth open.

Beating drums echoed again in the distance.

Chapter 46

T he shadow creature poured into Reid's mouth. With Heather and Danny, it looked like the creature had willingly climbed into their bodies. But with Reid, it looked like *he* was devouring *it*, forcing the demon inside against its will as it wriggled and flailed about.

Reid grabbed the shoulders of the Shadow, and instead of his hands going through, they held firm. To Alex's awe, Reid held tight onto the Shadow, something, none of them had been able to do before. Had their rules changed? Had Reid figured something out? Why was this happening?

And it seemed Alex wasn't the only surprised one.

The little winged beasts stopped dancing and clapping. Behind the Shadow, they stood, frozen. Then all their mouths opened at the same time and they screamed a hideous sound which filled the room and drowned out the crackling fire. It seemed that even the flames gave pause to their cries. And like synchronized swimmers, the beasts lurched in perfect harmony, toward the Shadow. Their little claws grasped onto any shred of it they could, trying to pull it back. When that failed, half of them attacked Reid, using their claws and teeth to rip at his shoes and ankles. Their beaks tore into his arms and slashed at his cheeks. His shoes were the first to go, then the bottom of his jeans around his ankles and calves. The little blur of demons lurched forth over and over, and streaks of blood dripped from innumerable wounds.

Alex reached out for Reid, whose body was slack, held up only by the darkness encircling him. Each time Alex tried to reach though the whirl of flying demons, he was zapped by cold electricity. His fingers became numb, and there was nothing he could do to get through to Reid.

Still, the creature continued down, down into Reid until all that remained were wisps of feet and claws dangling out of his mouth. The mix of shadows and fire continued to hold its barricade around Reid, propping his body up.

And then the storm began to die down. Within seconds, the creature disappeared inside Reid and the mass that had circled and held him up began to slow and fall away, like a tornado losing its power. He swayed once and folded forward to the floor. His body convulsed and then stopped. It all stopped.

Silence.

THE FIRE that'd been burning so fiercely, went out with a *poof*. The floor, the ceiling, the walls, all extinguished as though no fire had ever existed. But the remnants,—

stains of smoke and ash remained everywhere. There was no shadow creature, no tiny rats with wings, no nothing. Just Alex and Reid alone in the house, which they had finally affected.

There was no light coming from within the room, but light was coming in through the cracks in the front door. The door that hadn't been there. It was daylight outside. Through the cracks in the burned door brilliant rays of light streamed through. One ray of light was brighter than all the others and fell across Reid's body, giving him an ethereal and serene countenance.

Alex reached out to him, his hand cutting through the beam of light. Reid felt icy and panic washed over Alex at the possibility of his friend being dead. He slapped one of his tingly numb hands on Reid's neck and checked for a pulse. It was there, faint, but he was alive.

"Reid!" Tears welled up in Alex's eyes. "Reeeeiiiid!" He bawled, choked on a sob, then fought to compose himself. "Reid," he whispered. "Reid, I think it's over." He swallowed the tears and realized his throat was still on fire.

He was still on fire. Still sick.

He could only see out of one of his eyes. The other stung and felt clouded over. Alex wondered if it was red like Danny's had been, if the fire was burning inside it. He touched it. It was puffy, hot, and swelling shut. His temple ached. The room started to swim, but everything looked as it did when they'd first entered. The table, stools, and bench were all perfectly put together and exactly where they'd found them. It didn't make any sense, but Alex was too sick to be able to think it through. His focus was drawn back to the fireplace, where a faint memory of ash still smoldered inside. The walls looked like they had when the five of them had first entered the house, and the only thing that held a char was the front door.

He poked and pushed Reid, but he wouldn't budge.

So Alex leaned over and shouted in his face. "Wake up! Reid!"

He didn't respond.

Everything was spinning. Alex had to close his eyes and rest, just for a moment. Even though he knew he should stay awake, he curled up on the floor next to his friend and started to drift. The floor didn't move but Alex was convinced he was on a boat, his body rocking and swaying. His stomach churned, but he was too tired to vomit.

That's when he heard the banging and the voices.

And then he blacked out.

PART II

1991

Chapter 47

Not everyone has the stuff inside, the makings of a hero. You can want, you can try, you can do your best, but sometimes it's not enough. That's just reality. And reality sucks.

Alex and his friends had stepped into that house as five feisty, know-it-all, nothing-can-hurt-me, everyday kids. Everything was a joke, a game. Good times for all.

No real concept of fear, pain, suffering, or death. The house—the Shadow—reached down inside them, yanked out all hope and replaced it with despair.

Since Alex escaped that house, he'd heard the stories about others over the past few hundred years who'd braved that house and never made it out. Other stories suggested the house wasn't even a house at all. And stranger stories suggested that the town resides inside the house, in some strange vortex or alternate plane of existence. Murmurs, rumors, fireside tales, whispers on the wind. He couldn't say if those stories were true or not, but he was sure he was the only one who'd entered and made it out alive.

Well, technically, that wasn't accurate. Reid made it out alive, too, but Alex didn't count him. Not in his state.

So Alex was the lucky one.

But he didn't feel lucky. He felt cursed.

He was barely standing, yet that house still stood. Probably always would.

Four years.

That's how long it had been since they'd gone into that damned house. Some days, it felt like an eternity ago. And some nights, Alex woke up in a cold sweat, thinking he was trapped inside. He still was, in a way though. He would never be able to forget it, live it down. Not in this shithole town. A place where everyone knows everybody else. That's part of the reason why this day was such a big day. *Gotta let go. Gotta get out.*

ALEX BRUSHED past the last tree into the clearing, and froze. It was just a house after all, wasn't it? Why did it still hold so much power over him?

Daylight was his only friend in this task. There was no way he could've come during the night. On an early summer morning, the sunlight pushed through the trees, and the heat from it pressed at the back of Alex's neck, but he welcomed it. Anything to fight off the creepy chills that the memory this house brought him.

"It's been four years" he said.

The air seemed to yank the words away from him, and Alex doubted if he'd ever said them. He stepped a few feet closer and glared at the house before him. Weather-beaten, rundown wooden walls that had to be infested with termites. A makeshift door, boarded-up haphazardly. A smudged window. All of it seemed to mirror how worn-out Alex felt.

The longer he looked, the more he was sure the house was leaning to the left.

"Finally sinking back down into the hell you came from, I see."

Again, his words fell away too quickly, as if the dead air had eaten them.

A breeze ruffled his hair, but no tree, branch, or leaf moved an inch. He ran a hand through his hair and felt the scar at the edge of his temple. The souvenir he never wanted.

Unblinking, he stood in front of the house and waited. The longer he stared at it, the more he realized it wasn't leaning at all. In fact, it appeared to strand straighter and taller than it had before.

No matter.

Alex wouldn't be deterred.

It would all be over soon.

He took several deliberate steps toward the door, stepping into the shadow of the house. And just like four years ago when they'd all come to invade the house, Alex noticed the distinct absence of sound, of life.

Minutes before, as he'd pushed through the woods to get to this point, morning birds had chirped and flapped. Even a hare had bounced across his path. Gnats had buzzed and tickled at his nose and ears, causing him to keep swishing his hands around his face.

But now there was nothing.

As if death was in the air.

The stillness, the quiet called back jumbled memories from four years ago. He looked to his right and imagined Danny sitting in the dirt, wincing at his bloody elbow. Such a baby. *God, I miss that baby.* Clint would lend him a hand up, then stop to set his glasses right on his nose.

Alex pictured the rest of them, standing around bickering, all of them afraid to do what they were about to do. Heather, the toughest of the tough, tagging along behind them. He could almost hear her wise-ass comments. *"Who else would it be, dickweed?"* Alex swallowed down a giggle. Tough little shit, she was.

He swung a backpack off his shoulder and set it in the dirt in front of him. One by one, he pulled out the contents—four Molotov cocktails—and set them in a row, on the ground.

He could see an image of Reid cheering him on. *"Oh, shit! You're about to burn this bitch down! You're a crazy son-of-a-bitch."*

Alex shook a fist at the house. "You took everything from me!" His voice cracked. "But you're still here. Just me and you, here. And this can't end until only one of us is left. I'm done with you. Done with your curse. Done with it all."

He lit one of the Molotov cocktails. "This is for Danny!" He flung it at the house.

The glass shattered and flames erupted.

"And this is for Clint!" He lit another and threw it as high as he could.

It crashed down on the rooftop and spread a trail of flames.

He stifled a cry, but the tears overcame him.

"This...this is for Heather, you piece of shit!" He flung it at the window.

Just saying her name was like a knife thrust through his already frail heart, and his eyes became clouded with tears.

He threw the last at the front door. "This is for Reid!"

Once it hit the front door, the whole house shuddered and a wild pulse ripped through the air. It thrust outward and hit Alex like a linebacker, knocking him to the ground. He paid it no mind and got to his knees, his body racked with sobs, tears obscuring his vision as the flames rose into the sky. The heat of it sought to encompass him. He wiped the tears, rose to his feet and stepped backward.

The house was engulfed in flames. Alex had accomplished what he'd set out to do.

"We're done here." He spit at the house.

He turned and walked away. Didn't look back.

If he had, he'd have seen the flames turning into thick black smoke, then dying away.

Chapter 48

Alex pulled his weathered, yellow Z28 Camaro into the same parking spot he slid into every time he visited. Sad to think, in almost four years the hospice center was consistently so devoid of compassionate visitors that the parking lot was always vacant. Despite that, he always chose the same spot, fifth row to remember the five of them that went inside the house, and the first spot to remind himself that he's the last man standing.

He put the car in park but left it running. Couldn't quite bring himself to turn it off, not yet.

His fingers twitched as he fumbled around in the console, searching for a pack of smokes. That's just one more thing that'd changed since back then. Filthy habit, but it gave him some peace, a moment's fucking reprieve in a world of tension. He flicked the lighter and sparked the cig to life. Long inhale. Even longer exhale, hoping to steel his courage and calm his nerves.

How many times had he been here? A couple

hundred, at least. Not so often lately, but in the past four years, these visits had become a crucial part of his life. Reid was, after all, the only one who understood Alex and knew what they'd all been through.

Music blared on the radio. A little rock to rattle his bones.

"Can't hold onto you.
You've gone so far away.
Nothing left I can do.
Nothing can make me stay.
All I have left are these scars.
Battled, burned and bruised.
Though I wonder where you are,
it's time for me to choose."

The lyrics slapped him hard in the face and he brought his hand to the scar on his temple. After flipping through the stations, he came across song after song that set his nerves to frazzled.

"Oh, no, it still burns inside
from memories I can't hide.
Haunting me when I'm awake.
Never forget your face.
Never forget your face."

Alex cringed. "Hate to admit it," he told the radio, "but I'd kill for some mindless pop right about now, like that New Kids On The Block garbage."

He turned the knob, faster and faster, skipping through the stations. Unsatisfied, he flicked the tuner off and inhaled the rest of his cigarette.

Still none the calmer, he reached for the door handle. *On three, open that door. One, two, three.* He pushed it open. The humid late summer air crept over him. He shook his head. Not yet. He slammed the door shut and reached for the pack again.

As he lit up the second smoke, he realized how exhausted he was. He hadn't sleep much the night before. It was like the last four years had come screaming back at him during the night and all he could do was replay it over and over.

THE INFO on Alex's rescue had been hazy, and no one wanted to clear it up for him. More like they covered it up.

The last thing he remembered from the house was trying to cling to consciousness right after Reid had sucked that creature up inside. There were voices and banging, and he could've sworn he'd heard the sound of beating drums.

It was all in his head, he'd thought. Delusions and fevered hopes of help and rescue. But it had happened. The fire department busted open that door, the one they could never seem to find from the inside.

Alex had woken up in a hospital bed, IV stuck in his arm, nurses and doctors buzzing about, monitor beeping, mom crying. In and out of consciousness he went for two days. Fevered, tired, dizzy, confused. Lungs burned and skin felt raw, like it was kissed by fire. Shadows seemed to be lurking about in the dark when he was alone, even behind his eyelids when they were closed. Something Alex couldn't see but knew was there. Out of the corner of his eye...

There were times he'd wake up screaming and bolt upright, terrified he was still in that house and the shadow was closing in. Sometimes he'd open his eyes and swear he'd saw Heather sitting in the chair in the corner, just staring at him. Her dark curls pulled back into a ponytail or a loose bun like the way their mom would wear her hair to keep it out of her face. She looked so grown-up, so tired, so like their mother.

But Alex had been sick, with a temperature of 104 degrees, they'd said. Every time he tried to tell someone about the shadows, the house, he was met with stern hushes and more medicine. And every time they drugged him, when he closed his eyes he'd see that darkness, that creature creeping into the room. He wondered if the medicine they gave him was more for their sake than his. So they wouldn't have to be confronted by what'd happened, all the terror, death, fear, and evil. Each time they drugged him, he was sure he wouldn't ever wake up again. That it would finally get him, once and for all. There were moments he fought sleep, and there were other moments he couldn't do anything but give in. At least then, the terror would be over. Finally.

He was too helpless, but it shouldn't be that way. Not anymore. Not now that he was on the outside.

But once something like that fear creeps inside, it's almost impossible to get it out. Alex was still trying. He was tired of trying.

THE SMOKE from his cigarette was so thick he couldn't see through the windshield, so Alex rolled down the car window and the smoke slowly dissipated, filtering out of the car and into the warm air.

He ran his hand along the frayed, diarrhea-colored cloth seat, feeling each burn mark. The car was as worn and tattered as his nerves. He pushed his finger inside one of the holes and tugged until it opened wider. How many times had he nodded off or daydreamed in this damn car with a lit cigarette in his hand?

Sleep had become an enemy. When he fell asleep, he'd see their faces. Sometimes they were still intact. Those were the good days. And other times, they were nothing more than ashes.

An ash fell from his cig, into his lap and burned through his Levi's jeans. Almost passively he watched as the ash burned away those jeans, forming a perfect, tiny circle. He slapped at his leg and to put it out.

Yet another burn. Almost didn't feel it anymore.

Chapter 49

F or two days, Alex tossed and turned in that hospital bed, burning, aching, fevered. No goddamned clue which way was up or down. No idea of what was real and what wasn't. When he started to feel better, he tried to talk about what'd happened, but no one would listen.

That was when Alex began to understand that telling the truth wasn't all it was cracked up to be. When the truth makes people uncomfortable, you tell them what they want to hear, or better yet, you say nothing at all.

Through Alex's fevered state, he knew his mom, dad, and big brother, Mike, had come, but something felt strange. They sat or stood far away from the bed, never kissed him on the forehead, never held his hand, never a finger through his hair. As if they were afraid to get too close. Afraid of *him*.

Alex had always made fun of Heather because she kept a diary. He'd teased her and told her only girly girls did that. But no words could express how glad he was, in the end, that she had that diary. After Clint, Danny, Reid and Alex didn't show up for their sleepovers, panic ensued. But they'd always pulled stunts like that. So it wasn't until Alex's parents realized Heather was missing, too, that the real worry started.

They searched her room and found her diary under her pillow, with the full confession of where they all were about to go and what they were about to do.

They found Alex and Reid two days after the five of them went into that house. Just two fucking days. With all they'd gone through inside, it seemed like two years.

They searched that tiny one-roomed house and found nothing. No Danny, no Clint, no Heather. They did find something odd, though. Three piles of ashes. But no burnt clothes or remnants of who those ashes belonged to.

There was an unspoken consensus of what'd happened. They didn't need Alex's story, his truth. The house was evil. Hush, hush, no one talk about it or go near it. That's the way it had always been, and now it seemed obvious that's the way it was always going to be.

Everyone knew. It was just too bad that Alex and the rest hadn't listened.

Just talking about it was an invitation for something else evil to happen. The entire town swept the whole goddamned thing under the rug because they were scared. As though not talking about it would make things safer, take back what'd happened. Or worse yet, act as if they'd never even existed at all.

But Heather, Clint, and Danny had existed. They had lived and died, and what remained of their lives were nothing but piles of ashes.

And still, no one told Alex what'd happened to Reid. Every time he asked, they ignored him or hurriedly leave the room.

Until one night when they thought he was sleeping. He'd overheard two nurses chirping like birds outside his open door, about *the cursed duo*.

That night, he found out that everyone was afraid of him, and that Reid had made it out alive.

The two nurses said the police had barricaded the house's door again. That everyone was too afraid to go near it or do anything more to it. Everyone knew better than to try, they'd said. Only bad things happened to those who spent too much time near it, and God help anyone who tried to go inside. It had been crazy enough with that one firefighter who'd raced inside the house to pull them out. And look what good that got him. The doctors had never seen third degree burns like that on a person who was never touched by fire. And the other fireman who went in with him, stark raving mad, that's what he got out of it. A babbling idiot afterwards, talking about shadows and ghosts and fires burning in the night. Should've left those two boys in the house, yes, they should have, those nurses had said.

AND OH, how afraid they were of Alex. The scar on his temple, the one the Shadow had marked him with, was the mark of the devil, they'd said.

Maybe it was.

And then they talked about Reid, his whole family and how they were all cursed. Mom dead from cancer. Dad an abusive alcoholic. And the kid, worst of them all. He was always a bad seed, but the state he came out of that house in…devil inside.

Alex listened, and discovered that Reid was in the hospital, down the hall.

So he waited for those old biddies to go away and dragged himself down the hall until he found Reid's room.

Alex thought he'd be relieved. Thought maybe Reid would be okay. But as when walked into his friend's room, the temperature plummeted, like someone had left the window open on a crisp December morning. But this was August and no window was open. So Alex watched in amazement as his breath appeared before him when he exhaled.

Once Alex got closer to the bed, he wanted to cover Reid up, shield him from the cold, but he noticed that with each step toward Reid, the temperature got colder. Alex almost turned to go find a nurse and tell them to turn the fucking heat on for him, but he thought better of it. Besides, he had a feeling that the cold was something more unnatural than a thermostat problem.

As he leaned over to get a closer look, he reached for the blankets, and that's when he noticed Reid's eyes were open. He was blankly staring at the ceiling. When Alex pulled the blankets up higher on his chest, Reid's hand flew up so quick that Alex didn't see them before he felt a grip so tight around his forearm he gasped. Like a claw, Reid's hand locked on him, fingertips pressing into his flesh like they were made of steel.

Alex tried to calm him down and get him to let go, but Reid's hand remained like a vice grip, eyes unblinking, still staring at the ceiling. Those eyes…looked wrong.

They're darker, grayer. Empty.

Alex's heart thudded. All he'd wanted to do was get to Reid, and now all he wanted was to run away. *This is not my friend. This is not Reid. There's something else inside.*

~

THE CIGARETTE DANGLED from Alex's lip while he spaced out, trapped reliving the past. Another ash dropped and missed this time, ending up in between his legs, on the car seat. *Whatever.* As it singed the fabric, Alex regarded it detachedly. He pulled the cigarette from his mouth and tapped it out the window to flick off the ashes. A light breeze carried them off.

Fuck this.

He knew he was being a big baby. The sooner he went in there, the sooner he could go and be done with all of it, put the past behind.

Before he could talk himself out of it, he flung the car door open and jumped out, but his feet refused to go any further, like they were stuck in cement. He closed his eyes and summoned his old friend's voice, the one that used to bully and shame him. He needed some of that now. He could hear him saying, *"Quit being such a pussy."* He could see the look in his eyes, the way his brow furrowed when he got all pushy like that. His eyebrows would tilt down into a "*V*", all mean-like.

Alex kicked a foot backwards into the car door and it slammed shut. The finality of it startled him. Nowhere to go but forward.

While shuffling across the pavement, he looked up at the morning sky. Beautiful. A hot, humid summer day was already in the works.

Pink rays streaked across the sky, bleeding into red.

An old saying popped into his head.

Red sky at night, sailor's delight.

Red sky in the morning, sailor's warning.

He never really knew what that meant—something about a hot day. *Fuck, I'm no sailor. But I do vividly remember the last time I saw a sky as dramatic as this.*

ALEX WAS STILL in the hospital, four days after the rescue, when the fever finally broke. He was alone in his room, looking off into the morning sky.

That day, he found Mike's note. The note that said goodbye, that he was off to college and couldn't wait any longer. He'd waited too long already. He was glad Alex would be okay, blah, blah, blah. But he'd left without saying goodbye face-to-face.

Four years later and Alex still hadn't seen him. But Alex knew the truth.

Mike was afraid of him. They all were. Even though he was rescued and given a second chance, life would never be the same. People would never be the same. Alex would never be the same—alone forever.

The realization had made him so angry, so hurt that he scrambled down the hall, searching for familiarity, for someone who knew him. Someone who wasn't afraid of him.

Chapter 50

Self-pity gripped Alex's heart as he stepped into Reid's room the second time. And like the last time, the temperature became frigid. Each small step brought an even bigger chill, especially with a light hospital gown flapping open behind him as he walked. The air sliced through his skin, his nerves, his mind. He didn't know what to expect, but with each step he became less sure that this was where he wanted to be. Perhaps alone was better than what he was walking into.

He hesitated.

Something wasn't right.

Treading lightly, he suddenly felt afraid to wake Reid. At his bedside, Alex leaned over to get a closer look. He thanked the heavens that Reid's eyes were closed this time. Last time, they looked so wrong. *Maybe I only imagined it.*

Even though Reid was catatonic, Alex had to hope

his friend was still inside, the only person in the world who really knew him and what happened.

Reid's eyes flung open, and Alex realized he hadn't imagined it the first time. Those weren't his eyes. Empty, dark. They didn't acknowledge Alex but stared straight up at the ceiling once more.

Alex tried to take a step back, but his body locked with fear.

And then Reid's face crinkled up as if he was in excruciating pain and about to scream. His mouth fell open, but there was no sound or movement.

That's when it truly hit Alex that Reid was gone. He no longer knew this person, the body before him. Something bad happened in that house when he stepped in front of Alex. That thing went inside him, had it ever come back out?

His feet finally decided to work and Alex stepped back and bumped into something that hadn't been there before.

Memories came rushing back—shadows, bird-devils darting about.

Fingers gripped his shoulder and all he could picture were those gray claws, digging in. The flames encircled the room. The shadow on the ceiling...

Alex turned his head to look at those fingers on his shoulder and saw red.

Nail polish.

It was just the nurse. Good thing, too. Alex was exhausted, and being around Reid was now the last thing he wanted. She helped him back to his room, scolding the whole way, telling him that being up and about so soon was likely to make him catch his death. Alex almost laughed at that. How many times in that house had he almost been caught by death? And being in that room with Reid, having him silently screaming, staring out with those eyes—Alex knew death was already there.

ALEX SHOOK his head and the memory away, then strode across the parking lot, toward the door. He didn't want to see that pretty pink sky any longer. By the time he made it to the second row of cars, the sunlight had crept across the sky, sending a ray off the silver car in front of him and temporarily blinding him. He blinked to fight off the effect and came to a dead halt.

As his vision cleared, a girl climbed out of the car. Dark curls fell across her shoulders.

Alex's heart leapt until he heard her speak.

"What ah ya starin' at?" Her voice was sharp with a Boston accent.

Alex just stared at her, mouth agape.

"Well?" She put her hand on her hip and she leaned to the side.

"Uh, nothing. Sorry." His voice cracked. "You just look like someone—I mean, for a sec I thought you were someone…" He swallowed down the lump in his throat. "I used to know." Tears threatened his eyes and he held them back.

She shook her head, rolled her eyes and walked away, curls bouncing over her shoulders with each step.

That girl clearly didn't know him, or she never would have made eye contact. Never would've uttered a word or even looked in his direction.

YOU'D THINK Alex had been marked by the devil himself the way people looked at him and talked about him behind his back. People would cross the street just to avoid him. No one ever made eye contact, and if they did by accident, they'd quickly avert their eyes. It was worse at school. While walking to classes, it looked like Moses parting the Red Sea, except not so holy. The hordes of kids split to either side of the halls, afraid of getting close enough to touch Alex. Every now and then, someone would bump shoulders with him accidentally and lose their shit, frantically wiping at their arms to remove whatever poison he had. No telling what kind of madness he'd pass on to them.

No friends, no one to joke or fight with, no dates, no nothing. Like oil and water, Alex and the rest of the town. When you initially shake the two, it might look like they're coming together, but they always separate again.

BEADS OF SWEAT formed on his forehead as Alex relived those memories. He ran his hand across the marked side of his temple. The fine line of the scar, still there. Always would be, like a brand, a warning to anyone who might be dumb enough to get too close. As he stood outside the hospice, sweating, he couldn't shake those awful thoughts which pulled him back in.

STAY BACK—HE'S marked, cursed, tainted.

His own brother, Mike, just around the corner at UMass, was too busy to call or visit. Fuck, even a letter now and then would've sufficed. It was a shitty excuse. Alex had reached out numerous times, mailed letters, called, but he never got a reply. Mike had crossed Alex off his list the day he wrote that goodbye letter. His own brother.

And then there was Alex's dad. His excuse for keeping his distance was that he worked so much and he was tired all the time. He worked hard for a living to support his family, send Mike to school, and hopefully Alex at some point, too. If he were lucky enough, Alex would go far, far away.

Peace and quiet when he wasn't working, that's what his dad needed. He'd come home, kick off his shoes, hop into his recliner, and stare at the boob-tube for hours. When he wasn't doing that, he had his nose buried in the newspaper, pretending Alex wasn't there. It was such a quiet house. No one spoke to each other anymore. Weary glances were the extent of it.

Like robots, they'd wake, eat breakfast, go to work or school, come home, eat, sleep. Rinse, repeat.

His Mom was the worst of them all, though. Alex could take Mike hiding at school, Dad hiding in the paper or lost in the TV. But Mom hurt his heart the most.

Because Mom *would* look at him.

But it seemed that she either didn't see Alex for who he really was or was afraid of what she might find, so she always had to keep an eye. Those eyes of hers seemed to be asking, *Why you? Why are you still here and she isn't? You fool. You should've known better. Everyone knows better.*

Random bullshit, is what Alex wanted to say. Luck of the draw, if there were luck to it at all. *Fucking Russian roulette, that's why I'm still here.*

It was so close to being him, he wanted to tell her. A bend in the hallway, a blind corner and they got twisted up. That creature reached out for Alex and got caught in those curls of hers.

Or had it chosen her? Either way, Alex would never tell his mom. He couldn't, anyway. No one wanted the true story. Hush, hush, no stories of monsters and shadows and evil houses. Even though they knew, they'd never admit it. The entire town swept the whole thing under the rug.

Alex didn't want to think about any of it, but that's all he ever did.

It's all they did, too. He saw it in their eyes, their stance, their avoidance. Alex, the constant reminder of sadness, death, evil.

In the past four years since he'd come home, his Mom had aged ten years. She'd chopped off her lovely locks, real short, like a boy. Probably because she just didn't care anymore and had no energy to put in the effort. It was graying more and more every day. When the grays first started coming in, Alex remembered that Heather would poke fun at her and she'd dye it. No more Heather. No more hair color.

She'd stopped wearing makeup, too, and she never used to leave the house to get toilet paper without putting on some mascara or lipstick. But what was the point now?

She rarely dressed up anymore, just trudged around the house in ragged sweats and a baggy tee, with the rattiest, most tattered slippers Alex had ever seen. Those things bugged him the most.

He wanted to throw them away and buy her a new pair, but he knew she'd never wear them, never accept them from him. Gifts from the devil—no way, no how. And the worst thing of all was that she was on anti-depressants, walking around like a freaking zombie. But Alex really couldn't blame her for that. She'd lost her little girl. One day Heather was there, bright and full of life. The next, nothing but a pile of ashes and a painful memory.

But Alex had lost her, too. Did anyone ever think about that? Alex had watched her die and lived with the guilt every day that it should've been him. He should've been able to save her. The thought of it choked him with tears every time.

But no anti-depressants for Alex. He had to be clear and aware so that he could get through school and get outta this town.

That's why he'd started smoking. When he got too stressed, when the memories were too much to bear, it was nicotine for Alex. Everyone needs a vice.

A MCDONALD'S bag floated across the parking lot, toward Alex. He pulled his right foot back and let it rip. Sent the thing sailing straight up into the air. He threw his arms up and shouted, "Three points. It's good! Patriots win, Patriots win!" He spun around and flipped-off the air.

Then he shrugged, dug his hands in his pocket and continued walking.

Alex couldn't play organized sports anymore. All those years of athletic skill and training, down the stinking toilet. No one wanted to touch him, let alone throw him a ball. Solitaire was about as sporty as it got for Alex.

So he did the only thing he could—put his nose deep in books. His whole world became studies. His grades had always been good, but now they exceeded expectations. And he worked so hard that he made his wishes and his parent's come true. He got accepted into UC Berkeley. Just about as far away as he could get. And of course, his parents were all too happy to pay and send him off if that meant they no longer had to live with a burden, the cursed one.

Guess all his dad's hard work had paid off. Maybe once Alex was gone, Dad and Mom would talk again. Maybe he'd take her out, or at least buy her a new pair of fucking slippers.

Chapter 51

Alex made it to the front door of the hospice, finally.

He couldn't put it off forever.

Instead of opening the door, he leaned against the building and lit another cigarette. Today was gonna be one of those one pack-of-smokes kind of days.

The only time he wasn't thinking was when he was smoking. On the inhale, there was no room left for anything else inside him. And on the exhale, all bad thoughts, memories, feelings went out with it. It was his only relief. Problem was, it was only temporary.

He took a long drag and watched the ash eat away at the cigarette. *Burn baby, burn.* His fingers were starting to feel the heat already. This one wasn't going to last long.

"You going in, or are you just here to smoke?" said a familiar voice.

Alex looked up to see Mr. Thompson, Reid's dad, holding the door on his way out. He raised his eyebrows at Alex and pushed the door further open, indicating the entrance by tipping his head to the side.

"Not ready yet."

"Haven't seen you around here in a while." Mr. Thompson stepped out of the doorway and let the door swing shut. "Heard a rumor you were moving on. That true?"

"M-hmm. Got accepted into UC Berkeley. I'm outta this place in four days."

"Good for you." He sounded sincere.

Guilt crept up on Alex. "I can't be here anymore. Everyone knows me, knows what—"

"I'm not faulting you. I think it's good. You should. You've got a bad rap here and it's not right. Now you can start over fresh."

Alex tossed the nub of the cig onto the ground and mashed it into the pavement. "Then why do I still feel so guilty?"

Mr. Thompson laughed. "Don't I know guilt." He shook his head and stared at Alex's dead cigarette. "I'll never forgive myself for everything I did to him. Everything I put him through. I should've been tossing the ball around with him, not hitting him."

"But you're sorry?"

Alex could see the lines on Mr. Thompson's face. There were more there now than the last time he saw him. Brow wrinkled with concern, mouth creased with sadness. Made him look way older than his forty-three years.

"I'll be sorry 'til the day I die. But that don't make it all better. Nothin's ever gonna take back what I did to him."

Alex didn't know what to say. It took Reid's terrible

state to wake his father up and for him to realize how much he loved his only son. How much pain and anger he'd held onto all those years. Since Alex and Reid came out of that house, he was a changed man. Visited Reid every day. He read to him, told him stories, talked to him. Sat there by his bedside every goddamned day.

"I blamed him for his mother's death. I don't know why. Why did I take it out on him? He was just...a boy," he whispered.

Alex was pretty sure Reid's father never knew what had really happened between Reid and his mother. Never knew what she had asked of him. And even though Reid always thought his father knew, it turned out it was just his guilt eating at him. Just one more secret for Alex to keep. The list was getting longer every day.

Alex reached for another cigarette.

"Why don't you go see him?" Mr. Thompson reached out and stopped him from lighting it up.

"How is he today?"

"One-hundred percent unresponsive. He's in bed. I just finished reading him *The Old Man and the Sea*. I hope he liked it. It was one of my favorites."

Alex put the smoke back in the pack. "I'm sure he did. It's a good one."

"You know," Mr. Thompson leaned against the wall next to Alex, crossing his arms, "yesterday I coulda swore I saw him smile at me. Is that weird for me to think that?"

"Nah. Maybe he did. Or maybe you just want him to so badly you saw what wasn't there."

Alex immediately wished he hadn't said that last

part. Why'd he have to dash his hopes that someday Reid would wake up and be Reid again?

Mr. Thompson was the only person since the rescue who'd treated Alex like a normal human being. The only one who talked to him, listened to him, and looked at him without fear in his eyes. Never in a million years would Alex have guessed it would be him. But people can change. In the end, he was the only one to keep Alex sane.

∽

ALEX HAD MADE a mistake one night, two years ago, by confiding in Reid. He'd thought they were alone. He was sitting in Reid's room, talking about Heather, Clint, and Danny, sobbing over all they'd gone through and how everyone left him alone, when Reid's dad walked in.

Reid had been propped up to a sitting position, in a chair facing out the window. Alex sat in the chair next to him, just unloading everything.

He never heard Mr. Thompson come in, but a gentle hand gripped his shoulder.

Alex jumped and tried hard to wipe away the tears. Mr. Thompson was so calm. So unlike the man Alex had known in the past. He was patient and kind. He sat down on Reid's bed and asked Alex to tell him the story. The real story. After everything Alex had been through and everyone he'd tried to talk to, including his own family, here was Reid's dad, ready to listen.

So Alex told him everything.

. . .

SINCE THEN, he was someone Alex could talk to and someone who'd talk back, unlike Reid. It helped a lot. Life's weird like that. Unexpected as fuck.

~

THE LOOK on Mr. Thompson's face after Alex's thoughtless remark about him imagining Reid's reactions was like a puppy who'd got slapped on the nose, and Alex felt terrible for saying something so cold.

"Sorry. That wasn't cool of me to say." Alex cringed. "I never would've made it out of that house if not for Reid. He saved me. For that I'll always be thankful...and feel guilty. I was a goner, for sure, but he stepped in. He's a goddamned hero. And this," Alex pointed to the shitty hospice building, "this is what he gets for it. It's not right."

"The world isn't right or fair, Alex. You know that." Mr. Thompson pushed off the wall, swung around to face Alex and looked him dead in the eye. "I screwed up so badly with him." He choked on the words, then cleared his throat. "I've told him I'm sorry a million times. I don't know if I can help him, Alex. I don't know if he'll ever wake up. There are moments I want to hug him, hold his hand, kiss his forehead, but then I wonder, after all we've been through, if my touch would give him solace or frighten him. I don't know how to comfort him." He looked away. "No matter what, he never acknowledges my presence, my voice. Me."

Heavy sadness filled Mr. Thompson's bloodshot eyes, permanently darkened with baggy circles underneath. That's how he'd looked every day Alex had seen him in the past four years. Probably never even slept anymore.

"You can't do that to yourself," Alex said. "You're here for him. I'm sure he knows it. But you gotta take care of yourself. For him, if not yourself."

The weight in Mr. Thomson's eyes only grew heavier.

And it weighed on Alex, too, because he wasn't sure that Reid knew. Wasn't sure if he knew anything at all. Most days, he laid in a bed and would go weeks without a movement or a peep, and then one day he'd just start screaming as if the devil was on his heels. Other times he'd swing his arms like he was fighting an invisible foe.

Sometimes it was just his eyes, they'd dart about the room, like chasing ghosts. But those weren't his eyes anymore. They were so much grayer, so much darker as though someone had turned the lights out.

Moments when Alex stared into Reid's eyes, he wondered what Heather saw that day in the house when she'd asked him, *"Does it burn in the dark?"* He sure as hell hoped it didn't.

It was possible Reid didn't understand Alex when he talked to him. But he tried anyway. He had to. It was the least he could do. He talked about when they were kids, the happier days. Things they'd done, games they played, things they'd seen. Tried to always keep it positive. Never mentioned that house, the sadness, the pain, what every day was like for Alex since they got rescued. He tried until it hurt too much to keep trying.

It was like Reid's body was this strange shell and he was trapped inside.

So often, Alex hoped he was unaware. That he just floated around in there, blissfully ignorant of everything they'd been through and everything he was going through now. Alex prayed he was swaddled in soft clouds, bouncing and floating through a deep blue sky, impervious to all the sadness and pain around him, unaware of where his body truly lay. Alex didn't want to think of the nightmare it must be if Reid was aware but unable to do anything about it all. That was too much to bear. A prisoner behind dark walls.

Trapped inside.

Watching.

Waiting.

Mr. Thompson chuckled. "I think it's good you're going. You're so young. You deserve a chance. Forget all about this town, if you can."

"I want to. I'll try, but I'll never forget Reid. He's—"

Mr. Thompson placed a hand on Alex's shoulder. "He's your best friend, and he'd be happy about school. He'd be proud of you, Alex."

Alex blushed. "Thanks."

"I'm proud of you, too, for what it's worth. I know it's not easy." He backed up a few steps and turned around to walk away. Then he looked back over his shoulder. "Take care of yourself."

"You too, Mr. Thompson."

It was now or never. Alex got his lazy ass off the wall and reached for the door.

Chapter 52

An unwatched TV buzzed in the corner of the lobby. An orderly flitted about with busywork, opened the blinds and let the morning sunshine sneak through. The red and pink sky had dwindled, an orange-gold light taking its place. It added a warm feeling to the lobby, if that was possible. Drab colors were everywhere—a dirty tan carpet, worn thin from too many footsteps. Boring beige walls which could've used a touch of paint several years ago. A couple of brown wooden chairs and yellow lamps, along with a yellow table. So much for decorating with cheer. It was like they didn't want anyone to feel too much in that place. Just plain and mediocre.

Made Alex want to fucking puke. But maybe that was the countless cigarettes on an empty stomach. Or maybe it was from the anticipation of what he was there to do.

The attendant waved Alex through reception without making eye contact. As he walked past her, he had a wicked urge to shout *Boo!* just to see how far she'd jump and how loud she'd scream. Resisting that urge, he made for the elevator. As the doors closed, he had a second of panic about being confined in such a small space. Moments like that happened frequently, after the house, but he had to keep on going.

Alex pushed the button for the third floor and it lit up. He took a deep breath as he listened to the cables above, lifting the metal box up to his destination. He dug his fingers into his pocket, fondling the pack of smokes but curbed the urge to take one out.

The elevator jarred to a stop and relief washed over Alex like an autumn breeze as the doors opened and spilled him out into the hallway.

Twenty-two paces from the elevator to Reid's room. He counted the steps one last time as he proceeded down the hall.

Hesitating at the door, he grabbed onto the frame and poked only his head through.

"Hey, buddy, it's me. Alex."

No response. *Didn't expect one.*

Alex swayed back and forth in the frame and then let go, momentum pushing him into the room.

Reid was lying in bed and his eyes were open.

"Good morning to you," Alex whispered. "Ready for today?" He bit his lip. "It's a big fucking day, you know."

Not a blink.

"I ran into your dad outside. Had a quick chat."

Alex darted his gaze around the room and it landed on the Red Sox calendar he'd bought Reid for his birthday. At least it covered up part of the drab wallpaper and added a splash of life and color. Fresh flowers sat on the bedside table, most likely from Reid's dad. White, yellow, and pink bulbs. A little more cheer. His pillows and bedspread were that blue everyone assumes is a boy's favorite color—dark like a sky right before a storm.

Today seemed impossible. Alex had always been able to talk to Reid when they were kids and even after he became catatonic. Alex imagined his voice, his response to whatever he'd say.

"SAW a girl in the parking lot. She had some seriously curly hair. Looked a lot like Heather." Alex paused. "Or maybe she didn't, I dunno."

"*Heather's gone*," Alex imagined he'd say.

"Yeah, I know she's gone, but…never mind."

"*It's okay to remember them. All of them.*"

"I know, I know. But man, it hurts."

"*Life hurts.*"

"You got that fucking right." Alex strolled over to his bedside and sat down.

"Why is it always so cold in here?" The closer Alex got to him, the chillier the air felt.

"*It ain't the room, it's what inside, dumbass.*"

Alex rubbed his arms to chase the goosebumps away.

"So I got some shit to tell ya. Big news, man."

"*You don't say.*"

"And I'm sorry I haven't been around in a while. Things have been hectic, to say the least."

"*Stop making excuses, bitch.*" He'd have a shit-eating grin on his face.

Alex laughed a little at the thought of his chiding ways. "I'm having a hard time getting the words out."

The bed creaked when Alex shifted his weight. Still, Reid didn't move.

"For Christ's sake, just spit it out, already!"

"Yeah. Right, then."

Alex sat there and stared at him. Tried to see the friend that used to be there, before the house. His thick brown hair was cut way too short. *Reid would never go for that if he were...awake. Looks dumb. Looks like they want to do as little maintenance on him as possible.* The more he looked, the less that person in front of him was Reid. Where his skin used to have the brightness and softness of early teen years, it now had a macabre pallor, like he was always about to break into a sickly sweat. Almost didn't look like skin anymore. Alex had the revolting urge to touch it but stopped himself. No, what was in front of him wasn't really Reid. Some sort of Reid-shaped shell, but what was inside? What had really shut him down like that? What had turned out all the lights?

Alex shuddered. His mind flashed back to those last moments in the house, Reid pushing him aside and taking the creature inside himself, its form fighting the whole way down.

Perhaps some questions were better left unanswered.

Before Alex knew what was happening, a tear ran down his face and landed on the bed. Before he could wipe it away, another snuck out, and then a goddamned pipe burst. He couldn't stop the tears. Couldn't even see, they were coming so fast.

"I'm sorry. I'm so...so sorry." A stream of snot leaked out of Alex's nose, and he brought his sleeve up and rubbed it away. "It shouldn't be like this." His voice grew louder. "It should be me in that bed, not you. You son of a bitch. Why did you have to go and be the hero?" He lowered his voice. "Why—"

He took a deep breath, glanced around the room and realized he'd left the door open. So much for privacy. He got up and shut it softly, then leaned his head against the door, not yet ready to let go of the handle. He spoke to the door instead of Reid.

"Always thought we'd be doing this together. Some big scholarships to play ball somewhere. Our tickets out. Kids are dumb, huh?" He pushed off the door and turned around. "We thought a lot of dumb things." He plopped into the chair beside the bed. "College, girls, parties. Not this, not this."

He gripped the armrests and squeezed.

"I've said so many things to you over these past four years. It's hard, you know? And I'm not saying I have it harder than you. I hope you never thought I was complaining. I'm thankful for the chance you gave me. For all you did for me. For what you tried to do for them, too."

His fingers were starting to hurt. He loosened his grip and flexed his fingers. Nothing felt comfortable as he shifted from side to side in his chair. He began tapping his foot on the floor.

"I can't keep still. This is so hard."

He forced his foot still and sensed a twitch starting in his eye before spreading to his temple, like one of those facial tics that no one can see. But maybe he was just imagining it.

Lightning bolt zapped him right behind the eye and

made him cringe. He brought his hand to his temple and rubbed at the scar. *Fucking thing stung.*

The room warmed. The air grew thick and heavy, crawling over Alex, pressing down on his chest as he breathed in. A trickle of sweat beaded above his top lip. *What's with the shift in temperature? Maybe it's just the stress. Yeah, the stress.*

As he thought about that, he looked at Reid's face and swore it was getting flushed. When he leaned closer, he saw Reid's brow beading up with sweat.

Fear washed over Alex.

He took another heavy breath in.

"I gotta go, man. I can't take this town anymore. I don't wanna leave you, but...I can't stand the way they all look at me, the way they treat me. Like I'm poison. Like breathing the same air as me might do something bad to them." The shirt on his back began to cling as sweat ran down his neck and between his shoulder blades. "My own family is afraid of me. So I'm leaving in four days. Off to school in California. Far away. A fresh start. You gave me a chance and I gotta take it. I know you understand."

The sweat ran down his back, to the crack of his ass, and slipped into his jeans.

"So fucking hot in here, man."

Alex got up and went to the window to crack it open. He flipped up the locks and pulled. Nothing. This time, he propped his hands on the glass and pushed up. Still nothing.

"This goddamn place. Really? Can't even get the window open."

He tried one more time and gave up.

Covered in sweat and feeling like the hot air was

pushing at him from all sides, Alex turned back to Reid in the bed and gasped.

His eyes were squeezed shut like he was fighting to keep them that way, and his face was beet red.

"What's wrong? Should I get the nurse?"

Alex peeled the blankets away from his sweaty friend and found Reid's hands balled up into fists. He was clenching so hard his knuckles were white.

"Does it hurt? I'm gonna get the nurse, hang on."

Alex flew across the room, to the door and turned the knob, but nothing happened. He turned again and yanked, but the door still wouldn't give. Both hands now on it, he twisted madly, pulling, but all in vain. Panic gripped him. It started in his gut, like evil butterflies racing through, and tore up his throat, making it hard to breathe. A sharp pain shot through his temple and he buckled to his knees.

Chapter 53

Alex turned to face Reid in the bed. He was sitting upright, eyes wide in fear.

From the corner of his eye, Alex saw a shadow sweep across the wall.

It was gone as soon as he turned his head. *Probably never there in the first place.* Now wasn't time to get scared or distracted.

Reid sat there, frozen. Alex had seen him move before—that's not what freaked him out. He'd seen him scream, moan, throw up his arms and flail them about, but nothing like this. Something was different. *Wrong.*

Heat inundated the room. Swept over it like humidity on the hottest of New England summer days. Not twenty minutes before, it was freezing cold. Goosebumps had stood on Alex's arms and he could see his own breath in front of him. Now it was damp, sweaty. In an instant, Alex felt like he was flung back inside that awful house again. He breathed in that heavy air and found the distinct smell of fire tickling his nose hairs.

The window was stuck closed. The door wouldn't budge either. And no matter how he tried to shake the feeling, he knew a shadow was lurking close by.

A dagger-like pain stabbed at his temple and made him wince and squeeze his eyes shut. When he opened his eyes, his peripheral vision was fucked. The pain shot behind his eye and clouded it, creating a permanent shadow across the side of his vision. Every time he turned to see it fully, it was always just out of sight.

Darkness fell upon the room as if the sun had ducked behind a dark cloud and threatened to never come out again. If Alex hadn't known it was morning, he'd have sworn the sun had just set.

"Reid. Hey, what's going on?"

Alex cautiously stepped closer to the bed.

"It's something bad, isn't it?"

Beside the bed, he reached out toward his friend's shoulder, and that's when he noticed Reid's eyes. Worms. Worms made of fire raced into them. The whites of his eyes were now colored with squirming red lines creeping over and through. Alex touched Reid's shoulder and then yanked his hand back. Reid was scorching hot. Alex stared at his palm as a blister began to bubble.

Sweat covered Reid's body, his pajamas clinging to his form. His mouth began to move, but no sound escaped his lips.

"No, no, no!" Alex backed away and ran to the door. Flung his body against it. "Help! Someone help us! I'm stuck. We're stuck inside. Open the door!" Alex pounded away with his fist and then started kicking the door, too. "Help! Please!"

. . .

Inside

ALEX TURNED BACK TO REID. The hospital room was gone. Drab wallpaper replaced by dark wood. The walls looked as if they'd been burned. Like they did that last day...

"No!" Alex screamed. He searched for the Red Sox poster that he knew should be on the wall, but there was nothing.

That wasn't exactly true—there was something. Cobwebs hung from the corners, draping to the floor.

"No!"

The cobwebs swayed with the power of that word.

Alex spun around and found himself staring into a fireplace. It flickered to life. He backed up a few steps and tripped over something. His head slammed into the floor and he moaned from the pain.

As the dizziness subsided, Alex pulled himself into sitting position and realized he'd tripped over Reid's body. He was laying on his back, staring at the ceiling. Alex scrambled to his knees and leaned over his friend, whose eyes had gone from red to black. So cold and empty, devoid of any light or life. Black holes.

Not possible. They were just in Reid's room in that shitty old hospice. This couldn't be.

The smell of fire turned into the burning odor of smoke and pressed on Alex's lungs. Fear wrapped around his body, but his mind refused to give up. He begged his legs and arms to move. It happened slowly, but his body obeyed. He grabbed Reid from under the armpits and dragged him away from the fire, which was pushing out black smoke at an alarming rate. Looked like someone had thrown plastic into the fire. It was smoldering, with the tiniest flame inside. Alex's lungs burned with each caustic breath.

Reid's body tensed and it felt as if his weight had doubled. He was too heavy to drag, like a bag of bricks. And that's when he started convulsing. The shaking was so violent it pushed Alex away from him. Reid flung backwards against the floor, back to a laying position. His body bucked and twitched, and the sound of his feet and head hitting the floor made Alex's teeth rattle. On his knees, Alex bent over him and placed his hands under Reid's head to protect him from smashing his brains out. From upside down, Alex watched his face wrinkle, making him look much older. Reid closed his eyes, bucked one more time, then flung them open again, his body motionless. The blacks of his eyes betrayed what was inside. A shadow crept from the left eye to the right and then disappeared.

He thrust his head back and Alex let him go. Reid's mouth fell open and

a sound escaped, deep and guttural, like it came from his stomach.

"Reid!" Alex screamed.

Reid's mouth opened unnaturally wide, and Alex could barely see his friend in front of him anymore, just some misshapen thing laying on the floor, like a snake unhinging its jaw to consume large prey.

A VOICE SCRAPED Alex's eardrums from the inside. *Kill him. Kill Reid. Don't let it out!*

Those words frightened Alex to his core. He spun his head from side to side, searching for some kind of weapon. But would he use it if he found one? To defend himself, or to kill his friend?

It's coming. You must do it. Kill him!

Inside

How could he kill his friend? Instinct told him if he didn't, something worse would happen.

I shouldn't have gone back there. Should've left the house alone. Shouldn't have lit the match and tried to burn it all out, erase it once and for all.

Reid continued to make sickly sounds, and Alex saw something moving inside. From his stomach, it looked as if clawed hands were scraping, trying to push through the skin. Paralyzed by fear, Alex watched as those claws trailed up his chest, pushing frantically to get out. Up they dragged, until he saw those skinny fingers poking inside his neck, up to his jawline.

Reid moaned louder and flung his hands up to his neck. Looked like he was choking himself.

Alex didn't know what to do, and that voice inside continued to pressure him.

Kill him now!

Those sharp fingers and spindly hands slowly emerged from Reid's mouth, claws reaching out of his jaw and digging into his cheeks, prying his mouth wider still.

The smoky mass began to pull itself out of his mouth. It slithered up the inside of Reid's body until it pried itself from within his mouth. A long, skinny head emerged, eyes like caverns that seemed to look right through Alex, promising to swallow him up if he stared into them too long. The long torso came next, billowing out of his mouth like unwieldy black smoke.

Blood trailed down Reid's cheeks and face where the claws had dug in. Like hot lava coming out of a volcano, those wounds erupted, spilling too much blood too quickly.

Last, it pulled its legs and feet from within Reid,

335

long and unformed, more like wisps of smoke trailing behind. It shot up to the ceiling and reached back behind its body to dig its claws into the ceiling, where it hung over Reid, looking down on him.

Alex reached for his friend again, and Reid's hand shot up so quickly that Alex never saw it. He clenched Alex's wrist. Never turned his stare away from the shadow, but for the first time in four years, he was coherent.

"I tried." His voice sounded raw. He winced with each word. "I held on as long as I could. I took it inside, trapped it."

Reid and the creature continued to stare at each other.

"But I'm so tired. It's stronger than me. I thought I was dark enough, rotten enough inside to hold it. I'm sorry I made us come here, to this house. I'm sorry about Danny, Clint, and Heather." Tears streamed down his face, mixing with the blood on his cheeks. "I thought I was better than the myth. Thought we could prove it wrong or overcome it because of King Philip."

"KP," Alex whispered.

"I'm sorry to you, Alex. We shouldn't have come here. We were never meant to leave this house. And now I know we never will."

Chapter 54

The creature let out a hideous scream that ripped through Alex's body. He flung his hands to his ears, but nothing could block the sound or the pain.

Faster than Alex could blink, the creature descended upon Reid. It draped over him, covering him in shadow, and melted into his body, seeping its shadowy form through his skin. After it disappeared inside him, there was silence.

Then Reid began to writhe, clawing at his stomach, and bellowed. The sound shook the room, and Alex couldn't tell if it came from Reid or the Shadow.

Alex scrambled to get to his feet, aghast at the sight in front of him.

Reid clawed holes through his pajamas, then his skin. Red streaks dripped from his flesh. Then something poured out from Reid's stomach wounds and face lacerations. Dark gray trails of smoke. The Shadow was burning him from the inside. The sounds of sizzling flesh filled the air, followed by a horrid smell. Alex pulled his hand over his nose and fought the urge to vomit.

He couldn't watch any more. Couldn't bear to see yet another friend in a pile of ashes. He had to get out.

As Alex headed for the door, flames shot up and covered the walls, licking up to the ceiling.

Unmistakable chanting emanated from the evil little creatures that appeared, dancing within the flames.

"Watching…"

"Waiting…"

They clapped and flapped their wings, jumping and spinning around Alex.

"Watching…"

Reid's screams began to die down and the flames enveloped his body, leaving Alex alone.

He lurched for the door, but there was no handle. It had never been replaced after they were rescued. Boards were nailed over his exit. He turned around to search for something to break through with. Where Reid had lain just minutes before, the flames pushed back, revealing Reid's burned body. Charred ashes were all that remained.

"No!"

Where Reid's remains were, the flames shot back up, hiding the evidence. Alex followed a trail of flames that moved about the floor like a serpent. From the where Reid was to a spot in front of the fireplace, the serpentine flame slithered, then pushed back once again.

Lying to the right of the fireplace, Clint's body was preserved in ash.

"No!"

Alex tried to look away once again, but the flame darted to the left of the fireplace, and pushed back a spot that revealed Danny's burned body.

"No!"

The sound of a baby crying filled the air and swept around Alex in waves. Each breath he took pulled the sound closer, each cry sicklier and more desperate.

The little winged creatures leapt and curled through the flames as if in anticipation or celebration. Welcome to the party.

Alex went back to the door and began to kick frantically. Just boards. Surely he could bust through if he kept kicking. With all his strength, he kicked and pounded hands the boards, yet nothing would give. He might as well have been slamming his head into concrete, for all it got him.

A familiar voice whispered, "Shadow puppets."

"No," Alex whispered back.

He clawed his fingernails into the wooden boards, but it wasn't making any difference. He kicked and punched and scraped until his fingernails bled, but nothing would budge the stubborn boards. He knew it wasn't the boards that were strong, it was the cursed house.

Broken and bloody, he finally stopped banging and kicking, and pressed his forehead to the boards.

"Look, birds."

Alex knew Heather's voice anywhere. His heart wrenched in pain. He didn't want to turn around, but he had to.

"Hey, dickweed," she whispered.

Alex wanted to laugh. She was such a smart-ass. But he didn't laugh, didn't have time to.

"Run!" she screamed.

Alex turned around, wanting so badly to see Heather's face, her curls bouncing as she walked toward him, but it wasn't Heather.

The Shadow was there, its smoky shape looming over Alex.

Heather's voice was gone and all he could hear was Reid's voice as the shadow closed in.

"None of us were ever meant to leave this house."

The heat was overwhelming. Alex could feel his blood heating like liquid fire.

He stepped back and felt the boards behind him. Nowhere to go.

"And now I know we never will," said Reid's voice.

The house swelled in flames which burned higher up the walls and covered the ceiling. The little creatures swam in the flames, watching as the Shadow closed in on Alex. It reached its long-fingered claws out to him and he froze. There was nowhere for him to go. Never had been.

The Shadow was now back where it belonged—home. It locked its eyes on his, empty black voids pulling him inside, hypnotizing him, paralyzing him. Locked in its gaze, Alex had no will of his own. His jaws jerked open, mouth wide. The Shadow reached those hands out and tenderly grasped his cheeks, and Alex tried hard to picture his sister once more. The demon shifted its head to the side, sizing him up, then sprang forth and forced its form into Alex's mouth, down his throat, into every part of his body. Along the way, it lit a fire, burning everything it touched, coursing through his veins like molten lava and setting his blood aflame. Alex tried to scream but instead choked on the Shadow, the smoke, the fire burning inside his body. He squeezed his eyes shut and imagined Heather's smiling face as the Shadow pushed deeper inside. He opened his eyes and pretended to see Heather's curly dark hair instead of the smoky tendrils hanging from his mouth. His vision shut down, shrouded by an inky, weighty mass that oozed all around him. The world was becoming smoke and fire and ash. There was nothing to do but burn. Part of Alex was relieved. The fight had been too hard. The burden he'd lived with too great. If nothing else, he'd be with his friends once again.

His fiery gut cramped and twisted, and he buckled to the floor. The heat inside was too intense, melting away everything that was Alex. The hairs on his head began to eat into his skull, making them feel like hot, squirming worms. His skin cracked open all over and the fire leapt out of every crevice it had created. It burned and burned until there was nothing left of Alex to burn.

~

THE HOUSE SAT ALONE, *deep in the woods, dark and quiet. Its old wooden door and window boarded up once more.*

Invisible from the old dirt path, the house was hidden from view. But everyone knew where it was. Everyone knew what it was.

Invisible footsteps paced the floor. Darkness shifted. A crackle from a dead fire sounded from the fireplace, though no spark danced within it.

Tiny wings flapped from somewhere inside the house, slowed,

and settled in.
The house was at rest once more.
And waiting...

About the Author

D.M. Siciliano is a lover of all things creative. From the moment she could speak growing up in Massachusetts, she had a passion for flair and drama, putting on concerts for anyone who might be remotely interested (and even for those who weren't). A storyteller by nature, she first pursued her young dream of becoming a famous singing diva while living in Arizona. She soon found that stage-life wasn't the only form of storytelling she craved, so she dropped the mic and picked up a pencil instead. She still hasn't given up on her diva-ness and hopes that her pencil stays as sharp as her tongue.

A dark sense of humor and curiosity for haunted houses and things out of the ordinary led her down the path of completing her first novel, while several other projects are constantly floating around in her head and her laptop daily, and sometimes keeping her up much too late at night (occasionally forcing her to turn a nightlight on).

She now lives in Northern California with her two furbabies, Cezare and Michaleto.

The Gang Needs Your Help

Did you enjoy Inside*? Reviews keep books alive . . .*

The gang needs your help! Help them by leaving your review on either GoodReads or the digital storefront of your choosing.

They thank you!

The Parliament House

Made in the USA
Monee, IL
11 January 2020